UPON THE DEWY GROUND

THE SEQUEL TO "A LARK OVER NEW YORK"

By

Bill Harrod

Copyright © Bill Harrod 2023
This book is sold subject to the condition that it shall not, by way of trade or otherwise, be lent, resold, hired out, or otherwise circulated without the publisher's prior consent in any form of binding or cover other than that in which it is published and without a similar condition including this condition being imposed on the subsequent publisher.
The moral right of Bill Harrod has been asserted.

This is a work of fiction. Names, characters, businesses, organizations, places, events and incidents either are the product of the author's imagination or are used fictitiously. Any resemblance to actual persons, living or dead, events, or locales is entirely coincidental.

To all our family members,
who are all treasures to my darling wife Sylvia and I.

CONTENTS

Chapter 1 .... *1*
Chapter 2 .... *12*
Chapter 3 .... *33*
Chapter 4 .... *41*
Chapter 5 .... *44*
Chapter 6 .... *53*
Chapter 7 .... *60*
Chapter 8 .... *64*
Chapter 9 .... *70*
Chapter 10 .... *75*
Chapter 11 .... *83*
Chapter 12 .... *89*
Chapter 13 .... *92*
Chapter 14 .... *98*
Chapter 15 .... *108*
Chapter 16 .... *114*
Chapter 17 .... *118*
Chapter 18 .... *121*
Chapter 19 .... *128*
Chapter 20 .... *135*
Chapter 21 .... *139*
Chapter 22 .... *147*
Chapter 23 .... *158*
Chapter 24 .... *162*
Chapter 25 .... *165*
Chapter 26 .... *171*
Chapter 27 .... *177*
Chapter 28 .... *180*
Chapter 29 .... *187*
Chapter 30 .... *191*
Chapter 31 .... *196*
Chapter 32 .... *204*
Chapter 33 .... *212*
Chapter 34 .... *222*

Chapter 35 .... *226*
Chapter 36 .... *230*
Chapter 37 .... *235*
Chapter 38 .... *238*
Chapter 39 .... *243*
Chapter 40 .... *247*
Chapter 41 .... *253*
ABOUT THE AUTHOR 260

To Jenny Rainbow (jenny-rainbow.pixels.com) who has kindly allowed me to use her photograph named *'Hidden Glade in Fairy Rhododendron Woods'*, for the cover of my book.

Chapter 1

County Durham, 1881

Shinwell Hall stood high above Weardale, overlooking the town of Standale which nestled lower down the valley. The Hall, situated high enough up the fell to be above the smoke from the industrial chimneys, commanded an impressive view of the land beyond the fells. The Palladian style structure had been home to Chris and Jemima Paxton since moving from Durham City in 1863, two years after the birth of their son, Miles Thomas. The three-story house with its arched windows to the front, stood in three hundred acres of parkland. The carefully chosen site occupied an area where the land plateaued before gently sloping into the valley. The arched entrance was recessed and to the side were bay windows to the ground floor. The castellated flat roof was set off all around with intervals of stone balustrading.

Extra forestation had matured over the years, forming interlinking avenues of trees for walking, driving, or riding. The Grand Drive took a circular route around the park of just under two miles. The Grand Avenue ran diagonally across the parkland, forming a straight gallop of five furlongs; a short distance but long enough to assess the abilities of any good horse. To the front were rolling lawns leading down to a ha-ha, designed to keep out the local red deer.

The banqueting hall was exquisite in design, boasting high ceilings, intricate cornicing, and fluted pilasters. Other ornate plasterwork decorated the walls and ceilings. Edward Solesby, the previous owner had brought Italian artisans over to create the work. The floor was of polished mahogany, making this room the grandest in the house. It would not have been the Paxtons choice in design; too ostentatious they thought. Despite the lavish banqueting hall, the property came on the market at a price Chris Paxton could hardly refuse. Edward Solesby must have planned to entertain his wealthy friends in lavish style before his 'Icarus moment' brought him crashing down to earth and his loss was Chris Paxton's gain. Despite its grandeur, this room was the least used room in the house, but it came to life at Christmas time when the Paxtons invited all the children from the village to the 'Big House,' where a tea party was laid on for them followed by a magic show. The rest of the house comprised thirty main rooms. The rooms on the front of the house, while of a lesser specification than that of the banqueting hall, were superior to those at the rear. This variation in opulence indicated the progress of Edward Solesby's financial demise.

Also, to the rear, was stabling for twelve horses, a tack room and feed barn. In the centre of the stable block was the coach house and above the coach house was the mews accommodation for the groom. In the centre of the stable yard stood a dovecote built in keeping with the rest of the house. Other buildings on the estate included a gardener's cottage, and a lodge house where Thompson lived. He held a dual role of odd-job man and coachman. In total, the Paxtons employed twenty household staff. Edward Solesby was a successful lead mine industrialist who had owned several lead mines in the Alston area of the North Pennines. Unfortunately, he had lost his fortune on high-risk investments making it necessary to sell the estate to cut his losses. Included with the property was an option to buy into a mining opportunity, subject to sample boring. Chris Paxton, spotting a great financial opportunity, had bought the property and the mining option, in 1861. Jemima had named the house 'Shinwell Hall' after the small market town of Shinwell in Norfolk, where she and Chris had first met. Following the example of Lord Armstrong of Cragside Hall, Chris Paxton had electric lighting installed. He had repaired a derelict watermill on the estate and cleared the millrace. A natural spring, which emanated high up the fell, fed the millpond. With these repairs made good, he had installed a Siemen's dynamo, similar to that at Cragside.

*

Jemima Paxton sat half-turned in the window seat gazing out over Weardale; her left leg tucked under her. A poetry book she had been reading, lay beside her. In another life, she had been 'Mimi Martin – The Norfolk Lark,' world famous mezzo-soprano; now retired. She looked out over a landscape of green pastureland rising gradually until merging with the scrub and purple heather clad fells.

As she sat there, she mused over her past life. She thought back to 1855 and that chance meeting with Chris Paxton when she had sung at the wedding of his friend Jeremy Bolton in the small market town of Shinwell in Norfolk. They had quickly fallen in love and the following year, they were married. She remembered her husband's enthusiasm on first hearing her sing and his plans for her becoming a professional singer. She remembered appearing in 1858 at The Theatre Royal in Newcastle the first large theatre she had performed in under her stage name of 'Mimi Martin – The Norfolk Lark.' She could still hear the applause ringing in her ears as she remembered that first feeling of adulation as the members of the audience took her to their hearts. How her audience had adored her, *I am on my way*, she had thought at the time. Continuing her musing, she remembered how in the following year, she appeared in the opera *The Bohemian Girl*,' in the role of 'Arline,' at the Drury Lane Theatre in London's West End. She remembered at the end of the West End run, taking the production to Broadway, in New York. With her husband's mentoring, her singing voice had developed into that of a beautiful mezzo-soprano and her career had blossomed. She remembered how in five heady years Chris Paxton had taken her from being a humble 'wedding singer' to her appearance on Broadway. The New York run ended abruptly when rumours of civil war between the abolitionist states in the north and the Confederate states in the south, became increasingly a reality.

A planned tour of the United States throughout 1861, culminating in Boston, Massachusetts, failed to materialize and they returned to England at the end of the New York run. Shortly after their return, Jemima discovered she was pregnant with their first child. Early in her pregnancy, she decided she would go into semi-retirement for at least five years after the birth of their child. She wanted to be there for her baby during the formative years; first smile – first tooth – first steps unaided – first word; all these things she would miss if she were on tour, and she had wanted assurance that she would be there with her baby for all these 'firsts.' And so, she entered into a self-imposed exile from the stage; her husband warning her at the time of the possibility that her adoring public could quickly forget 'Mimi Martin' if she was absent for so long. After much thought, her mind was made up. *I will review the situation year by year*, she could hear herself saying.

During the following years, contrary to her husband's fears, her agent had received numerous requests from leading West End impresarios for her to come out of retirement, indicating her popularity had not waned. Five years later in 1866, on the advice of her husband and her agent and with their son Miles Thomas, going off to boarding school, she had indeed, returned to the stage.

Her return tour of the provinces had followed the same route as her first successful tour, back in 1858, culminating in London's West End. Her audiences had welcomed her back with open arms. It was as if she had not been away. As the years passed, and after several successful European tours and royal command performances in front of most of the royal houses throughout Europe, she had amassed a huge fortune. Over the last few years, her husband had encouraged her to reduce her workload. At the time, she had thought he was more tired of touring than she was and so, in 1880 she had made her final bow. As she reminisced, her mind went back to her farewell performance, at the theatre that had been the venue of her first great success, The Haymarket Theatre, in the West End. The crowd had given her a tremendous send-off. Eventually after three encores, the last of which was a final rendition of – 'I dreamt I walked in Marble Halls' from *The Bohemian Girl* and several curtain calls, she had entered retirement.

*

As Jemima sat, thinking over her present situation, with all the touring over, she realised she was spending most of her time at home and that the house was too big for them. Their son was in his final year in medical school at Edinburgh University and these days her husband spent most of his free time with his racehorses.

To fill his free time left by Jemima's retirement, he had taken up the sport of kings, and now he was so engrossed in his new-found interest that these days, he spent most of his time between his racehorses and his business interests. His racehorses were in training with Fraser Copeland at his centre situated over the southern county border at Richmond in North Yorkshire. Ten years ago, Chris Paxton had entered partnership with Oliver Bell, a local coal owner, and they had sunk a shaft down to the five-quarter seam of coal to the southwest of Gateshead. They had brought sinkers from Germany for the skilled work and had used Irish immigrants for the labouring. The assumption that there was coal below the fells had proved to be correct, and the exploratory bore holes having initially penetrated the overlying magnesian limestone, had struck fine quality coal, five feet eight inches thick and approximately five hundred feet below the surface. It was good coking coal for firing the blast furnaces of the Bessemer process employed at Consett in the manufacture of steel from molten pig iron.

Many of the Irish labourers, employed in the sinking of the mine, stayed on as coalminers and occupied the temporary accommodation, built for them during the establishment of the mine. They named the mine West Fell Colliery. As it developed, more houses were built near the pit, forming a new village comprising one hundred and twenty dwelling houses, made up of four terraces of thirty homes on each terrace. The village, as with most other mining villages took the name of the colliery and so West Fell Village came to be. The original Irishmen, who cut the first sods when sinking the shaft, moved from their temporary accommodation into new houses and once reunited with their families, they quickly integrated within the community of the newly established village of West Fell.

Compared to other mining communities, the houses at West Fell were of substantial construction. In some mining villages, especially where the pit was long established, the colliery houses, neglected over the years, were now little more than hovels with dirt floors. In building their pit village, Chris Paxton and his partner Oliver Bell, had had each dwelling fitted with flagstone floors and each serviced with a cold-water tap placed in the kitchen. A natural spring on the fells, fed the tap in each house. The same spring fed the watermill that provided the electricity for the Hall. Gravity fed the water to each dwelling.

In the kitchen was a fireplace, on one side of which was a set-pot for boiling water and on the other side was an oven for doing the baking. The miner's wife took great pride in the big range and every week she religiously polished it with black-lead until she could see her face in it. The houses also had a back yard where the woman of the house could wash and dry the clothes using a poss-tub and poss-stick.

The tub was made of galvanised steel. The stick was a heavy implement fashioned from wood. It had a heavy cylindrical wooden block, rounded at the end. Attached to the block was a shaft with a crosspiece handle, made to a comfortable length according to the wife's height, so that it came roughly to her waist. The miner's wife would fill her tub with hot water and soap. Into the tub, she would immerse her dirty washing. With her tub prepared she would adopt a two-handed action of raising the poss-stick in front of her and bringing it down with force into the tub thus pounding the dirt out of the clothes. While effective, it was quite arduous to implement, especially where the laundry for a large family was concerned. At the far end of the back yard, away from the house, a coal shed, and a dry ash midden stood side by side.

The backyard was also a place where the children of the household would play games of tops and whips, and five stones, where a flat surface was important. Also, in the backyard of every house, was a hook on the wall from which, hung a zinc bath, used by the miners of the house on their return home from the pit. The children had to leave the kitchen during male bath times and likewise the males during female bath times. Bathing took place in front of the fire, where it was warm, and the system worked very well. The fire burned in the grate throughout winter and summer. It burnt out during the night and was re-lit each morning. The man of the house would remove the ash from the grate daily and deposit it in the ash midden. Coal for the fire was readily available as each miner received an allocation of concessionary coal. Chris Paxton and his partner, Oliver Bell had deliberately improved the specifications of their employees' accommodation; not out of social conscience, but purely to attract the workforce they needed to work their mine.

New mines were opening throughout County Durham and Northumberland to fire the industrial revolution. Miners and their families were arriving from other parts of the country. Nearly every village in the area had its pit: the village having evolved around the pit. Cornish tin and copper miners, made redundant at the worked-out mines in Cornwall and agricultural workers, coaxed from the land with the word of higher wages also settled locally. Word spread that the West Fell Pit was a good place to work, and soon a village had sprung up near the pithead. They built a Primitive Methodist chapel in 1875 and six years later in 1881 juxtaposed, an alehouse named

'The Infantryman', after the landlord Sam Bailes, who was a veteran of the 68th Regiment of Foot, now part of the newly formed Durham Light Infantry. The children of the village attended a school run by two women teachers, Miss Rowe, and Miss Adamson, both spinsters of the parish and both sticklers for discipline. They could both wield a cane with equal vigour, a fact that many of their male students could vouch for; or should that be *'ouch for'*. The school met Monday to Friday in the vestry of the Methodist Church.

*

Jemima sat thinking over her present situation and she realised most of her time was spent at home. Like the house, her life was empty. Their son was in his final year in medical school in Edinburgh and her husband spent most of his free time with his racehorses. He had ambitions to own a three-year-old filly good enough to win the Oaks, the fillies classic, run at Epsom; then breed from her. The best he had achieved with his horses so far, was winning a modest handicap for moderate horses at Mandale Marshes, situated in a loop of the River Tees, near Stockton. Nevertheless, he lived in hope. Meanwhile, Jemima was spending much of her time in her own company, and how she missed the stage. For years, she had lived off the adulation of her audiences. They had been her life. Now with that vital artery cut, she felt her lifeblood slowly draining away. She needed something to occupy her time; something to staunch the flow before it became a life-threatening haemorrhage. After so much aspiration when she was younger, she now found herself totally without ambition.

She averted her eyes from the view across the fells and picked up the book of poems that lay on the seat next to her. As she did so, it fell open at a poem by William Wordsworth entitled, 'To the Skylark.' She began reading the words in front of her. She thought, in her present situation, they were very apt. After all, she *was* 'The Norfolk Lark.'

> *Ethereal minstrel! Pilgrim of the sky!*
> *Dost thou despise the earth where cares abound?*
> *Or, while the wings aspire, are heart and eye*
> *Both with thy nest upon the dewy ground?*
> *Thy nest which thou canst drop into at will,*
> *Those quivering wings composed that music still!*

She read the words and realised the similarity between Wordsworth's skylark and herself; had she not *'returned to earth, her wings composed, that music still.'* Away from the stage, what would her *'wings' aspire to now*? She felt desperate for something to occupy her, now that she had put those highflying years behind her and now, returned to *'her nest upon the dewy ground.'*

*

Chris Paxton's involvement with the mine, up until his wife's retirement from the stage was minimal and he still had not descended to the dark depths to the coalface workings of the colliery, although he had visited the manager's office on several occasions. He left the running of the mine to his partner, their manager, and their viewer. The manager made all the executive decisions on the day-to-day running of the mine, hiring and firing, adopting policy and conducting mine legislation. The viewer was usually a qualified mining engineer, and he would liaise with the landowners who owned the mineral rights to the coal seams that passed under their land. It would be the viewer's responsibility to negotiate the royalties paid to the landowners. Several collieries would come under the authority of the same viewer; but each colliery had its own manager. Chris Paxton still did not intend to get his hands dirty, that was his reason for not joining his father's foundry and engineering works, on graduating from Cambridge University with a degree in music, but that is another story.

*

Travellers in the early eighteenth century, journeying across the fells of Weardale, would have found their eyes drawn across the verdant countryside of County Durham towards the magnificent sight of Durham Cathedral in the far distance. A sight that on a clear day in the past, would have drawn many a pilgrim to this man-made structure, spurring them on to make that final effort to reach their goal; to pay homage at the tomb of Saint Cuthbert. Travellers in the 1880's, making the same journey, would experience a vista pockmarked by many mines and factories belching out their smoke into the atmosphere, making a view of Durham Cathedral in the distance exceedingly difficult indeed. Ironically, it was the Dean and Chapter of Durham Cathedral to whom Chris Paxton and his partner Oliver Bell paid royalties on every ton of coal removed from beneath the land owned by the Bishops of Durham.

This area in the Northeast of England until the passing of the Durham County Palatine Act of 1836 was unique, in that here, the King of the Realm did not rule; it was the powerful Prince Bishops. The difference between the 'king' of County Durham in those days, and the king sitting on his throne in London was the headwear. The king in London wore a crown and the 'king' in Durham wore a mitre. It was widely claimed that the Bishop of Durham's throne in Durham Cathedral was the *highest throne in Christendom*.

This area, bordered in the north by the River Tyne and to the south by the River Tees, was the County Palatine of Durham. Through the centre of the county the River Wear meandered, before flowing into the North Sea at Sunderland. The bishops had the power to levy their own taxes, hold their own parliament, promote justices to administer their own laws and collect the revenue from the mine owners who mined the coal beneath their territories.

*

Jemima heard the door behind her open and pivoting on her seat, she saw it was her husband.

'Hello Darling, reading again?' he asked on entering.

'Oh hello,' Jemima replied adding, 'what kind of day did you have at the races?' trying to sound interested. Her husband had attended the horse race meeting held on the Town Moor at Newcastle, where his two-year-old filly, Indian Empress, had been competing.

'How did the 'Empress' run?' she enquired with a minimum of interest.

'She finished fourth in a field of eight; a most encouraging run for her first attempt. She found it all very strange early on. Once she realised what it was all about, she settled nicely after halfway. Considering she was an April foal and still a baby, she did well,' he replied enthusiastically.

'What was Jed Smyth's opinion of her performance?' Jemima asked. Jed Smyth being the jockey who rode Chris Paxton's horses.

'He thinks she will be better over a longer distance; she put in her best work in the closing stages of the race. If anyone knows, Jed Smyth does. He is a fine judge and on dismounting said the filly was the best horse he has ridden for me,' her husband said, enthusiastically.

Jemima knew the jockey's comment was vastly different from saying she was the best filly he had ever ridden, per se. *That is what any jockey would say to the owner.*

'Well, we shall see,' she replied optimistically.

Chapter 2

1884

Today, Jemima Paxton was unusually elated, an emotion she did not experience often since her retirement. Her son was coming home from his studies in Edinburgh and her husband had given his racehorse trainer strict instructions not to enter any of his horses on the weekend of their son's homecoming. This time Miles was coming home to stay, having completed his final year at Edinburgh University. Dr Miles Paxton, with his medical qualifications gained, had his own ideas for the future. The carriage transporting Miles Paxton from Gateshead railway station, pulled up at the portico to Shinwell Hall. There, waiting to greet him were his parents. His mother could not wait for him to alight from the carriage, and she rushed forward, even opening the door before the coach had stopped and holding it open for him while he alighted.

'How are you my darling? Did you have a good journey from Edinburgh?' Jemima asked, and almost in the same breath, 'Thompson, see to the trunk.'

By now, Chris Paxton had joined them.

'Hello, Dr Paxton, how are you,' and shook his son firmly by the hand.

'I am very well, thank you Father,' and he turned to his mother and kissed her on the cheek.

'Hello Mama. I had a most enjoyable journey, thank you. The railway follows the Northumbrian coast for a lot of the way, through beautiful scenery and all those coastal castles. The wonder is, how the Scots could ever have had the audacity to even contemplate invasion.'

He turned back to his father, 'I'm hoping you may be able to use your influence to get me a place in a practice, somewhere local father, possibly as a junior doctor for starters. I have learned so much while I have been away, and I cannot wait to put some of my ideas into practice.' he said, enthusiastically.

'That is for the future Miles, but for now let us have an aperitif before we eat.'

Jemima sensed his enthusiasm could mean he would be spending lots of time with father and his horses and feared she may not fit into their future schemes.

'Let us go inside and have some lunch. Sally has arranged for Cook to prepare some nice cold game pie,' Jemima said.

Sally Binney, who Jemima had alluded to, had arrived in Durham from Norfolk, following the death of her husband to help Jemima's mother Frances, run her boarding house. Sally's late husband, George Binney had lost his life while running trials on a steam plough at Renton House Farm in Norfolk in 1864. A shackle pin had sheared and on breaking, the wire rope had snaked as the tension was released and with the shackle still attached, had struck George Binney violently on the temple. He died almost immediately from a brain haemorrhage. They had been married for eleven years. The following year, Jemima's mother, Frances, had suffered a cancer and she died a year later. Poor Sally: fate could not have been more cruel. In two years, she had lost her husband and her best friend, and she was only forty-seven years old. Sally and Frances had met when the latter arrived at Renton House Farm as maid to Hannah Hayward, wife of the farm bailiff, and Sally had been bridesmaid at the wedding of Jemima's parents.

When Frances died, she left the boarding house to her two older sons John and Edward. This was with the approval of Jemima and her youngest brother Daniel Jr. They had both fared well, Jemima with her successful career on the stage and Daniel who was a qualified mechanical engineer. He was in partnership with his Uncle Peter Paxton and together they headed the Paxton Foundry and Engineering Company, founded by Miles Paxton, Chris, and Peters' father. Chris, on graduating from Cambridge, had opted out of the family business. His interests lay in the arts. Having studied music at university and an accomplished pianist, he had accompanied his wife and he was her musical director throughout her successful singing career.

Shortly after their inheritance, Edward had purchased his brother's share of the boarding house and he and his wife Lucy had taken on the running of the business. John, like his father Dan before him, had preferred the outdoors and he was quite happy working as a platelayer on the railway and he did not intend to change his job. Maintaining the track of the Great Northern Railway suited his lifestyle. He and his wife Elsie lived in a rail-side cottage near the crossing at Cuthbert's Well, five miles southwest of Durham City. While he loved his sister and immensely proud of her achievements, he was a simple man who never discussed his sister's fame with his workmates.

With the changes at the boarding house, Sally Binney found herself surplus to requirements, once again she was in a state of crisis. Jemima, who had decided to return to the stage when her son, then aged five, had gone off to boarding school, came up with a solution to Sally's dilemma when she offered her the position as her dresser. As a result, Sally had travelled throughout Europe with the famous soprano. When she finally retired from the stage, Jemima insisted that Sally should stay on as general manager of the household staff. She had her own quarters in the east wing of the grand house. The Paxtons regarded her as a family member and as such she enjoyed a secure future.

*

In the mining village of West Fell, another mother was preparing for a big event in her son's life but without any feeling of elation. Today she was putting up two lots of bread and jam in her husband's 'bait tin', for today, their twelve-year-old son was accompanying his father on a first visit underground to see what to expect should he follow in his father's footsteps and make his living down the pit. If he could read a passage from the Bible and print his name, he could leave school at the end of the present school term. His father had arranged with the colliery manager for his son Tommy to go underground to spend a shift with him. Alice Cogon had strong misgivings about her son following his father down the pit; after all, he was still a 'bairn,' who in her eyes, was not mature enough for pit work. Like most miners' wives, they hoped their sons would aspire to greater things and not go down the pit like their fathers. She knew her son wanted to continue his studies and his heart was not in the pits. Very few mothers had their dreams realised and most lads followed their fathers into the pits, but Alice Cogon knew it was not for their lad.

'What's a bairn like our Tommy goin' to do down the pit, Joe?'

'It'll do him no harm Alice; it'll be an experience for the lad and who knows – when he sees what it's like down there it might scare the life out of him, and he won't want any part of it.'

'Ee! Don't talk like that Joe; yer temptin' fate. I don't want life frightened out of him, neither down the pit nor anywhere else for that matter. I want the life in him for a long, long time. I'll never settle 'til y' both walk through that door again, safely home from that hellhole.'

Her husband's attempt at reassurance had not helped. If anything, it had made her feel worse. 'I know you want the best for the lad, but I don't want y' fillin' his head with notions above his station. Name me one lad from round here that has stayed out of the pits and made somethin' o' themselves. Look at Arthur Turnbull's lad, Ben. He stayed out of the pits and the best he's done for himself is roamin' round on the fells repairin' dry stonewalls for the hill farmers who can ill afford to pay him, and half the time they don't. Durin' the winter months, he cannot get any work done for the weather other than diggin' sheep out of snowdrifts. Y' know what it gets like, up there on the high fells in the winter,' Joe Cogon reminded her.

'That be as it may, but at least Ben Turnbull is happy doin' what he's doin' and that's what I want for our Tommy – to be happy doing what he wants to do. Not all the lads that stay at bank are goin' to end up as fells men.'

*

Joe Cogon opened his 'bait tin', took out a slice of jam and bread, and handed it to his son. 'Get that down y' son. You'll not taste better jam and bread than that,' he promised. 'Jam and bread always tastes better down the pit than at bank,' Joe said, and many other miners would agree, because the jam kept the bread moist it was easy on a dry throat. 'Well son, what do y' think of working down here?' Joe asked.

'It's all very interesting Dad,' Tommy replied, 'but I felt a bit queasy comin' down in the cage, it's a wonder you didn't hear me knees knockin' and me ears went funny. I thought they were goin' to burst, until they popped,' he said, adding, 'I know now what y' mean about the jam and bread,' and he held his half-eaten sandwich up for all to see.

'Oh aye, I heard a noise son, but I thought it was just the cage skeets rattlin' on the guides,' Joe joked. 'Never mind lad you'll soon get used to that before y' put y' first week in. Everybody goes through that for the first time. Ask any of the lads here.' Joe added, reassuringly.

'Why yes, we've all gone through that son, mind you it's that long since I did, I'd forgotten all about it,' Old Geordie Hodgson, the deputy overman said, adding, 'Come on lads, let's have y' back on the job. Y've had y' baits and a bit crack at the kist.'

The word crack Old Geordie had used was the Durham miners' version of the Irish word craic, meaning news or gossip and the kist was mining talk for the large wooden chest in which the deputy kept replacement picks and shovels. Over the years, the 'kist' had become synonymous with the meeting point where the deputy would detail the workforce to their various places of work within the district over which he was in charge.

The men rose to return to the coalface in the North Winning and Tommy was about to follow his Dad when Geordie Hodgson took hold of his jacket sleeve. 'You come wi' me Tommy, for the rest of the shift. I'll look after him for y' Joe,' he shouted to Tommy's dad. Y' dad' and the other lads are goin' to be up to their eyes in work to get their quotas out before the end of the shift. I've got a bit of inspectin' to do before the next shift comes in, it'll be good experience for y. We'll check the regulator door back-by to see if enough air is gettin' through and check that old workin' in the West Winnin'. Work had ceased in there when they hit a fault. We need to make sure it isn't leachin' firedamp into the airway,' Old Geordie explained.

They set off together, Tommy asking question after question of Geordie. Geordie had taken an instant liking to the lad, and he thought he would make a good pitman, like his dad.

'What's a regulator door Mr Hodgson?'

'It's a door with a slidin' panel in the middle which can be adjusted to allow control of the airflow, lad,' Geordie explained.

'How do y' know when there's gas in a place?'

'By, Tommy, you've got an inquisitive mind, lad; but that's not a bad thing. Keep that up and you'll do well. Never be frightened to find things out Tommy. Read as much as you can and ask as many questions as you can and store it all up in your mind. You never know when you might need it. Keep it pigeonholed up there until one day you do,' the old pitman advised, and he knocked on Tommy's head as he delivered his sermon. They passed the entrance to an old working to the right.

'In that heading, the men had to pull out, when they hit the Whin Dyke,' Geordie said, pointing with his yardstick. 'We'll have to go down there when we come back and test for gas. Ah'll show you how to do the test then. First, we must check the regulator door.'

The Whin Dyke that Geordie had alluded to, was a fault of fine-grained basalt that passed through the strata interrupting the coal layers. Two roof timbers, placed in a criss-cross fashion across the entrance, supported a sign with the message, 'KEEP OUT', sternly suggesting that venturing beyond this point could be a foolhardy decision, especially for a young lad on his first trip underground in a coal mine. They continued past the old working. 'We'll soon be at the regulator door,' Geordie said rather abstractly; his mind was elsewhere. 'We should be able to see Bobby Anderson's lamp shining through the regulator panel aperture. He's the trapper lad on back shift. I hope he's goin' about his business down there,' he added threateningly, and he gesticulated once more with his stick in the direction ahead. They reached the regulator door and George Hodgson rapped on the door with the butt of his stick. The noise caused the trapper lad to jump up from his 'cracket' sending it flying in his haste. A coal hewer would sit on a cracket at the coalface to be more comfortable when wielding his coal pick. Bobby Anderson's cracket would not be used for its rightful purpose for a few more years. Bobby, at sixteen, had to gain a bit more pit sense working back-by before graduating as a hewer at the coalface. He quickly pulled the door open. The deputy and his young attendant passed through, and the trapper lad closed the door behind them.

'Good mornin' Mr Hodgson how are y'?' he said trying to curry favour with his boss.

'Are you sure you weren't asleep when I was in-by Bobby Anderson? I'll have y' guts for garters if y' were,' Old Geordie warned. It was Bobby's job to open and close the door, allowing the coal tubs to pass through. A small recess had been hewn out as a refuge into which the trapper-lad could enter until the pony and tub had passed through. All trapper lads found it difficult to stay awake throughout their shift, during periods of inactivity, sometimes they worked a twelve-hour shift.

'No Mr Hodgson, I never was,' Bobby said, trying to be as convincing as possible, knowing he was safe in the fact that Old Geordie would never know if he had been asleep or not. On approaching the regulator door, Geordie Hodgson couldn't see any light from Bobby's lamp on approaching the door and realised the sliding panel in the middle of the door was completely closed. 'Who the hell has shut that regulator? 'George Hodgson shouted, and he struck the regulator door with his stick in anger. Y haven't shut it because it was draughty and ye were feelin' a bit cold, have y'?'

'No! Not me Mr Hodgson. Ah know how important it is for it to be open when need be, and I know better than to touch it. Ah always take notice how it is when I start me shift and that's the way I found it. Please believe me. Honestly, on my Mam's life,' he pleaded.

Tommy took all this in and noticed how Mr Hodgson's attitude had changed and wondered if his anger about the regulator-setting would spill over onto himself, after all, he would be with him for the rest of the shift.

'Let's get that open straight away; I can't believe some daft sod would do a trick like that,' Geordie said and after adjusting the regulator to three parts open, he took off his hat and scratching the back of his head, he said, 'Well I've seen nothin' like that all the time I've worked in the pits. Come on Tommy, let's get goin'; we've got more work to do and quick. We need to get into that old workin' down the West Winnin' and check that the gas hasn't leached out while that regulator door was shut.'

Young and inexperienced in pit work as Tommy was, he sensed the concern and urgency in Geordie Hodgson's voice, and the importance of their next actions.

They reached the old working and went in as far as the abandoned face. Where there should have been coal at the face there was nothing but grey stone. He also noticed the stone sloped towards him at the base of the fault and the coal at either side looked like cinders.

Geordie Hodgson, despite his urgency, talked as he adjusted his safety lamp. 'This is a fault lad; the strata were interrupted by something durin' the formation. This fault was formed by the magma from an ancient volcano, and this is called the Whin Dyke. His explanation was both brief and hurried.

'But that's enough of that. We've more important things to do down here,' he said with a sense of urgency. He turned the flame of his safety lamp down to the test cap, just above the wick. What little light there was in the chamber dimmed further. Holding his lamp by the base and keeping it vertical, he carefully raised it high into the top of the working, knowing that firedamp was lighter than air and that would be where the gas would collect. The lamp flame quickly flared up inside the gauze cylinder with a blue flash, extinguishing the flame instantly indicating there was a high concentration of gas present in the old working. 'Quick Tommy we have to put up a brattice (canvas screen) at the junction to stop the firedamp from getting into the main airway.' Working together Geordie and his young helper soon had the brattice in place and they were making their way back in-by when there was a loud roar as the air, instead of coming at them steadily from behind, it hit them full in the face with a force that knocked them both off their feet. 'Are you all right lad?' Geordie shouted as he picked himself up, feeling for his stick as he did so. Neither could see the other; their lights extinguished with the force of the blast. Unseen swirling dust filled their throats and nostrils.

'I've banged me shoulder, but I think it'll be alright,' Tommy replied shakily.

'You wait here Tommy; don't move until I come back for y.' Do y' hear? One more thing before I leave y', have y' got a hankie in y' pocket?' Geordie asked anxiously. Tommy put his hand in his ragged pocket and pulled out a hankie.

'I have Mr Hodgson – me mam must have put it there,' and he dangled it in front of him, forgetting his companion could not see it in the dark. 'Good lad, now tie it round your mouth.' Geordie paused, and he could hear the rustle of cloth as he tied the hanky.

'That's done Mr Hodgson,' Tommy said in a muffled voice. Geordie adjusted the neckerchief, which all deputies wore, and pulled it up around his mouth.

'Right lad, I'm off back to get Bobby Anderson's lamp so I can go in-by and see how the lads are in the North Winnin.' Stay right there and don't move until I get back for y.' You should be safe so long as y'stay still. Don't sit down, stay upright in case of poisonous blackdamp, it's heavier than air and collects at floor level. Ah'll be back for y', son.'

Geordie, like all the old miners, knew about the different gasses present in gaseous pits. It was imperative for the officials, who had studied mining engineering, to understand the various gasses prevalent in a coal mine. Tommy could hear Geordie Hodgson tap-tapping with his stick on the upright roof supports as he shuffled off into the darkness. The sound of Geordie's presence in the dark abyss gradually faded into an eerie silence leaving Tommy alone and in total darkness.

Meanwhile, Geordie went along the airway feeling his way back-by as best he could until he could see the glow from Bobby Anderson's lamp, but no glow from Bobby's lamp lit the aperture, when George Hodgson reached the regulator door. On opening the door, he found Bobby was sitting on his 'cracket' by the regulator door.

'Bobby, I've got t' take your lamp son. I've got to get in-by to see how the men are in the North Winnin'.'

'What's happened like, Mr Hodgson. The air freshened on my face, and I thought me lamp was goin' out. Luckily, it didn't,' Bobby said.

Taking the lamp Geordie said, 'Stay here Bobby 'til I get back and don't wander off in the dark.'

'I won't Mr Hodgson. I'll wait here like y' say,' Bobby promised, straining his eyes as he watched Geordie Hodgson and the light from the commandeered lamp fade into the black distance.

Geordie Hodgson once again reached the spot where he had left little Tommy Cogon. 'Don't forget what ah told y' Tommy lad. I'll be back for y' ah promise.' The further he went into the mine the more acrid the atmosphere became, and the devastation more severe. In the half-light, he struggled to clamber over a mishmash of broken timbers, which had become wedged in the gallery forming a tight barrier. The explosion had blown out all the roof supports, and it was dangerous to attempt any further progress. He was also aware of the danger of the possibility of afterdamp, a mixture of carbon monoxide and other gasses produced after a firedamp explosion. He clambered up the tangle of jammed props and other debris and with the limited light; he reached out as far as he could into the darkness, tracing the roof with his stick. His stick met no obstacles, telling Geordie that a vast area of the roof ahead was now unsupported and in an extremely dangerous state and he had to retreat as quickly as he could, through the mishmash of broken timbers. As he struggled to drag himself back, he halted and listened; a cracking noise was coming from in-by. He knew the cracking noise was coming from the few pit props that had survived the initial blast and were now taking all the strain from the unsupported roof. The cracking of splitting wood yielding to the strain generated by the closing roof above and heat from a raging fire below was becoming more frequent. Despite his urgency to retreat from the place, he paused briefly and listened. The roof was no longer 'talking,' it was 'growling angrily' as if it knew it was getting the upper hand in its fight against man's plunder of the Earth's bounty. Free of any restriction, gravity was taking over, and the roof was slowly coming in to meet the floor. Suddenly, a rumbling noise like that of loud thunder, followed by another rush of air, dust, and smoke, told George Hodgson that the roof, further in-by had collapsed. His mining experience told him, there was no hope for the twelve men in the workings. He once again was in complete darkness. Turning, he retraced his steps as best he could in the dark, skinning his knees and hands frequently, as he blindly staggered and crawled in desperate haste, back to where he left Tommy Cogon. He had to ignore the scrapes and knocks he suffered as he fumbled his way back. His stick was lost on the hurried return journey. He was unable to retrieve his stick in the dark. He'd had that yardstick since qualifying as a deputy, three years after his marriage.

*

Tommy Cogon leaned against a prop trying to ease his aching shoulder as he stood in the pitch-black gallery waiting for the return of deputy Hodgson. The idea of sliding down the prop and sitting on the floor tempted him. Remembering the deputy's warning he quickly dispelled the notion. He had his eyes tightly closed. On opening his eyes, he realised it made no difference it was pitch-black. He was not afraid of the dark, but this was different; he was terrified. He strained his ears for any sound of Mr Hodgson coming back with the men. In his naivety, he still thought the deputy would return with the men including his father, but the only sounds his strained ears were hearing was the menacing creaking of the timbers. In this environment, the senses seemed more acute. The smells, the sounds, and the loneliness during the periods of silence, broken intermittently by the eerie creaking of the straining timbers, all this was alien to him. He was terrified and shook like a leaf. A seasoned collier would know that the timbers moaned all the time and through time, everyone got used to these everyday sounds of the pit. To a little twelve-year-old, on his first experience underground it was petrifying. He did not have the men here to reassure him that what he could hear was 'normal.' Even though he was in pitch-black darkness. He blinked instinctively as if the sun shone in his eyes. He thought of his Dad again and found himself praying inwardly for his father's safe return. He still could not hear any sound coming from in-by. He strained harder to catch any sound other than the timbers, which he thought, in his boyish, terrified state, were becoming more menacing. Still there was no sound of the deputy and his men. 'Please God; don't let anything happen to Mr Hodgson and the men. Please let them get out safely,' he found himself saying out loud, between sobs that were now so deep they hurt his chest.

He listened intently yet again, for the tap tapping of Geordie Hodgson's stick but no sound met his strained ears. Silly thoughts began to fill his mind. Will he ever see his mam and dad again? Or daylight for that matter, or the flowers, or the animals and birds on the fells; he thought he would perish alone in this terrible place, with nobody left to get him out. He wondered what death would be like. Would it be just like falling asleep – never to wake again? Would he go to Heaven or Hell? He searched his mind for any wrongdoings he had committed. He remembered he had stolen a penny chew once when he was at Gateshead with his mam.' They had been in a sweet shop called 'The Chocolate Box.' He remembered it was like a wonderland in there and he had sneaked the chocolate covered toffee bar into his pocket and he had got away with it. His mother was unaware of what he had done; if she had, she would have killed him; he thought. On reflection, it would have been better than dying down here. Thinking back, he could even taste the toffee bar, as he remembered eating it in secret. He had climbed high up on the fell, to be as far away as possible from the village, to be out of sight. He remembered dropping down in the heather when he was far enough away to eat his stolen confectionary without detection; he would have travelled farther up the fell, but he could not resist the thought of the chocolate-covered toffee any longer. He laid on his back among the purple heather, taking care to reduce his outline against the skyline. In his mind's eye, he remembered vividly, taking the toffee bar from his pocket and his disappointment when on removing the wrapper he discovered the heat of his body had melted the chocolate coating. Not wanting to waste any, he had licked the waxed paper wrapper clean, before starting on the toffee. He turned the wrapper over and the image of a cow licking its lips smiled up at him. Still relishing the sweet taste of toffee and chocolate, he reluctantly tore the wrapper into small pieces hoping the evidence of his theft was gone forever.

He *had* thought of keeping the wrapper as a sort of trophy; instead, he flung the fragmented 'trophy' into the air; the bits carried, on the wind. The sweet buttery smell drifted up his nostrils as he slowly put the toffee bar to his mouth. He wanted to savour the moment for which he had incriminated himself.

Tommy returned to reality and the crisis he now faced down in West Fell pit. *Was this a big enough crime to stop him from entering Heaven?* he asked himself with trepidation. *Was he now paying the penalty for his wrongdoing?* Then his mind posed another more serious question. *Was he halfway to Hell in this God forsaken place and did the Devil have first claim on him, down here in the dark?* After all, his mam referred to it as *'that Hell hole.'* Had he somehow trespassed into the Devil's territory once he had stepped out of the cage. He thought about the Lord's Prayer and ran through it in his mind for 'protection.' He got to the bit *'Forgive us our trespasses'* and realised there was no such arrangement with the Devil. Shifting his back against the thick wooden prop to make his bruised shoulder more comfortable, he realised the air was becoming warmer and he was now sweating heavily. He removed his arms from the ragged jacket, struggling with the injured shoulder. He let the old garment drop to the floor knowing he had discarded it for the last time. It was at that moment when he parted company with that old tweed jacket, he was conscious of the fact that never again would he be pulling that jacket on to go down the pit. His shirt was sticking to his back like a hot poultice. He knew if he should survive this ordeal, he would never again come back down a pit, ever.

Just when he had given up all hope, he heard a shuffling noise coming from in-by.

'Is that you Mr Hodgson?' Tommy shouted.

'Aye lad it is,' Geordie Hodgson replied breathlessly. Keeping his head down, he walked slowly as he felt for Tommy in the dark. His outstretched arm blindly described an arc in front of him. Geordie's searching hand contacted Tommy's sweaty arm. Sliding his hand down the lad's arm, he grabbed Tommy's wrist.

'Come on lad, we've got no light again. I lost it in-by when the top came down. We have to move as quickly as we can in the dark; there's a fire ragin' in the North Winnin' and it's heading this way. With a bit of luck, the top comin' in, might form a barrier and stop the fire from spreadin'. We must get that regulator shut to try to stifle that fire and hopefully it will burn itself out, or this pit is doomed,' Geordie said urgently.

The thought of the fire in the North Winning made up Tommy's mind. He knew now this is where Hell is; me mam was right all along - it is a Hell hole down here.

'What about me dad, Mr Hodgson?'

'I won't try to lie to y', son. I fear y' dad has probably gone to his maker.'

'I hope he has Mr Hodgson, and the Devil hasn't got him first,' but Tommy was not very hopeful. He thought his dad and his mates had got too close to the Devil in the North Winning and had paid the penalty.

In the darkness, Geordie could hear Tommy sobbing deeply. They fumbled their way as quickly as they could towards the shaft bottom and safety. As they torturously struggled along, Geordie dragged Tommy up from the floor for the umpteenth time. As he did so, he caught the familiar whiff of a sweaty pit pony wafting in on the incoming air.

'Tommy lad, our prayers have been answered,' Geordie said, his voice more relaxed than of late. In the dark, they felt in front of them, as the sweaty smell got stronger. Geordie's hand contacted the moist back of the pony. It was still warm, suggesting that the driver had recently done a runner in the direction of the shaft bottom thinking he would make better progress on his own, selfishly leaving his pony to its own devices. Geordie traced his hands along the reins until he found the pony tethered to one of the roof supports. The pony was still tacked up and the limbers were still in place. Moving the pony forward a couple of paces until he thought its little hooves were clear of the tack and traces.

'Steady boy, whoa now,' Geordie said, as he carefully loosened the knot in the reins. The last thing he wanted at this stage, was for the pony to bolt before he got little Tommy across the pony's back. He knew the little pony was their best hope of survival and he did not want to lose him now.

'Lay still Tommy and keep your head down over his neck; we know he's not going to strike his head on the baulks, he's not tall enough otherwise he wouldn't be down here.' The height of each pony and the headroom in the district, determined the area of the mine to which each pony worked. Baulks, (pronounced 'barks' by the miners), were the thick crosspieces of timber supporting the roof.

'He'll find his way back to the shaft bottom and his stable, even in the dark, 'Geordie predicted. Once he had Tommy lying across the pony's back, Geordie laid himself across the pony's rump and they set off down the gallery making quicker progress than they had thus far. After a while, the pony suddenly began to slow down until he was reluctant to move. Keeping a tight hold of the reins in the dark, Geordie reached down with his left leg until it touched the ground and he dismounted from the pony. Reaching blindly in front of him, with his arm fully outstretched, his hand contacted the wooden regulator door. The little pony had sensed the obstacle ahead even in the dark.

'Are y' there Bobby son?' Geordie Hodgson called out in the dark; but there was no reply and he called out once more but there was still no reply. 'I reckon Bobby's gone out-by with that driver whose pony this is,' he said, more to himself than to Tommy. His hand searched across the middle of the door for the regulator panel. He soon found it and firmly slid it fully shut, his plan being to stifle the flow of oxygen to the fire once the trapdoor was fully closed. He maneuvered the pony through the open door. Once through the regulator door Geordie closed it tightly behind them. He lay across the ponies rump with the fresh air from the surface now quickening into their faces.

The little pony quickened his stride almost to a trot and Geordie had to subdue the little pony's enthusiasm before he and his little companion were bounced off his back and onto the pit floor.

'Whoa, steady boy!' Geordie yelled, and the little pony slowed to a steady pace again.

After what seemed an age, they eventually saw light ahead in the distance. The pony sensed he was getting near to the stables and his feed and quickened his stride again. Geordie hung on tighter, clutching tighter to Tommy, he let the pony have its head. Two hundred more yards or so and they reached the shaft bottom and safety. Billy Simpson, the driver who should have been responsible for the pony carrying Tommy Cogon and George Hodgson to safety came to meet them. On seeing his pony coming towards him, he grabbed the reins and brought him to a halt.

'There now Darkie, steady boy, steady now,' Billy Simpson said calmly.

The pony came to a sudden halt almost dumping the two 'riders' over his neck. Billy rubbed the pony's muzzle with the palm of his hand.

'Good as gold this one Geordie,' Billy said. The little pony stood shifting his hooves on the spot, affectionately pushing his face into Billy's midriff.

'Darkie did y' say Billy; that's his name is it. A pony never had a better name. Is anybody injured?' Geordie asked, addressing all the gathered miners.

'Don't think so,' said a chorus of voices.

'Apart from one or two with cuts and bruises,' someone said.

Geordie again addressed the miners. 'I'm afraid I can't say the same for the twelve souls in the North Winnin.' I tried to get through to them, but it was hopeless. The top was gone, and a fire was ragin.' I got as far as I could, but all the supports were blown out wi' the blast and I could hear and smell the fire. If it is any consolation, they wouldn't have suffered. It would have been instant.' He was looking at little Tommy when he made this telling remark.

'God rest their souls,' Sydney Marr, a Methodist local preacher added.

'Take your pony round to the stables Billy. He'll be brought up with the rest of them once things are sorted. Y' realise I can report y' for abandonin' him underground,' Geordie said half-jokingly, 'but unbeknown to you, it was the best mistake you'll make in your life; but for your action or lack of it and the grace of God, me and young Tommy here, have made it back.'

Tommy could hear murmurings going through the crowd of men.

'Is that Joe Cogon's lad?'

'Aye it is,' he heard another voice answer.

'What's that young 'un doin' down here anyway?' another one asked.

'Same as most of us here have done, come down with our dads, just for a look around before we made our minds up.'

'Ah bet he's made his mind up now then,' another said cynically, quickly adding, 'sorry about your dad son,' on realising Tommy stood close to him.

Tommy felt self-conscious as he listened to all the reference to him being down the pit at time of the disaster and he hoped the men did not blame his dad for bringing him into the pit. Despite all the camaraderie shown to one another, he felt like an outsider that did not belong in the pit at that moment.

'The powers that be, will decide what to do about the ponies in the stables. They'll have other priorities to deal with first. But they'll be taken care of,' said Geordie Hodgson.

*

After several journeys, up and down the shaft, the cage brought the last of the survivors to the surface to greetings from their relieved families. The families of the twelve victims of the tragedy, including Alice Cogon, who stood cuddling Tommy, stared vacantly at the pit shaft. The last man to step from the cage was George Hodgson, no more living beings would be stepping from that cage alive, except for the horse keepers and the ponies from the stables.

With every living being now out of the pit, a working party was set up to seal off the downcast shaft with a large timber cover, preventing fresh air entering the mine and feeding the fire. They shut down the extractor fan drawing the spent air from the up-cast shaft, to deprive the fire in the North Winning of oxygen in the hope it would eventually burn out.

After several days, they opened the cover on the downcast shaft slightly and restarted the extractor fan on the up-cast shaft. They assessed air samples taken from the up-cast shaft until the results proved wholesome enough to indicate that the fire had abated and that the air exiting the pit was fresh enough so as not to present any threat to life.

*

Charles Lambton, the viewer, led the party that went into the pit to retrieve the bodies of the victims. They progressed from the shaft bottom and made their way into the North Winning. They came to the regulator door, which Bobby Anderson had been operating on the day of the tragedy and they found the regulator within the door, closed. Charles Lambton opened the regulator fully to allow the maximum flow of air into the airway to keep any residual gasses at bay and the air ahead of the party fresh. They proceeded further in-by and came to the point where Geordie Hodgson and his young helper had put up the brattice cloth at the entrance to the West Winning and it was still intact. Shortly after passing the derelict West Winning, the party reached the barrier of criss-crossed baulks and props, which had hampered George Hodgson in his attempt to get to his trapped men. Removing enough of the timber to afford access further down the gallery they reached the point where the roof had undergone total collapse. A solid wall of stone faced them, and they knew immediately that they had a major operation ahead of them to penetrate this vast obstacle.

They stopped for the day and returned to the surface to plan the strategy required to overcome the barrier of stone. They knew they needed a team of the best stone-men employed at the pit. There was no shortage of volunteers to undertake the task. They wanted to retrieve the bodies of their dead colleagues and they needed the pit back in production to earn their livelihoods. It took them four whole weeks working round the clock to drive a tunnel through the stone between them and the destroyed North Winning face. They used the derelict West Winning, down which to stow the stone removed from the area of obstruction. On breaking through the stone barrier, the devastation that met them was chilling. All the timber had gone except for odd half-burnt timbers that were miraculously still in situation. The retrieval party made much quicker progress now, replacing the missing timbers as they went. Although the air coming into the working was fresh, the acrid smell of smoke was intense but as they got closer to what had been the coalface there was worse waiting for them. A group of charred human remains, some one-on-top of each other, stunned their senses. They counted the bodies as best they could. They couldn't agree between them whether there were seven or eight as at this stage they dare not touch them in case of further disintegration. Nearest to what remained of the coalface there were only charred body parts. They assumed these were the remains of the other four or was it five miners. It was a most macabre sight that met them and some of these hardened miners were vomiting at the sight before them, others were even crying. After the initial shock, they soon realised they had a job to do.

They had brought body bags down with them, made from tarpaulin. None of the bodies was readily recognisable and they started on the bodies that were most complete and with four limbs intact. They found among the remains of one body, a snuffbox with the initials L P, Laurence Pringle. Two more had engraved pocket watches revealing the owner's name, one of which had been a gift – *From, Mam and Dad on your twenty-first birthday, 20-03-83*; it had seen little over a year's service. The other had been his grandfather's watch, handed down to him on his grandfather's death. Both watches showed times within two minutes of each other; one showed 1.13 and the other 1.15, as the time of the initial blast. They continued with their gory task until they had tentatively identified eight of the bodies. The other four bodies they made up from the jumble of remains, allocating the body parts until they made some sort of match. There, amidst the scene of such a cruel ending, lay the remains of these poor souls. Until a short while ago they had been powerful men, full of vitality; qualities needed to be good hewers of coal, now sewn-up in makeshift bags. All the men present on the retrieval mission, agreed to a pact of secrecy concerning the dubious assessment of the remains of the four men working closest to the blast. The four bags containing their alleged remains carried no guarantee that they were 'as labelled.' One of these bags carried a label bearing the name, 'Joe Cogon.'

Chapter 3

The inquest presided over by Coroner, Daniel Dean, on the deaths of the twelve miners killed in the explosion at West Fell pit took place on the second Monday in September 1884, in 'The Coach and Horses' hotel in Gateshead. None of the jury, compiled from local businessmen, had any mining experience. In effect, the victims of the disaster and more importantly, their dependents, had no representation at the hearing. The coroner, Daniel Dean, had presided over several other disasters in the past, all of which he had returned verdicts that were favourable to the mine owners. Some cynics even went so far as to suggest he was in the pay of the owners. Coroner Dean further fuelled this opinion at the outset of the hearing, when he categorically stated that he would not recognise James Outram, a young solicitor, as the representative of the dead miners and their dependents. After several attempts by James Outram to interject during the early hearing, Daniel Dean's patience had reached its limit and leaning forward in his chair and looking menacingly in the direction of the young solicitor, he declared; 'It is unfortunate that the victims are not here to speak for themselves, for they were the only people who were working in the North Winning at the time of the explosion. On the strength of that, may I remind you Mr Outram, with due deference, that neither you nor anyone else who was not underground on the day the explosion occurred with such devastating effect, will be allowed to influence, or persuade the findings of my court. If you continue to attempt to subvert my authority, I will have no recourse but to have you removed from this building.'

The coroner resumed his hearing by allowing Charles Lambton, the viewer for West Fell colliery, and qualified in mining engineering, to give evidence, even though he had not been underground at the time of the explosion. He had led the group whose grim task had been to retrieve the bodies and make sure the pit was safe to return to full production. He confirmed that on reaching the regulator door, they found it fully closed. He described what he and his men had found on reaching the source of the explosion, making no specific reference to the 'four bags.' Charles Lambton also said in his evidence that he believed there had been a secondary explosion, more violent than the first and in rapid succession, brought about by the disturbance of the coal dust into the atmosphere of the mine, in effect, a coal dust explosion.

'Has this theory of yours been expounded, Mr Lambton?'

'As of now, no sir,' Lambton confessed.

'Then in that case, I cannot accept your theory as fact and as such I will disregard it as purely supposition at this stage.'

But one piece of evidence that Lambton mentioned, and which Coroner Dean had picked up on, was that a Davy lamp was found lying on its side next to one the bodies. It was a known fact that the Davy lamp, if not kept upright would malfunction and overheat, possibly being, in the opinion of Coroner Dean, the root cause of the initial explosion.

*

It was patently obvious to anyone who had a modicum of pit-sense, that the force of such a blast would knock everything over within the vicinity of that explosion and beyond. Nevertheless, as Coroner Dean at other explosion inquests over which he had presided, made great issue of the fact that a Davy lamp found on its side was once more the opportunity to berate the Davy lamp, blaming it for the primary cause of the tragedy.

George Hodgson and Bobby Anderson both gave evidence concerning the regulator door. Bobby Anderson swore under oath that he found the regulator closed when he commenced his duties on the back shift and it had remained closed until Deputy Hodgson had opened it later, on his examination halfway through the back shift. George Hodgson in his evidence corroborated what Bobby Anderson had said in as much as he, George Hodgson, had opened the regulator to three parts of its full capacity, halfway through the back shift. He said he closed the regulator fully after the explosion to prevent the air from feeding the fire.

'Tell me Mr Hodgson, to get to your district did you not have to pass through the regulator door in question at the start of your shift?' the coroner queried.

George Hodgson pondered the question and after realising the coroner had touched on a vital point, he reluctantly spoke knowing he had been in the wrong. 'I hadn't noticed, if I had, I would have opened it then.'

'Well, I suggest in your capacity as deputy, a position of responsibility, you should have noticed, Mr Hodgson.'

Also, under oath, the fore shift trapper lad, David Griffin, had contradictorily stated that he had left the regulator three parts open when he had finished his shift. With a state of stalemate existing between the evidence of the two young trappers, the coroner moved quickly on. He cared not which one of the two lads was to blame, he had his cause for the build-up of gas, and he concentrated the rest of his enquiry on the Davy safety lamp. It was a known fact among the mining community that the Davy lamp by design, was prone to malfunction if not kept upright, or if the inner gauze sheath became rusted. Coroner Dean knew this to be fact and had shown his lack of faith in Davy's design in the past and had used this fact in other enquiries, over which he had presided. Nevertheless, the miners at this pit preferred it over any other. He had his human error, in as much as the regulator should have been seventy-five per cent open and as such, this had played a major part in the tragedy. This left many people pointing their fingers at Bobby Anderson. Once again, the owners, exonerated of any blame, would be under no obligation to pay compensation to the dependents of the victims of the disaster. Yet again Coroner Dean had given the owners the verdict they wanted. His findings provoked several angry outbursts from the supporters of the widows and families of the dead men and those in the assembly who were supporters of fair play.

*

In summing up, Coroner Dean said, 'The erroneous setting of the air regulator door had caused a large build-up of volatile gas in the North Winning working and that the Davy lamp found on its side had ignited the gas causing death and devastation, proving once again, the Davy lamp was fundamentally unsafe in its design, and not fit for purpose in a gaseous mine like West Fell. As a result, this in his opinion, had contributed to the death of the twelve victims.'

This was not the first time this coroner had shown his dislike of the Davy safety lamp. The coroner once more reminded the court that Charles Lambton's theory on a 'coal dust explosion,' was unfounded and as such was inadmissible. If this evidence was indeed admissible, he still emphasised that in his opinion the Davy lamp had functioned as the catalyst that triggered off the explosion with devastating effect and the verdict on the death of the twelve victims was that of accidental death.

*

On leaving the 'Coach and Horses' hotel, Chris Paxton passed a knot of people gathered around a young man whom he recognised as the young solicitor, James Outram. Shouts of 'fix', emanated from the group and Outram stepped out in front of him, stopping him in his tracks. 'That was not a proper inquest; it was shambolic sir; serving no purpose but to exonerate you and your partner of all responsibility. Why Coroner Dean would not allow me to represent these good people fails me. Surely, they have a right to some say in any decision as to the cause of the deaths of their loved ones. Is that not, sir, what a coroner's court should be all about? The fact that the men bought the Davy lamps out of their own money on the advice of *your* viewer and *your* manager for use in *your* pit, must place some onus on you and your partner, does it not? The very same lamp sir, that Coroner Dean was so critical of in his summing up.'

Chris Paxton could find no answer to the young solicitor's protestations. And all he could say at that moment was, 'I am so sorry, terribly sorry. I remind you that the men had bought the Davy lamps themselves as some miners buy their own candles in non-gaseous mines; now if you will excuse me,' and he walked on to his waiting carriage.

'Not as sorry as we are,' he heard someone reply above the hubbub of angry derisive voices as they hurled verbal abuse after him.

'Will you and your partner be advising the use of the 'Geordie' lamp in future?' James Outram shouted after him, but the question went unanswered, Chris Paxton deliberately avoiding being the subject of any further confrontation on the matter.

*

On the journey back from Gateshead, Chris Paxton could not rid his mind of the young solicitor's reasoning and he had to agree, he had a point over the partners support for the Davy lamp and they should, in future consider a change to the 'Geordie' lamp, or to give its proper name the George Stephenson lamp, when the mine returned to production.

He arrived back at Shinwell Hall and headed straight to the library. 'I need a drink', he said as he entered, to no one in particular. He made a beeline to the large sideboard where a variety of cut crystal decanters stood on a silver tray. He selected a Cognac and poured a large measure into a brandy glass. He settled himself into a wing-backed chair by the fireplace. Taking a swig of brandy, he let it slowly trickle down his throat as he ruminated over the recent inquest. He cupped the glass between both hands and swirled it in a circular motion, warming the brandy to body temperature. He stared vaguely at the pattern of the fine mahogany top of a small drum table with its sunburst inlay, as he tried to recall the description given by Charles Lambton, of the scene that befell him and his men on reaching the coalface in the North Winning. Without any experience of conditions underground, he found this exceedingly difficult. Coming out of his macabre reverie, he watched the sparkling light as it diffused through the brandy, the cut pattern in the glass intermittently sent flashes of rainbow colours across the surface of the drum table next to him. He took another sip of the warming brandy, relishing both the bouquet and the palate.

'I'm glad that's over with,' he said to his wife, who on hearing him return, had followed him into the library and sat in a matching chair opposite her husband.

'Sorry darling, can I get you something?' he asked, raising his glass in her direction.

'No, not for me thanks, it's too early for me but I can understand your need,' she said, adding, 'how did it go?'

'Harrowing,' he replied. 'Almost as bad as the funeral; seeing all those grieving people again was most upsetting. It is obvious to all who attended the inquest, that it will take a long time for the dependents to get over this,' he continued, staring into his glass as he tried to assess what effect this tragedy would have on those widows and children. 'It's the young trapper boy, Robert Anderson, or Bobby as he is commonly known, for whom I feel sorry. There were many people in that coroner's court today, who believe he was responsible for the build-up of gas that killed those men.'

'And do you believe him?' Jemima asked.

'I would like to give him the benefit of the doubt, but it is always going to be one of those imponderables. He swears the regulator was closed completely on starting his shift and by the same measure, the trapper boy on the previous shift also swears he left the door regulated to seventy-five per cent open and there you have it.'

'What does Oliver Bell think of the outcome?' Oliver Bell, her husband's partner in the business operation at West Fell pit had advised Chris to stay away. Despite this, he had chosen to ignore his partner's advice.

'I haven't spoken to him on the subject and like most pit owners when these tragedies occur, they do not want the responsibility and the ramifications that would entail, so like the rest of the owners, he will be pleased with the outcome and as far as he is concerned, that will be the end of the matter. I know he will be anxious about how long the pit will be idle,' he said.

'And you?' his wife asked.

'I am genuinely concerned about the victims' dependents. You know I have no knowledge of the day-to-day happenings at the pit. I leave all that to the viewer and manager. But I will do all I can to see the dependents don't suffer unnecessarily, even though I may not be popular with the other owners,' he said.

'Is that wise? You could find yourself ostracised by the other pit owners. Don't get me wrong, I am with you on this, but it is going to be difficult.'

'I will have to take that chance. But I can't leave them to their own devices. From what I understand, the general rule of thumb in cases like this is that the owners will allow the widow to remain in the tied house if there are other boys in the family coming on, ready to go down the pit and make good hewers of coal.'

'I have an idea of my own. I will give my services free of charge to a charity concert at the Theatre Royal, Newcastle.'

'Are you sure that is what you want, Jemima?'

'I have never been so sure about anything in my life. We will make enquiries of Donald Forbes the manager of the Theatre Royal. I have filled the place before and I will fill it again once the public realise the proceeds go to boost the disaster fund. They are generous people in the Northeast – they look after one another especially in adversity. Leave this to me; the lark will leave her nest upon the dewy ground and rise again,' Jemima said enthusiastically.

*

The following Monday, Jemima and Chris got in touch with the management at 'The Theatre Royal', to discuss the possibility of putting on the charity concert in aid of the families of the dead miners of West Fell colliery.

'The theatre will not incur any cost as I will hire the theatre for the concert at my own expense,' Jemima promised.

'That won't be necessary Miss Martin,' manager Donald Forbes said using Jemima's stage name. 'Leave it with me I have an idea. In mid-November, we have a week of variety, when we could incorporate your concert into the Saturday night at the end of the week. I can't see any problem. It will be so good to see you gracing our stage again, they loved you here.'

*

The charity concert had proved a huge success. It had been a sell-out of over one thousand seats and Mimi Martin had brought the house down. Even though she hadn't performed for over four years, she was in great voice and the audience would not let her leave the stage. Again, as she took the umpteenth bow, she felt the adulation of an audience that had enjoyed her performance and she felt invigorated. The other performers who appeared on the variety bill all gave their performance money to the disaster fund. In all, the fund benefited the sum of £420 and Jemima and Chris made the sum up to £480. This handsome sum provided each dependent family with £40. The earnings of the miners who had perished, had averaged approximately twenty-six shillings per week; this sum equating to almost eight months wages in each case. It would never bring their loved ones back, but it would keep the wolf from the door for a little while.

Chapter 4

Jemima and Chris Paxton sat in the library of Shinwell Hall, he was reading *'The General Stud Book'* and she had taken up once more her copy of *'The Book of English Verse.'* Putting down his reading material, Chris Paxton was the first to break the silence between them.

'I have been thinking Jemima, about the business of what happens to the dependents of miners after, if; God forbid, their loved ones lose their lives at the pit or indeed, those that die in service of natural causes. Or as often happens, they become too old for the rigours of pit work.'

'In what respect my dear?'

'Well, I am thinking mainly of what can be done in the case of Alice Cogon and her son Thomas, and what will happen to the rest of the dependents of the disaster when their disaster fund money runs out, which won't be too far distant.'

'And have you come up with a solution?'

'I have an idea, but will it be a solution? Only time will tell.'

'So, what is this idea of yours? Come on, spit it out; I'm dying to hear what is on your mind.'

'Well before I give you all the facts, I will say this, I intend to put it before Oliver Bell only for the fact that he is my partner and as my partner he has a right to know of my intentions.'

'Come on Chris, please you are destroying me with your delay. You have me on tenterhooks with suspense.'

'Whether Oliver agrees or not, I have made up my mind and I will go it alone with my plan if needs be. I intend to build another six houses solely for the widows and the dependents, of miners killed or who die of natural causes while in service, or miners who have become too infirm through age, illness, or injury, to continue working at the mine. We will keep the dwellings simple in design to keep the cost down. We can build more as and when the need arises.'

'This is a very radical move Chris. I do not think you have the makings of a mine owner. You have too much of a conscience to sleep in your bed at night when things are going wrong for your employees.'

'I am inclined to agree with you darling. It was an eye-opener to injustice for me, when I attended the inquest on the twelve miners killed in the explosion. Just a couple of days since, one of the miners at West Fell pushed a pamphlet into my hand, written by Thomas Burt the Liberal MP for Morpeth and the representative of the Northumberland Miners. In that pamphlet, he states that John Wilson, Secretary of the Durham Miners Association, shares his views on many issues. Rather strange reading matter for a Durham County mine owner, you might think, and you would be right in thinking such thoughts. Maybe I should relinquish my share in West Fell colliery and move into politics on the Liberal ticket. I must admit the thought is not new to my mind. Do you know that since John Wilson's involvement with the Durham Miners Association, the coal owners of the Northeast now deem him unemployable, simply because they see him as a threat to their fortunes and not as a man of strong principles. Fortunately, for him and his family, he is now working full-time for the Association and the miners now pay his wages from their contributions. From what I hear, he could be the next working-class MP to take his seat in Westminster.

William Gladstone's Representation of the People Act, on ratification at the end of the year will enfranchise many miners and other working-class people, owning land worth more than £10. These people will need representation, whom until now, have had no representation whatsoever. I only hope that the present Liberal Party will be able to provide them with that representation. If not, then maybe a new party will emerge that will do the job in their best interest.' Chris Paxton expounded.

'I think you have much soul searching to do Chris before you are much older.'

'Do not concern yourself on my part my dear, I think politics would be too time-consuming and I would be away from you and Miles too much should I be fortunate enough to win a seat in parliament. Those journeys to London even using the modern railways would be too much for me to bear. So, I think we can rule that one out straight away, but Miles and I have other ideas besides the miners' housing which I explained to you. We had an interesting conversation the other night on the matter, and he has a plan in mind; something like a hospital fund for the miners, to cover sickness and hospitalisation. Let us say, a kind of health service, of which Miles has already indicated to me, his interest in such an endeavour. It is an idea he has nursed since qualifying from medical school. At the moment, it is only in the embryo stage. We need to do more planning first. But once established it would be an ideal opportunity for Miles to put his qualifications to good use.'

'Well, I am sure you will do whatever you think fit darling,' Jemima said. She thought of adding, 'one thing at a time,' but she declined.

Chris Paxton got up and placed his book back on the shelf. Excusing himself, he was about to leave the room when his wife spoke. 'One moment darling, I too have been giving some thought to Alice Cogon's future. We could possibly find something for her to do here, don't you think?'

I'm sure we can my dear, after all, the place is big enough. I will leave that to you. I'm sure, you will come up with something.'

'Well, it will be Christmas soon and we will need an extra pair of hands to help at the West Fell Children's Christmas Party.'

Chapter 5

1885

Chris and Miles Paxton were riding their hunters, Duke, and Warrior, in a fast workout on the five-furlong gallop. They reached the end of the gallop and brought their mounts to a jog trot. As they did so, they heard young, excited voices coming from the field at the end of the gallop. The field, which belonged to the colliery, butted onto the extreme edge of the Shinwell Hall estate. It was in this field that the head horse keeper kept the unbroken pit ponies on their arrival from Scotland. The two riders dismounted and walked their mounts up to the fence that separated the gallop from the field. They stood and watched as the two youths were enticing the unbroken ponies over to the fence with fists full of lush grass. Once a curious pony came alongside the fence in search of the grassy treat, the boys in turn jumped on the ponies' bare backs, and hanging on for grim life, they set off round the field at breakneck speed, hanging on to the ponies manes and riding only hands and heels.

'I recognise those two,' Chris Paxton said. 'The smaller of the two is Tommy Cogon, whose father was one of the victims of the explosion and indeed the boy *was* down the pit at the time of the disaster and survived.'

'Who is the other boy? You say you recognise him too, Father?'

'I do – he's Bobby Anderson, the trapper lad who was responsible for the controversial regulator door at the time of the disaster. Rightly or wrongly, many people in West Fell still attach blame on him for the explosion.'

The two lads had become great friends since that fateful day. The two ponies bucked and arched their backs violently as they attempted to dislodge the intruders from their backs.

Tommy soon went down the side of the pony and tucked himself into a ball as he rolled over and over before coming to rest up against the fence. He scrambled up the fence and sat on the top bar as he watched his friend attempt to master the black pony. He adopted a technique where he crouched over the pony's neck with his mouth near the pony's ear. His knees gripped the horse's withers, with his heels behind him where a saddle would be, had there been one. He whispered words of encouragement as he coaxed the unbroken pony first to a canter, then a trot and finally a walk as he headed back, proudly punching the air with his right hand extended high and his left hand gripping the pony's mane. He brought his charge to a halt in front of his mate.

'That's the way it's done Tommy,' he said haughtily.

Chris and Miles Paxton broke into warm applause at young Bobby Anderson's raw yet still accomplished equestrianism.

Realising they had been seen, they were about to take to their heels, but Chris Paxton called them back. They sheepishly made their way back to where Chris and Miles Paxton waited.

'That was no mean feat you pulled off there, young man. Where did you learn such skills?' Chris Paxton enquired.

'Nowhere, I just taught me self,' Bobby said. 'I just talk into their ears, nice and calm like.'

'That is a natural talent you have there, my lad, Chris Paxton said, adding, 'you are Robert Anderson are you not?'

'Aye, I am sir,' Bobby said and immediately wished he had given a false name. He knew he should not upset the mine owner in case he and his father should lose their jobs and the family, their home.

'Are you still working at the pit?'

'Aye I am sir, but I don't know whether I will be after what you've just seen us doin'. Also, I'm not happy since the disaster,' Bobby replied rather cautiously, wondering where the conversation was leading.

'Has it unnerved you?'

'No sir, nothing frightens me, but I'm blamed by many people for what happened that day.'

'Have you ever thought of putting your skills to better use?' Chris Paxton asked.

'No sir,' Bobby replied.

'Would you like to?'

'How d'y' mean?'

'How would you like to join a racing stable?'

'Aw man, y'r kiddin' sir.'

'I'm not, my lad. I mean every word.'

'I would love that sir. But who would have me?'

'Leave it to me. I will have a word with my trainer, Fraser Copeland, down at Richmond.'

'Not *the* Fraser Copeland?' Bobby said excitedly. But he'll never allow me near those thoroughbreds of his sir, let alone ride 'em; will he?'

'He will when I tell him of what we have witnessed today. You won't be a race rider straightaway you understand. Fraser Copeland will be the judge of that. You will have to start at the bottom and bottom being the operative word, 'mucking-out' at the stables for starters. Then you will have to work your way up. You will have to leave home and live-in at the stables. Talk it over with your parents and if you decide to go ahead, I will take you down to Richmond to meet Mr Copeland. I tell you what, young man, better still, how would you like to go to Thirsk races a week on Saturday? It is the first meeting of the new season, and we have a two-year-old filly running and the great Fred Archer will be riding at the meeting; sadly, not on my horse, more is the pity. It will give you an opportunity to meet Fraser Copeland and to discuss with him what working in a racing establishment entails. But it's up to Fraser Copeland; he will have the last say. It will give you the opportunity to see the professionals in action.'

'Eeh fancy goin' to the races and seein' Fred Archer ride. Are y' sure sir? Y' wouldn't kid us like that would y'?'

'I am serious young man. You and your friend here – it's Thomas Cogon, I believe – you shall be our guests. Dress in your Sunday best and I will send Thompson to pick you up outside 'The Infantryman', at nine o'clock en route for Gateshead railway station to catch the train to Thirsk. What shift are you on tomorrow?' Chris Paxton asked Bobby.

'Ah'm on back shift,' Bobby replied.

'Good then you can come up to the house tomorrow evening and you can ride one of our hunters; see how you shape up on a real horse,' Chris Paxton suggested.

'Oh, that would be great. Can Tommy come as well?'

'Of course. We still have my son's Welsh pony Star, he is a safe ride for a young rider like Tommy, and you can ride Silver, a grey twelve-year-old mare who is a real schoolmistress. Anything you don't know she will teach you herself. Miles graduated from Star to the hunters as he became more competent in the saddle.'

'That's very kind of y' sir,' Bobby replied eagerly. 'Say thanks Tommy,' and he gave his young friend a stiff nudge in the ribs.

'Thanks, Mr Paxton,' Tommy responded, rubbing his ribs at the same time.

'See you two tomorrow evening then. And after your ride, we will have some tea. I'll get cook to bake some biscuits for you.'

'Eeh, that would be a real treat. You're too kind, Mr Paxton,' Tommy muttered, shyly.

'Nobody has ever shown us such kindness,' Bobby added.

Chris and Miles Paxton remounted, wheeled their horses around and trotted off back up the five-furlong gallop.

'You are becoming an old sentimentalist,' Miles Paxton shouted across to his father, adding, 'I hope you know what you have let yourself in for.'

'They deserve it. Indeed, they need a break, and I am determined to give them just that, and it would really top the day off, if Jed Smyth rides Indian Empress into first place in the two-year-old fillies' race. In the meantime, I am looking forward to seeing young Bobby ride a real horse tomorrow evening.'

*

Bobby Anderson and Tommy Cogon headed back down to West Fell village hopping and skipping with glee, unable to believe what had just taken place.

'Nip me Tommy. Nip me hard, to prove I'm not dreamin' man,' Bobby Anderson said incredulously.

'No man, it's true enough, but I thought we were in for a beltin' with a ridin' crop, never mind ridin' the squire's horses and goin' to the races with him and Fraser Copeland,' Tommy Cogon replied.

'Aye and don't forget the tea and biscuits, tomorrow,' Bobby reminded his friend, adding 'Nobody'll believe us.'

*

The following evening the two young friends made their way to the Hall and reported to the stables. Thompson greeted them with an air of reluctance. 'Ain't ever known such a thing. I think the master has taken leave of his senses, invitin' the village scruffs up to the house.'

The pony and the hunter were all tacked up and tied to a hitching post in the stable yard together with Chris and Miles' hunters. 'You take care of them horses while they're in your charge and don't go doin' anything daft. I still say the master's mad.'

Across the stable yard came Chris Paxton and his son Miles. Thompson bowed and tipped his cap on seeing 'the master.' Casting a sheepish glance in their direction without making eye contact and hoping they had not caught any of his remarks.

'Thompson has got everything ready I see. Thank you, Thompson. Now then, are you two lads ready for a ride?' Chris Paxton asked.

They both nodded without speaking. 'Come now, have you suddenly lost your tongues?' Chris Paxton prompted, reassuringly.

'Aye, we are sir,' replied Bobby, ever ready to take the lead. Tommy was more reserved and quite prepared to take one step back from his more forward friend.

'Have you ever ridden other than bareback? Truthfully now, for I need to know for your own safety.'

'No sir, we haven't. But I'm sure it's goin' t' be comfier than the backs of them ponies,' Bobby opined.

'Right then let us have a little run through the tack and its uses. Just to familiarise you with the reins etcetera as they are your steering gear. We will go on a hack round the drive until we get to where it joins the five-furlong gallop and if you feel up to it Bobby, you can try a trot, then a canter and if I think it safe for you to continue, then a steady gallop.'

After the lads had received instruction from an unenthusiastic Thompson, on steering their mounts around the yard, Chris Paxton called them across to join them and he said, 'I think we can venture out now Thompson.'

'So be it Master,' Thompson replied, grudgingly.

The party of riders left the yard at a steady walking pace and when Chris Paxton was satisfied the two lads were comfortable, he upped the pace to a steady trot. The party of riders turned into the wooded area to the rear of the estate. Chris and Miles Paxton assumed a rear position where they could keep a diagnostic eye on the two lads and their mounts. Tommy was less synchronised with his pony than Bobby was, atop the grey mare, which is what Chris expected. He thought Bobby's style was something else. He and his horse were in complete unison, and he found it hard to believe that the lad had not had equestrian tuition. They continued at a leisurely trot until they reached the entrance to the five-furlong gallop where Chris called the two lads to a halt.

'Now then Bobby I want you to canter down the gallop. Give us time to get further down the gallop so we can view your ability and at my signal I want you to canter towards us and slowly bring Silver back to a trot and return to us.'

Leaving Bobby and his mount at the start of the gallop, they proceeded up the gallop until they were about a furlong and a half distant. They halted and assumed a position at the edge of the gallop and Chris Paxton signalled for Bobby to commence his canter. Bobby extended his arms and kicked the mare into action. He cantered toward the party ahead of him, struggling not with his mount, but with himself to maintain a canter, and not to break into a full gallop. He knew there and then this was what he wanted to do in the future. After passing the watching group Bobby reined his mare to a walk, turned her and jog-trotted back.

'How did that feel, Bobby? You certainly looked at home in the saddle for someone untrained.'

'I loved it, sir. When can I go at a gallop?'

'Do you feel you are up to it?'

'I'd like to give it a go.'

'Right you are. But the first time you feel things are not going right, you pull her up, do you hear?'

'Are you sure you are doing the right thing here father. The lad is very inexperienced', Miles Paxton said, showing his concern.

'I think the lad has shown enough natural ability so far, to let him have a go. Let us say I am taking a calculated risk. I will stand by my beliefs; the boy has something special.'

'Can ah ask you something sir before I go back to the start? Can I shorten me stirrups? It'll allow me to get further up the horse's neck. I like to talk in the horse's ear when I'm ridin'. I'm no expert as y' know but I feel I can get the horse balanced better. That's just my idea of things. It's my belief that that's how I stayed on the backs of them unbroken pit ponies,' Bobby said, trying not to sound too clever.

'Count me out of this one father; on your shoulders, be this,' Miles Paxton stated with concern.

'I just want to see how good the lad really is,' his father replied, and he jumped down to adjust the lad's irons. He tightened the nearside stirrup leather two notches and went around the other side of Silver. 'How does that feel Bobby?' Chris asked as he hitched another two notches on the offside stirrup leathers.

'Give it one more,' Bobby suggested.

'Are you sure?' Chris Paxton asked, he reluctantly pulled another notch on the stirrup leather. 'How does that feel?'

Miles Paxton cringed at his father's encouragement of Bobby's reckless technique.

Bobby squeezed his knees into the area just below Silver's withers and pushed his legs back towards the horse's hindquarters. He felt comfortable and totally at one with his mount.

'Perfect sir,' Bobby replied.

'Now remember what I said. I want you and my mare back here safely. I'm taking a risk here Bobby. Nevertheless, I have faith in your ability,' he reminded the young man.

Bobby turned the mare, while Chris and Miles watched, as the young rider cantered back down the gallop.

'He certainly moves well father. I'll give you that. But I hope he comes back in one piece.'

From their viewpoint, Chris and Miles Paxton watched as Bobby turned the mare at the bottom of the gallop. He got his mount composed and started off back. By the time Bobby and Silver passed the watching group, Silver was travelling at a full gallop.

'Did you ever see anything like that in your life before Miles? It was like poetry in motion. I have never seen Silver travel at speed like that before. Just imagine that style in a close finish in a horse race.

The boy is a natural. I am getting him down to Richmond as soon as possible. Miles you have just seen my future jockey in action'

'I have to admit I share your enthusiasm. A most impressive demonstration Father, all he needs is experience in race riding and that is up to Fraser Copeland.'

'One thing I have no doubt about is that he will deal with the rough and tumble of the racecourse and show no fear,' Chris Paxton said confidently.

Bobby had re-joined the group with a wide smile across his face.

'How did that look sir?'

'Well Bobby, I would be telling lies if I said it wasn't different. I have never seen anyone ride so short. You certainly are unique in your style. It was my pleasure watching you and you can ride my horses any time you wish'

'Thanks sir. That's kind of you,' Bobby replied.

The group made their way back to Shinwell Hall, still picturing in their minds what they had just witnessed. In young Tommy's mind he pictured tea and biscuits.

Chapter 6

Come the Saturday, the two boys were extremely excited about attending Thirsk races. All spruced up in their Sunday best and their hair slicked down with Bobby's father's cheap pomade, they waited for Thompson to pick them up to take them to Gateshead railway station. They had to suffer much leg pulling from villagers as they stood outside 'The Infantryman' public house.

'You two young 'uns aren't waitin' for the pub to open are y' now; looking all scrubbed up like y' are. Are y' waitin' for y' girlfriends. Y' sure y' know its Saturday' and not Sunday?' reminded Mrs Newton and both lads reddened with embarrassment.

'I wish that Thompson fella would hurry up Tommy,' Bobby Anderson said.

'I'm thinkin' the squire was havin' us on,' Tommy Cogon replied.

'Or he's changed his mind,' Bobby retorted.

*

After a short while, a carriage appeared from around the corner, drawn by two fine horses in gleaming tack and polished hooves. The two lads climbed on board and took their places inside just as two pitmen, returning home off shift, their faces besmirched with coal grime, passed the coach.

'Bugger me Arthur; I've seen it all now. Is it the brightness of the sun after bein' down the pit or is that Bobby Anderson and Tommy Cogon, goin' off like toffs for the day?' Stan Parkin joked.

'No, that's them alright Stan, but I'd like to know where the pair o' them are off to, lookin' so fine,' Dave Simpson replied.

Being the elder of the two, Bobby took charge as usual and shouted, 'Drive on Thompson,' in a mock cultured voice, stifling a laugh as he did so.

'Thirsk races, here we come. Yippee!' Tommy shouted.

'Did y' hear that, Stan? Bloody hell, they're off to Thirsk races. How the hell has that come about and in such style?'

'Ah think the squire has been hittin' the claret a bit too much, Dave.'

*

Chris Paxton met the boys at Gateshead railway station and gave them each a third class return ticket to Thirsk. Take care of your tickets and I'll see you both when we get to Thirsk where we will walk the rest of the way to the course together. Chris had a quick word and slipped a sovereign into Bobby's palm.

'This will pay for your admission onto the course; buy a race card, get you a bite to eat, and remember, no gambling.'

'Right sir, we'll see you there,' Bobby said. Being the elder of the two, he took the lead in the day's events, as usual.

*

On arrival at Thirsk, Chris Paxton and his party made their way on the half mile walk from the station to the racecourse. Knowing their place, the two friends subserviently brought up the rear. At the racecourse entrance, Chris Paxton introduced the two lads to his trainer and his jockey Jed Smyth.

'These two young lads are employees of mine, both of whom survived the gas explosion at West Fell Colliery last year,' Chris Paxton said tentatively, not knowing what response the introduction might generate. There was a charged silence between the lads and the trainer and his jockey. Jed Smyth touched the peak of his cap and offered a weak bow, aimed mainly at Chris Paxton than the two lads. He acknowledged the two lads with a weak handshake and immediately wiped his hand instinctively, down the leg of his breeches.

Copeland remained noncommittal, but his silence spoke volumes. Chris Paxton realised he had done the wrong thing in inviting the lads to the races, as his trainer moved contemptuously on without saying a word. The opportunity for Bobby to meet Fraser Copeland informally, had passed and Chris Paxton knew it had not been a good idea. It would not all be lost as a day at the races would still stand the lads in good stead, especially young Bobby.

'After racing, I will meet you back at the railway station for the train back to Gateshead,' Chris Paxton instructed and quickly caught up with his trainer and jockey before they passed through the entrance to the course marked, 'Owners, Trainers and Jockeys.'

'We will sir. Thank you very much,' Bobby shouted after his mentor, as he disappeared through the gate. Bobby opened his palm and looked down at the sovereign.

'Bloody hell; ah've never had a sovereign before,' Bobby blasphemed.

'Y' still haven't,' Tommy reminded him,' adding, 'half that's mine, remember.'

*

Jed Smyth left the other two and headed for the jockey's tent before changing into his silks before weighing out for his ride in the first race.

'Was that wise Chris? For a moment, I thought you had lost your senses back there. Do you not think you are showing more concern for your employees than is necessary? Showing concern for them is one thing; socialising with them is another. I am trying to be as delicate as I can here, but two boys as young as those two, if you get my drift Chris. You could set tongues wagging.'

Chris Paxton ran his trainer's comments over in his mind. He felt uncomfortable, and he now regretted his actions. 'I can see your point of view Fraser, but it is done now. I'm determined not to let the opportunity pass and while agreeing with you, I had hoped you would give Robert Anderson the opportunity to meet you. I promise you, I have seen his style, albeit only once on a real horse. Nevertheless, I can assure you, the boy has a natural ability which needs nurturing, and you are the man to bring that out in him.'

'Send him down to Richmond and I will give him a formal interview. I will bear in mind that he comes recommended by your good self, Chris. One thing in his favour; I have employed several ex-pit lads over the years I have been training racehorses and none of them has been afraid of hard work. Now let us have a good afternoon of sport.'

'He has a natural way with the pit ponies, and I think he will make an important contribution to your workforce, and I would appreciate you giving him his chance. Now, as you say let us enjoy the sport and may 'Indian Empress' record her first win,' Chris Paxton replied.

*

The atmosphere of the racecourse excited the two newcomers to horse racing. The smell of the newly mown turf, the hustle and bustle of the crowd, this new experience excited the two companions, and they loved every minute of the time on the racecourse. The roar of 'they're off,' as the starter's flag dropped at the start of each race and again the rising crescendo as the horses passed the finishing post. Bobby took great interest in the styles of the jockeys, particularly the great Fred Archer, who was riding at Thirsk for the first time. Bobby knew he didn't venture this far north as a rule. What Bobby noticed as he studied the different jockey's riding styles was that there wasn't much difference between any of them at all except for Fred Archer. They all appeared to ride very upright, and they all went off pell-mell for the finishing post – it seemed to him that none of them had given much thought to race tactics and the ability of the horse beneath them; in other words, they applied no tactics to their race riding. It was now the fourth race on the card and Fred Archer had ridden two winners.

The next race on the card was special in as much as Chris Paxton's two-year-old filly, Indian Empress was running for the second time. They watched as Jed Smyth cantered his mount down to the six-furlong start, wearing the black and white silks adopted by Chris Paxton. Bobby Anderson looked in awe as these finely muscled animals moved at speed on the racecourse. Seeing these beautiful animals in action enthralled both the young lads. Bobby watched enraptured at every rippling muscle as the highly conditioned horses performed to the best of their ability.

The runners for the fourth race, on reaching the starting point, circled patiently at the start. The starter called them in and a shout from the grandstand on the opposite side of the course indicated that the race was underway. The lads strained their eyes and necks to make out Chris Paxton's black and white colours. With two furlongs to go, they could clearly make out the black and white colours at the head of affairs, leading by two lengths. Inside the final furlong with the members of the crowd who had backed the horses leading the charge to the finishing line yelling their encouragement, Indian Empress still had the edge on the rest of the runners. Bobby and Tommy jumped up and down as the first three horses passed the winning post almost together. The crowd waited anxiously until the race result appeared on the runners and rider's board. Indian Empress's race card number, seven, occupied third slot. The board also showed the distance between the first three was a short head and a neck. She had just been touched off in the last strides of the race.

'That was unlucky. I thought the boss's horse was goin' t' win it,' Tommy said.

'I think that Jed fella could have ridden a better race. He made too much of her early on. I'd have held her up longer and let her go in the closing stages of the race. He burnt her out before the last furlong.'

'What d' you know about race ridin' Bobby Anderson? It's the first time we've ever been t' the races,' Tommy protested.

'Maybe, but you wait, I've me own ideas of how to ride a racehorse. Another thing, all these jockeys ride too long in the stirrups and too upright in the saddle. Notice how short Fred Archer rides,' Bobby said confidently.

'Listen t' the expert; what would you know?' Tommy teased.

'You mark my words Tommy. I'm goin' to be a great jockey one day.'

Following the trip to Thirsk Races, Bobby Anderson was hooked on joining a racing stable and with Chris Paxton's assistance, he secured a place with Fraser Copeland at his stables at Richmond, as a stable hand.

Chris Paxton took on Tommy Cogon as a groom and under the supervision of Thompson, part of his duties was the exercising of the horses when they had not worked the day before and the maintenance of the harness, saddles, and carriages at the Hall stables. Jemima had created a position for Alice Cogon as the assistant cook to Mrs Davison or 'Davison' as the household knew her. As Tommy was the groom, he qualified for the accommodation in the mews above the stables, which was big enough for him and his mother. Now they could leave their colliery house in West Fell of their own accord; the threat of eviction removed.

*

It was Bobbie's first week at Richmond Gill stables, and he was 'mucking- out' a box with his back to the door when a tap on his shoulder surprised him. Turning around he saw Jed Smyth standing in front of him with a stern look on his face, to which Bobby didn't take too kindly.

'I hope you are making a good job of that, pit-lad,' he said menacingly, kicking a clump of manure over the area of the floor that Bobby had already cleaned.

'What's your problem?' Bobby retorted.

'You are... pit-yacker,' Jed Smyth replied.

'I'll ask you once, politely Smyth, don't call me that or next time I won't be so polite,' adding, 'you stick t' ridin' horses badly an' I'll stick to improvin' me style.'

'What style? You are like a monkey on a mangle with your knees up the horse's neck and your head round the horse's ears,' Jed Smyth replied, scathingly.

'Just wait and see, I'll soon 'ave your job, Smyth. I won't have t' improve much to better you.'

'In your dreams, pit-yacker.'

Before Jed Smyth had time to move, Bobby Anderson floored him with a right hook that sent the stable jockey sprawling face down in the manure-laden straw.

'Get out and leave me t' get on with me work. I did warn y',' Bobby reminded him.

Jed Smyth picked himself up and knocked loose muck from his jodhpurs.

Glaring at Bobby, and rubbing his jaw, he said, 'Don't think you are getting away with it. The boss will get to know about this.'

'Go ahead, I'll just deny it. Nobody saw what happened. It'll be my word against yours. But I'll tell y' somethin' Smyth, y' won't be callin' me 'pit-yacker' anymore and I do 'ave more style than you.'

Chapter 7

Chris Paxton's filly, Indian Empress had turned three years old on the first of January and Fraser Copeland was preparing her for her place in the line-up for the 1885 renewal of the fillies' classic, The Oaks, run over one and a half miles on the Derby course at Epsom Downs in June. The fact that Fraser Copeland had not summoned him to his office, since the incident with Jed Smyth, led Bobby Anderson to believe that he had got his message across. By the same measure, Jed Smyth while cagey whenever they met had got Bobby's message and had not once referred to him as a pit-yacker.' Indeed, in the time that Bobby had been at Richmond Gill Stables he was now riding work regularly, especially Chris Paxton's horses and especially his filly, Indian Empress. She was a beautiful chestnut and Bobby loved her. She was a saint on the gallops. When Bobby had completed his grooming of her, her coat gleamed, and her muscles rippled. She was ready for the Oaks at Epsom and Chris Paxton had arranged with Fraser Copeland for Bobby to travel down to Epsom on Thursday 4 June, with the filly in readiness for the big race the following day. As Copeland's stable jockey, much to Bobby Anderson's consternation, Jed Smyth as usual would have the ride on Indian Empress.

The following day, Bobby led Indian Empress to the course from the racecourse stables and housed her in the pre-parade ring where he carried out her final grooming and talked to her constantly to keep her as calm as possible. As the time for the race drew near, Bobby took his charge into the parade ring, calmly talking words of encouragement into Indian Empress's ear. She looked a picture. In the centre of the parade ring Bobby could see Chris Paxton, Fraser Copeland and Jed Smyth waiting for the bell to ring for the jockeys to 'get mounted.'

'Jed Smyth will be driving you from pillar to post, girl,' he whispered in Indian Empress's ear. Not the way I would do things at all, me beauty. I would take much more care of y' early on. I'd just get y' nicely settled towards the rear of the field until we got to Tattenham Corner. Then we would make our move as we hit the home straight and I would be up your neck. That would take pounds out of the saddle, makin' it easier for you, me darlin.' We would cut through them like a hot knife through butter. Indian Empress pricked her ears up and looked down at Bobby as if she understood every word Bobby was saying to her. It was a love affair between the horse and groom. Bobby glanced across to the centre of the parade ring and saw Fraser Copeland beckon him and Indian Empress to join them. Jed Smyth took the reins from Bobby and with a leg up from his trainer he was in the saddle.

'How is she in herself Bobby?' Chris Paxton asked.

'She's fine sir, she couldn't be better, cool as a cucumber. I only wish it were me up there in the saddle. I know we could win it for y'.'

'You'll get your chance Bobby. Just let me work a little longer convincing Fraser Copeland. I believe in you. But for the moment Jed Smyth is still the stable jockey.'

Jed Smyth must have heard the end of their conversation and he looked down from the saddle and once again gave Bobby one of his now familiar contemptuous glares as he left the paddock for the starting post. Jed Smyth was not a bad jockey, but he learnt to ride in the same old style as everyone else, like most of today's jockeys. Bobby being self-taught, riding the pit ponies bareback had created a style of riding that was unique to him.

He found a vantage point with the rest of the handlers from where they could view the race. It was impossible to see the start from ground level, but the usual roar from the crowd in the top tier of the grandstand, indicated to everyone else that the race was underway. The first Bobby saw of his filly sporting the black and white silks carried by Jed Smyth was at the top of the hill, before the descent into Tattenham Corner. Once again, the whole field had taken off like a cavalry charge. Bobby looked on in despair as he watched the final part of the race unfold. Coming around the final bend into the straight, Indian Empress was making no forward progress under the driving of Jed Smyth. As the race reached the final furlong, Jed Smyth frantically took up his whip, coming down heavily on Indian Empress's hindquarters without any response from the tiring filly.

'Put the bloody whip away y' fool. Can't y' see she's given her all.' Bobby yelled and several of the other stable lads looked round at him in surprise, muttering to themselves, knowing that if his trainer was within earshot of his outburst and there was a strong chance of facing discipline. Nevertheless, Bobby knew he was right, and he could not wait to replace Smyth in the saddle of Chris Paxton's horses. He watched totally dejected as his beloved charge trailed in eighth, in a field of ten runners.

Bobby met the horse and jockey as they came off the course. He slipped a lead rein through the ring of the bit as he led the pair back to the paddock. He glowered at Smyth as he took his sleeve and wiped whip welts from his filly's quarters. There was no exchange of words between Bobby and Jed Smyth on the walk back to the unsaddling enclosure. Bobby continued to glare at the stable jockey, but a sheepish Smyth averted Bobby's glowering looks. Bobby was seething that his master and mentor's dream was over for another year. On the approach to the unsaddling area, Fraser Copeland and Chris Paxton joined them.

'They just ran her off her legs sir,' he offered lamely, adding, 'she just didn't stay,' as an afterthought.

'Don't you think you all went off too quickly? Maybe you could have held her up instead of charging off like the rest,' Chris Paxton suggested, bearing in mind what Bobby Anderson had told him.

'She was well beaten four furlongs out sir. I would suggest her best distance maybe a mile,' Smyth suggested.

'Then why the hell did you take-up your whip on my horse in the last furlong of a twelve-furlong race?' Chris Paxton countered angrily and glanced towards Fraser Copeland as he did so, giving him a long stern look.

His trainer said nothing, content to allow Chris Paxton to continue the chastisement of his jockey. He concluded with his final scathing statement, 'That is the last time you will ride for me Smyth, a very disappointing performance on your part.'

Bobby Anderson listened in silence as he took over the care of Indian Empress in readiness for the long journey back to Yorkshire.

'Bobby, get as much practice in, on the gallops as you can, as you will be riding my horses in future.' He was looking at Copeland when he made his statement. 'If you don't approve Fraser then I am afraid I will have to find myself another trainer.'

Chapter 8

Alice Cogon entered the dining room where Jemima Paxton was having tea with Sally Binney. 'Excuse me Ma'am; there is a black man at the door who is enquiring after you.'

'Do you mean an unwashed miner, Alice?'

'No, he is black skinned and presented himself at the front entrance saying he met you in New York back in 1860 and that he knew your father Ma'am,' Alice explained.

'My goodness, Thomas Mays. It can't be after all these years. I will come with you Alice and greet him. Excuse me Sally.'

Alice re-opened the front door and there stood Thomas Mays.

'Mr Mays, come in, come in. After all this time, how good to see you again. Sorry we were slow to admit you into our home, but your arrival was announced rather cryptically.'

Thomas Mays stepped inside and shook Jemima's hand.

'Turning to Alice,' she said, 'could you set another place at the table for Mr Mays, please Alice? Let us go to the dining room; we were about to have tea, when you arrived,' Jemima Paxton explained.

'Oh, I am sorry for interrupting your meal. If you would rather I wait here, in the hall, it would be no problem,' the newcomer suggested.

'Not at all Thomas, please join us. You are more than welcome, and we can chat over our sandwiches and cake. What has brought you to Shinwell Hall and how did you find us?' Jemima asked, as they made their way to the dining room. On entering, Jemima and her Black visitor joined Sally Binney at the table where she was awaiting Jemima's return.

'Sally, this is Mr Thomas Mays, who has travelled all the way from America to be here with us. Sally was a great friend of my late mother Mr Mays, and we all treat her as one of the family.'

Turning to Sally, Thomas Mays offered his hand, 'My pleasure Ma'am, I'm sure.'

'I'm pleased to meet you Mr Mays. Jemima has told me of your chance meeting in New York, and of your association with her late father.'

'Now Thomas, what a pleasant surprise. Is this a holiday trip or is it business that has brought you back to us today?'

'I'm sorry to just drop in on you like this without any prior arrangement, but I did not know where you were living these days. I have to say; it took detective skills that I was not aware that I possessed. On arrival in England, I started my line of enquiry at the Haymarket Theatre. There, they gave me the address of your agent in London. I tracked him down and he told me that you had retired from the stage, and you were living at Shinwell Hall, near Standale, here in Durham County. Quite a place you have here. It is uncanny that I am here in the northeast of England on business at Robert Stephenson's locomotive works, in Newcastle upon Tyne, almost next door to you. I am here on behalf of the New York and Northern Railroad, to place an order for four new locomotives, which Robert Stephenson's company are building to our specifications. If they can come up with the goods, on the first off, then the contract is theirs. I have an appointment with their chief engineer at their works tomorrow. It will take a while to finalise. So, I'll be around for some time yet.'

Alice Cogon returned with an extra place setting for their visitor.

'Would you prefer tea or coffee Thomas?' Jemima enquired.

'Alice, could you clear this away and we will start again with Mr Mays as our guest.'

Alice Cogon returned to the kitchen.

'What was that all about, Alice,' Davison the cook asked.

'Seems a visitor has turned up from America of all places, and they're all startin' tea again.'

Amusingly, since taking up her position at Shinwell Hall, she had taken up a second accent, which she herself admitted was her 'posh' accent. This she kept for her employers and their visitors.

In the dining room, the conversation between Jemima and Thomas Mays continued. 'If you are here for a while you must be our guest. I refuse to let you book into a hotel when we have all the room here. It will be so pleasant to have someone stay, and we have so much catching up to do. So much has happened since we last met.'

'That is most kind of you, Jemima. Are you sure your husband won't mind?'

'These days, since I retired from the stage, he spends most of his time at the races or with his racehorses down at Richmond. Today he is at Catterick Bridge, he should be back about six or seven o'clock.'

'Has he many horses?' Thomas asked.

'He has four horses in training, all fillies, with Fraser Copeland, one of the leading trainers in the north of England and here we have three hunters and five working horses, plus our son Miles's pony which he has long outgrown. Even so, we don't have the heart to part with her. She is such a darling. Do you ride, Thomas?'

'I do indeed, Jemima; not as often as I would like to nowadays, I might say.'

'Then you should stay with us during your time in England. I think we can kit you out with some attire. Now let us have some tea,' Jemima declared.

With tea over, they removed to the winter room situated on the other side of the house, where it caught the sun. At this point in the proceedings, Sally Binney excused herself.

'If you don't mind Jemima, I will retire to my room until dinner. I have some letter writing I need to catch-up on.'

'Not at all Sally,' Jemima replied.

'It has been so nice to meet you Thomas,' Sally said, politely.

Thomas Mays stood, in response to Sally leaving. 'Likewise, I'm sure. It has been my pleasure Sally; until later,' he said.

*

Chris Paxton arrived home from the races at Catterick Bridge and was surprised to find their visitor from America. 'How long is it since that uncanny meeting in New York, Thomas? You don't look a year older than how I remember you.'

'It is almost twenty-five years ago, would you believe? You are looking good yourself Chris. As for me, I think I've put on a few pounds here and there, especially here,' and he patted his midriff. 'As I was telling your good lady, I'm here to buy locomotives; four in all, if Stephenson can meet our specifications.'

'I'm sure they will come up with the goods. They are world leaders. My brother and brother-in-law, do much business with Robert Stephenson's company, producing specialised castings at their foundry in Standale.'

'I have an appointment with Stevenson's production manager on Monday. That gives me all the weekend to enjoy you and Jemima's kind hospitality and to see some of the places of interest. By the way, how did you do at the races?'

'The races were competitive, with some exciting close finishes. I had no runners today. Although, I have a runner at High Gosforth Park, Newcastle tomorrow. She is a three-year-old filly called Indian Empress and I am giving a young local boy his first ride in public. He has some revolutionary ideas on how to race ride. He learnt his riding on the bare backs of the unbroken pit ponies when he was a boy. I have seen him carry out this feat on one occasion and I must say it was most impressive. He has also impressed my trainer Fraser Copeland on the gallops down at Richmond.'

'Are you sure you are doing the right thing darling?' Jemima asked, joining in on the conversation. 'What about Jed Smyth? How does he feel about losing the ride?'

'Jed Smyth, to whom my wife has referred, was my ex-jockey who rode the filly badly at Epsom in the Oaks, in the summer. He took-up the whip on my horse that had nothing left to give and I said then that he would not ride another horse of mine. To me the horse is paramount, and I am afraid Smyth has violated that criterion and has paid the penalty,' Chris Paxton said indignantly.

'Wow! That's some spot decision to make Chris if you don't mind me saying so. He must have put in one helluva bad performance that day, to suffer such wrath.'

'He certainly did. He never put the horse in the race with any chance. Therefore, I am giving Robert Anderson his chance. I am interested to see him put his new riding style into action.'

'What has he got that is so revolutionary Chris?' Thomas Mays asked, curious to learn more.

'Well, he rides much shorter than the other jockeys and he crouches high up the horse's withers, his legs angled towards the back end of his saddle. 'Would you believe, he talks to his mount throughout the race and having worked down my mine, he knows no fear. Not that he rides recklessly you understand.'

'I'm sure if you thought otherwise darling, he would not be replacing Jed Smyth tomorrow. You have whetted my appetite for the race, so I have decided to accompany you and Thomas to Newcastle tomorrow to see your protégé in action for myself,' Jemima Paxton stated.

'That would be wonderful my dear. I am sure I speak for both Thomas and I when I say we would be delighted with your company. Who knows, you could be 'Lady Luck,' Chris replied.

'I'll say hear, hear to that Jemima,' Thomas Mays added.

'Splendid, so be it, the races at High Gosforth Park it is then,' Chris Paxton declared. 'Oh! By the way, I heard from Frazer

Copeland, that Jed Smyth has been offered a job riding for a Maharaja in India. He is to take up the new post at the end of the current season.'

Chapter 9

Chris Paxton's party stood in the parade ring at 'High Gosforth Park', watching Indian Empress as she paraded prior to the third race on the card. It was the filly's first race since the Oaks at Epsom in June and her first on the recently established new racecourse on what was formerly the Brandling Family's estate and country home. In 1881, the Brandling family sold the whole 850-acre estate and house for £60,000 and the buyers founded the new racecourse called 'High Gosforth Park'.

Indian Empress looked a picture. She was definitely on her 'toes' and did little jog trots as she circled the parade ring. The group of jockeys left the weighing room and made their way to their relative connections gathered in little groups about the parade ring. Bobby Anderson dressed proudly in the now familiar black and white silks of Chris Paxton, spotted the Paxton group, and joined them in the centre of the ring. He touched the peak of his cap with his whip in acknowledgement. Fraser Copeland was the first to speak.

'I don't have to tell you how to ride your race today Bobby. This is the day we put your riding theory to the test. All I have to say is to bring yourself and the Empress back unharmed. Good luck to you both.'

'I will second that,' added Chris Paxton.

'Good luck from me too,' was Jemima's wishes. Thomas said nothing as he stood and listened to the connections wish their young rider good luck before he left the paddock.

Fraser Copeland gave Bobby a leg-up into the saddle and he circled the horse a couple of times to settle her before he went out onto the racecourse for the mile and a half start. 'How do those irons feel Bobby?' Fraser Copeland asked cautiously, knowing there were revolutionary changes in the adjustment of the stirrup leathers when Bobby was in the saddle.

It was a short canter to the mile and a half start, situated to the right of the stands. There were twelve runners taking part in the race, which was for maiden three-year-olds. Judged on looks alone, Indian Empress would have won already. The owners and trainer accompanied by Thomas Mays took their places in the grandstand and focused their eyes on the horses milling round at the start.

On the orders of the starter, the twelve runners formed a line and on achieving some semblance of a straight line, he dropped his flag, and the usual cry of 'they're off' came from the stands. Bobby Anderson was in no hurry to jump his filly off with the rest but was content to settle her in at the back of the field. The runners reached the far side of the course and still Bobby hadn't moved a muscle on Indian Empress. He was four lengths adrift as the field began the long sweeping turn before the straight. Ahead of him, the rest of the field still had a four lengths advantage. He leaned forward and stroked his filly's neck as he whispered in her ear, 'come on girl, this is where we start to race,' and he let out a minimum of rein. His horse immediately quickened her pace and quickly closed the gap between her and the rest of the field. As the field took the long left-hand turn into the straight, Bobby took-up a position on the inside rail. There were a lot of tired horses coming back to him and he soon passed four of the runners on the inside with his horse still on the bridle. Coming off the bend and into the straight there was still four furlongs to run.

As the runners turned into the straight Chris Paxton peered down the course in search of his black and white colours. He turned to

Fraser Copeland. 'Is he still in the saddle Fraser? He is crouched so low that it looks as if my horse is riderless?'

Bobby kept his inside position on the rails, so much so that at times his boot was rubbing the running rail, as he and his mount took the shortest route home. In front of him, jockeys were whirling their whips like windmills. As more horses tired, they began to drift to the right leaving a gap on the rails that Bobby could have driven a coach and four through. With two more furlongs to go, Bobby was about to move to win the race. Leaning high up his horse's neck, he talked to her again. 'Come on girl, this is it, let's go for it. You can do it,' and he shook his hands twice and let out more rein. In an instant, his mount shot forward and was soon up into second place alongside the brown, almost black favourite, Meldon. He knew then that he had the race in his hands. Indian Empress was going smoothly beneath him, and the winning post was getting nearer. He could now hear the roar of the crowd above the rattle of hooves as he pushed one final time with both arms alongside the horse's neck and his feet driving backwards, coaxing the maximum forward propulsion from his filly.

'One more time girl,' he shouted. His horse responded with a final supreme effort as she quickly left the favourite floundering in her wake. They passed the finishing line four lengths clear, with the third horse a further length away. Bobby returned to the winner's enclosure with the crowd's cheers ringing in his ears. He jumped from his horse's back and undid the saddle and saddlecloth. He stood proudly alongside his filly. Fraser Copeland was the first to congratulate him.

'Bobby that was some exhibition of horsemanship. I doubt if I have seen a better example of race riding. You were exceptional.'

'Thank you, sir. Thank you for having faith in me.'

'Well done Robert; I am sure, that had you ridden my filly at Epsom in the Oaks, as you said on the day, she would have won.'

Thomas Mays offered Bobby his congratulations.

'Well done Bobby. You have an exciting style, and you judged your race perfectly,' he said as he shook Bobby's hand.

Finally, Jemima shook Bobby's hand and kissed him on the cheek, saying, 'I enjoyed that,' taking Bobby somewhat by surprise.

'Thank you, Ma'am,' and Bobby, quickly left, red faced as he ran to weigh in, not knowing whether Jemima Paxton had meant the race or the kiss. He would ponder this over the next few days.

'That certainly was a revelation Chris,' Fraser Copeland said.

'It was a pleasure to watch. It was just as he predicted,' Chris Paxton replied.

'The kid sure has guts and determination. He'll go far,' Thomas Mays added.

During the following three weeks, Bobby Anderson went on to ride ten winners, much to the delight of Fraser Copeland, for whom he rode three. The other seven were for several different trainers, illustrating the young rider's popularity; trainers were scrambling for his services.

*

Two weeks after that memorable day at High Gosforth Park, Thomas Mays was returning to America after securing the production of the first two of the four locomotives ordered from Robert Stephenson's works in Newcastle. He was confident that he had negotiated a 'good deal' and that his company were getting a product that could not be beaten anywhere in the world. Jemima and Chris Paxton accompanied by their son Miles stood at the entrance to Shinwell Hall while Thomas Mays prepared to leave. Addressing Jemima and Chris, he said, 'I must thank you both for all your hospitality. You have turned what would have been a boring business trip into a most enjoyable experience,' he declared. He turned to Miles Paxton. 'I am extremely interested in the idea of a medical fund for the workers and their families at the mine. Your father has run through the basics with me, and it has much merit and a lot of integrity in the idea. I shall keep it in mind and good luck with that.'

'That's very kind of you sir; it's good to get an independent view on the scheme,' Miles Paxton replied.

'Well Thomas this is the sad part in all this. The time has come for our goodbyes,' Chris Paxton said, and he shook Thomas firmly by the hand. 'Remember you are always welcome here,' he added.

Turning to Jemima, Thomas Mays shook her hand gently and kissed her on both cheeks.

'I will no doubt be returning to England somewhere down the line to check on the progress made on our locomotives. So, I shall see you all again – God willing.'

'Well, as I said Thomas, you are always welcome here,' Chris Paxton reaffirmed.

The goodbyes completed, Thomas boarded the coach and took his seat facing forward. Thompson shook the reins once, 'walk on,' he ordered, and the two horses immediately responded. Thomas Mays was on his way and the small group watched a little while longer as the coach gathered speed down the long drive, and they turned and disappeared back inside the big house.

*

The young genius Bobby Anderson continued to flourish and on Epsom Downs the following June of 1886 Chris Paxton's faith in his young rider was rewarded when Bobby rode his three-year-old filly, Black Gold to victory in the Epsom Oaks. Chris Paxton's ambition had been realised by winning with a homebred filly and Bobby had ridden his first classic winner.

Chapter 10

1887

Bobby Anderson had gone from strength to strength over the past year and was now top jockey on the Northern circuit and he carried the title of 'Cock of the North.' He had several offers to go south to ride as retained jockey to several powerful owners including no less a person than the Prince of Wales. Despite this magnificent offer, Bobby had stayed faithful to the one man who had given him his first opportunity in life and his first classic winner.

*

Jemima Paxton had become more interested in the racing game and had bought two yearling colts of her own at the Doncaster sales. It was Jemima's idea to bring the young horses on at Shinwell Hall where Jemima could watch their early progress for herself. After breaking them in, they trained them on the five-furlong gallop before going to Fraser Copeland at Richmond. To meet horseracing protocol, Jemima Paxton registered the two colts in her husband's name, and they carried his colours in running, except instead of a black and white cap; the jockey on Jemima's colts wore a pink cap.

Shortly after the start of the new flat racing season, Bobby Anderson had taken a fall at Catterick Bridge, when his mount attempted to jump a path over the course. The horse had pitched on landing sending his rider over the horse's head; not surprisingly, considering how short Bobby rode. He suffered a dislocated collarbone and quite a lot of bruising. But other than that, he had got away with it. To aid his recuperation, the Paxtons had kindly invited Bobby to convalesce at Shinwell Hall. This gave him the opportunity to catch up with his pal Tommy Cogon and cast an eye over Jemima's two young colts.

*

Bobby was quite mobile again and could get around unaided. Without the tell-tale sign of his left arm slung up across his chest, it would appear there was nothing wrong. It was now Tommy's job to work the new colts on the five furlongs gallop. A job which he had taken to like a duck to water and, if asked, he would say it was the best part of his job. Bobby was here to observe Tommy teaching one of the young horses belonging to Jemima Paxton to gallop.

Jemima joined the two young friends in the stable yard.

'Good day Ma'am,' they said in unison and removed their caps. Bobby's shock of dark wavy hair fell across his brow and Jemima found herself drawn to Bobby's good looks. As a jockey, he was tall in stature, yet still light in weight and now subject to the open air since leaving the pit, the sun had bronzed him. Jemima found his fine features extremely attractive. Tommy mounted the older of Jemima's two young bay colts.

'Pardon my ignorance, which one is, this Tommy?' Jemima asked.

'Well, this one Ma'am is the elder of the two. Foaled in January he is two years old already and he is ready to run now. He will be your first runner once he has transferred to Mr Copeland's Richmond stables. You can recognise him by the heart-shaped white patch on his brow. As you haven't named him yet, we call him Star and your other colt, recognisable by the white stripe down his face, we call Stripe. Not very clever of us but it serves the purpose,' adding, 'stripe was an April foal and while he is officially two years old, as far as his racing career is concerned, he is not two until next month,' Tommy explained.

Tommy Cogon, riding Star, left the yard ahead of the other two and steadily cantered the colt to the far end of the five-furlong gallop. Jemima Paxton and Bobby Anderson made the short walk to the entrance to the five-furlong gallop and assumed a vantage point about a furlong from the end, to view the progress her colt was making. Tommy reined his horse to a halt at the end of the gallop turned and cantered back, passing Bobby and Jemima at a meaningful speed. They looked on as Tommy breezed up the two-year-old bay colt once more, increasing the speed almost to a gallop.

'He moves very nicely Ma'am, and he has good conformation, even at this stage of his development. Soon he'll be going into full training down at Richmond; there, he will put on more muscle. If I may say so, you have a nice colt there. I'll give him one more spin, just to see how good he feels and then we'll stop for the day.' Tommy shouted excitedly as he passed them once more as he cantered down for the final time to the bottom of the gallop.

'If he feels as good as he looks, I can't wait to get up on him,' Bobby shouted back.

'I still haven't named him. Have you any notion on the subject Bobby. After all, you will be riding him.'

'Oh, I'm not very clever at naming horses – I'm more inclined to riding them. How about you Ma'am; what have you got in mind?'

'I had considered 'Young Cavalier,' after you Bobby,' Jemima replied and tilted her head slightly, rather coquettishly.

'I am sorry Ma'am; how do you mean. I'm afraid you have lost me now.'

'Please, Bobby, call me Jemima; a young cavalier is a chivalrous man, especially one escorting a lady.'

Once again, Jemima had caused Bobby to colour up at what she had said, and his thoughts went back to their brief kiss in the unsaddling enclosure at Newcastle races following his first win on Indian Empress. Jemima had kissed him on the cheek saying, 'I enjoyed that,' and he had wondered what she really meant. Had she enjoyed the kiss or the race?

'May I ask if you have some lady whom you are sweet on Bobby?' She paused a while before continuing. 'The reason I ask is, if so, you should bring her to have dinner with us sometime soon.'

'I'm afraid I have no one in particular… er… Jemima.' He hesitated in his reply, feeling uncomfortable with the way the conversation was leading.

'Then in the meantime, we shall have you all to ourselves until the right young lady comes along,' Jemima Paxton suggested rather hurriedly, as Tommy Cogon walked his mount back towards them.

'I shall look forward to that, very much, but whether some young lady shall accompany me, we shall have to wait and see,' Bobby Anderson replied. A strange feeling crept inside him, and he found himself wishing Tommy hadn't got back to them so soon. He didn't know what was going on inside, but it felt good. Jemima Paxton also had a good feeling about her young jockey even though she knew she should be attempting to suppress it. He aroused feelings in her which she had almost forgotten about. Something inside was being rekindled for the first time since her retirement from the stage. At last, she felt alive.

'What sort of feeling did he give you today?' Bobby Anderson asked Tommy; but he was looking at Jemima when he asked the question, and a smile came across both their faces at the innuendo in his question.

'It's a bit early yet to say he is going to go far, but he's telling me something, and it feels good,' Tommy replied and once more Jemima cast a knowing smile in Bobby's direction.

'I like the look of him Tommy, what's he by?' Bobby asked, enquiring of the horse's breeding.

'His dam's line traces back to 'The Darley Arabian' and his sire has in his line the great 'Bay Middleton,' winner of the 1836 Derby.

'Born in the purple then Tommy.'

'Why aye man,' Tommy replied, just to show Bobby, who had lost his accent completely that Tommy had not lost his. Although Tommy's accent had also mellowed from that of the son of a Durham pitman, who had died in the West Fell mine disaster.

'How long are you here for?'

'As long as it takes to get this shoulder strong enough to race ride again; but I want to get back in the saddle as soon as I can. I have a title to maintain,' Bobby replied, referring to his title of 'Cock of the North.'

'When your shoulder gets stronger, we can bring the young 'uns up here together then,' Tommy suggested.

'I'll look forward to that,' Bobby said, adding, 'I hope that day's not far off.'

'Excuse me Ma'am. I'll see you both back at the stables,' Tommy said adding, 'I'll have to get this lad hosed down and dried off.' and he touched the peak of his cap and jogged the young horse back to the house, leaving the other two on their own.

Jemima and Bobby had continued walking up the gallop as they watched Tommy and the bay colt canter ahead before wheeling off to the left at the entrance of the five-furlong gallop in the direction of the stables.

'How old are you Bobby?' Jemima blurted out without thinking, taking Bobby aback and causing him to hesitate before answering.

'I'll be twenty in December.'

'My goodness, I am more than twice your age,' she said somewhat coyly, as if it had come as a surprise to her. 'In fact, I am old enough to be your mother,' she added, rather pensively as she calculated the years between them.

'How old are you actually Jemima?'

'I don't think I should answer that young man, but I will. I am forty-eight years old.'

'Goodness gracious, you certainly don't look that age at all.'

'Well, I'm afraid that is the case,' Jemima revealed.

'Time has certainly been kind to you; let me look at you,' Bobby said. He stepped in front of her and looked directly into her eyes.

'It must be all that stage make-up I have applied over the years,' Jemima said wistfully.

A breeze, heavily laden with the scent of the grass, freshly bruised by the horse's hooves, swept wisps of her brown hair across her face. Using his free hand, Bobby cleared the wayward hair from her face. The back of his fingers lingered briefly on her smooth cheek, and he looked directly into her eyes. Without any further hesitation, she kissed him passionately on the lips. Bobby did nothing to resist her advances as she wrapped her arms around him, taking care not to crush his damaged shoulder. After what was nothing more than a few heavily charged seconds, they broke their embrace and stood looking into each other's eyes. Jemima was the first to speak.

'Whatever was that about? I don't know what came over me. I must have taken leave of my senses. It can't happen again; it must not happen again.'

'Why not?' Bobby asked, bravely. The experience had excited him, despite Jemima's age she was still a tremendously attractive woman.

'I am a married woman, as you well know and as I said, I am old enough to be your mother and the wife of your employer, remember. We must be getting back to the house. My husband will be wondering where we are,' Jemima said nervously.

As she came to her senses, she quickened her pace to distance herself from the young jockey. Bobby had to run a few steps to catch up. He reached out for her hand and slowed her down. During the walk back to the house there was little conversation between the two. Jemima ran the recent happening over in her mind again, and to her surprise she found that the thought of what had taken place, instead of revolting her, she still found it exciting. On the other hand, Bobby Anderson, on his recollection of the brief incident, could not believe that he had been involved sexually with Jemima Paxton, even if it was nothing more than a kiss. He realised he had been fortunate to get away with what had happened, and it now worried him. After all, his career was at stake. Chris Paxton had given him his opportunity, and this was not the way to repay him by taking advantage of his wife. What if tomorrow she was remorseful and decided to tell her husband. He was running it through his mind, what had led to it. In his mind, he was working out a case in his defence. God forbid, that Jemima should indeed reveal the incident to her husband, blaming it all on his young jockey.

As if Jemima could read his mind she said, 'Don't worry Bobby, what happened back there will remain between the two of us. I led you on and I am sorry I compromised you in that way. I know it could be the end of your career if my husband finds out. Even if you were to deny it, the cynics would say there is never smoke without fire. But you have my word; there will be no revelation from me,' and she squeezed his hand. Bobby felt a little relieved at what Jemima said but he was not convinced that it would not come out with devastating consequence sometime in the future and he knew he would have to take care to stay on the right side of his employer's wife.

*

Shortly after the establishment of the Medical Scheme, Chris Paxton received a letter from Thomas Mays in America outlining his offer of $1,500 towards the building of the Medical Centre and Hospital. He made one proviso that they named it the 'Dan Swain Memorial Hospital,' in honour of Jemima's father; deliberately using the name Dan to differentiate between her father and her youngest brother. A suitable site, to the south of the Hall and at the same altitude above the valley floor, where the air was fresher, became the beginning of the new cottage hospital.

*

The new hospital opened in 1888 and initially it had six beds. There was room for further expansion to the hospital with added plans for a bathhouse to be used by the miners when they returned to the surface after their stint underground, situated closer to the pithead. The children and females of the village could use the baths on Sundays if they so wished, alternating with the aged miners who could no longer stand the rigours of pit work. This allowed the segregation of the sexes, and so the Medical Scheme, the first of its kind in the Northeast, came into existence.

Miles Paxton threw himself wholeheartedly into his role of Medical Officer, even mooting plans for a dental service and swimming baths but that was for the far future.

Chapter 11

1890

It was the Sunday after the race meeting at Elvet Racecourse in Durham City. It had been a good meeting for Jemima Paxton and Fraser Copeland. He had two winners, both ridden by Bobby Anderson, one of which was Young Cavalier one of Jemima's two three-year-old colts. Young Cavalier had been unbeaten the previous season as a two-year-old, winning three times; leaving Chris Paxton regretting he had not entered him in the Derby as a yearling. A race in which he thought Young Cavalier would have done well. Jemima had named her other colt, Secrecy. He was unraced as a two-year-old, and as yet he had never won as a three-year-old.

Chris Paxton had taken to his bed suffering from what he first thought was a fever brought on by an overindulgence in celebrating their success on the previous day at Durham. He had not come down for breakfast; instead, he had taken a light breakfast in his bedroom. He managed to eat a poached egg on toast, with a slice of toast and marmalade to follow. However, he failed to finish the slice of toast and marmalade.

'You should try to finish your food sir,' Alice Cogon advised him when she had answered the bell summoning her to her master's bedroom.

'Take the tray away Alice I think I have done well; at least I ate all of my poached egg.'

'Well, you know what they say, feed a cold, and starve a fever. So, I will let you off this time,' she said rather boldly.

'Could you bring me my newspaper Alice? I'll have a quick scan through the news and then settle down and try to sleep off this attack. I will spend today in bed and see how I feel tomorrow. Bearing in mind what you said about starving a fever would you tell cook not to include me for dinner and tell my wife of my plans for today.'

'I will indeed sir,' Alice replied. 'I hope you feel better tomorrow. Meanwhile if there is anything you need, just ring.'

*

Bobby Anderson had stayed overnight at Shinwell Hall following his successful race riding at Durham. He entered the dining room where Jemima was already having breakfast.

'Good morning Bobby how are you this morning?' she asked.

'To be honest, I feel a bit groggy; must be the brandy Mr Paxton and I consumed last night. After all, we were in a celebratory mood. And it *was* excellent brandy I might add.'

'My husband is also feeling ill. So much so, that he won't be down for breakfast this morning. He is spending the day in bed to shake off what he claims to be a fever. I think, like you, it is probably the brandy. Have some of those devilled kidneys for breakfast and a couple of cups of strong coffee; it should make you feel better. It's a fine morning and later we shall take a stroll through the grounds to clear your head,' Jemima suggested conspiratorially; realising her husband's incapacity would give her the opportunity to have time, alone with Bobby Anderson.

'That sounds like a splendid idea. If the devilled kidneys don't clear my head, your company certainly will,' and he gave Jemima a knowing smile.

They walked together through the park, until Jemima suggested to stop for a while. 'There is a nice clearing through here Bobby, just off the main walk. Let us stay a while here, it's a pleasant spot,' Jemima Paxton suggested, and she led him by the hand through an arbour of tall growing rhododendrons which formed a circle within the glade. 'I love it here Bobby,' as she looked up into the tops of the mature trees.

Filtered sunlight strained through the overhead canopy, dappling the glade below.

The large blooms of the rhododendrons, some as large as tea plates decorated the glade with their colours of purple, pink, and white. The fragrance of the blooms, mixed with that of the wild woodbine created a balmy potpourri.

Jemima decided to stay a while, much to Bobbie's surprise as the rays from the sun had not penetrated sufficiently to dry the dewy ground. She sunk slowly to the ground and sitting with her legs tucked under her. She patted the mossy carpet to the side of her. It was still damp, and her palm was wet. Undeterred by the ground conditions, she said, 'Come and sit by me here Bobby,'

'But it is wet Jemima. Do you think that is wise? After all you could catch your death.'

'The lad doth protest too much, methinks,' she replied, deliberately misquoting Shakespeare.

'What was that?' her words wasted on him. He was ignorant of the Bard, quoted correctly or misquoted.

'It was nothing, my dear. Just my facetiousness. Come now. Sit by me. I am feeling romantic, being so close to nature out here in our own little glade,' she said.

She was looking up to the treetops through half-closed eyes, as though in a trance like state, which made her appear to be under the influence of some drug; or was it 'lust.'

Bobby removed his tweed hacking jacket and stretched it out on the ground alongside Jemima. Getting Bobby's meaning and without a further word exchanged between them, she sidled across onto

Bobby's outspread garment. Once positioned, she leaned back resting on her elbows. Bobby reclined alongside her, resting on his left hip.

It was wet, but she did not care. She looked up into his eyes as he leaned over her. Jemima was the first to speak.

'How is the head?' she asked.

'What head?' Bobby said dismissively. 'Drinking in your beauty Jemima would be the draught to cure the worst of hangovers.'

'If, as you suggest, I do have such curative powers, then just to make sure, let me kiss you better.'

Bobby lay still as Jemima leaned forward and kissed him on the brow. 'How does that feel?'

'I'm feeling better already but I think I need further treatment,' he said, and a puppy-dog look crept over his face. 'Come here Nurse Jemima and increase the dosage.' He spread his arms wide, invitingly. Accepting his invitation readily she fell into his arms. Clasping her to him, he kissed her passionately on the lips. They held the embrace until Jemima, in a pang of conscience, broke away saying, 'Please Bobby, this is all wrong; if Chris were to find out, your career would be finished, and I hate to think what would happen to me.'

'I know you are right, but I have wanted you ever since that first innocent kiss on the cheek in the paddock at Newcastle races. You have probably forgotten about it by now. I don't want to bring age up, but I want you to know it means nothing to me; I fell in love with you the moment I met you.'

'I feel the same about you Bobby, but this is too dangerous. We are playing with fire.'

'We can have each other and if we are very careful, no one need find out,' he said, and he gently lowered her shoulders to the ground. He stared down into her face momentarily before kissing her fully on the lips. She parted her lips, inviting his tongue to explore within. As they kissed, the fingers of his right hand searched up inside her undergarments until he was stroking the soft flesh above her stocking tops. She eased her legs apart allowing his hand to explore further.

Their kiss lingered on and on and his errant fingers reached the hairy mound of flesh between her legs as he gained intimate knowledge of her body. They frantically tore at each other's clothing until they had gained access to the parts of their bodies, which until now had been deeply private. Breaking at last from the kiss, Bobby straddled her, and she wrapped her legs around his narrow waist...

The deed done, they laid back on the protective jacket staring up at the weak sunbeams that had struggled to penetrate the treetops high above them. They rearranged their clothing and headed back to the house.

'I love you so much Jemima; I must have you more often. I can't wait for the next time,' he confessed.

'Don't expect that to happen again,' she said remorsefully. 'Just one moment of complacency could eventually lead to our being caught out.'

The two, their act of impropriety over, were unaware that they were not alone.

Thompson had walked the gallop looking to retrieve a new shoe lost by his master's hunter, Duke. The horse had just been re-shod the previous week and being thrifty on his master's account, he was exercising more than enough sense of duty in his search for the missing horseshoe. This was Thompson's style – never one to miss an opportunity to curry favour with his master. Hearing whispered voices and thinking the voices may be those of poachers, catching them in the act would be a further chance to please his employer and he carefully parted the lowest branches of the rhododendrons. What he saw nearly caused him to gasp out loud. Controlling his surprise, and with a strangely pleasing, idle curiosity, he watched his mistress in a sexual act with the famous jockey, Bobby Anderson. He watched for no more than a couple of minutes; he needed to make his exit before they were aware of his presence. In that short time, he noticed a large birthmark on the inside of Jemima Paxton's thigh.

He hurried down the gallop in the direction of the house but once he was out of earshot of the couple, he cut through the woods out of sight of any followers. That knowledge could come in handy sometime in the future, he thought.

Chapter 12

Thomas Mays's letter arrived, announcing his return to England to supervise the second phase of the purchase of the two more locomotives in an order of four, for the New York and Northern Railroad. In his letter he had revealed to Chris and Jemima Paxton that he had married his housekeeper, Mary, and that he would like to bring his recently widowed stepdaughter Kate, to England, to recover from her recent bereavement. He also asked if they could both stay at Shinwell Hall instead of booking two separate rooms in a Newcastle hotel for the duration of the trip.

'We can hardly say no to him Jemima. After all, at the end of his last trip we told him he was always welcome here.'

'I agree, but he didn't have a stepdaughter in tow, or indeed a wife when he was here last. Fancy him marrying his housekeeper. That came as a surprise. He never mentioned any budding romance back in America when he was last here.'

'Well, it is hardly any of our business Jemima. Mind you, if there was nothing between them back in 1885, he hasn't hung about since. How old will he be Jemima?'

'He was sixteen when my father was murdered in 1850. That makes him fifty-five years old,' Jemima calculated.

'The sly old devil,' Chris Paxton said rather cynically.

'Well, it appears, we are once more obliged to accommodate Mr Mays. We have no other option,' Jemima admitted disappointedly.

'You don't seem too keen on the idea Jemima. Do I detect an air of regret in our offer of ongoing hospitality?'

'It's not that Chris. It's his stepdaughter being here as well; we know nothing of her, do we?'

'He is a convivial chap, is he not? I am sure she will display the same pleasant disposition.'

'What we are forgetting Chris, she is his stepdaughter not his daughter; she comes without any chance of inheritance of his natural traits. He states in his letter that she is not a child, she is a thirty-seven-year-old widow.'

'I see your point. maybe he could have done better by marrying the daughter,' Chris Paxton replied, acerbically. We are committed now. I will get a letter off to him tomorrow saying they are both welcome to stay as long as it takes. I fear we have no option my dear and let us not forget his generous gift of $1,500 towards the hospital.'

*

Thomas Mays duly arrived with his stepdaughter Kate Dooley, at Shinwell Hall. As was the custom on occasions such as this, the Paxton family, and their staff, waited in the large hallway to welcome their visitors. The large doors opened, and Thomas Mays entered with his stepdaughter a couple of paces behind him; she adopting a somewhat shy stance, not having met the waiting family before. Kate Dooley was about the same height as Jemima and was of similar build with the same shade of brown hair. She was an attractive woman with similar features to Jemima, except her face was more rounded and her complexion unlike Jemima's was quite pallid, due to having spent all her life living in New York city. With warm reunion greetings exchanged between Thomas Mays and the Paxton family, Thomas ushered his stepdaughter forward to meet them.

'And this,' he declared, 'is my stepdaughter, Kate Dooley. Unfortunately, Kate was widowed a year ago when her husband Richard died from consumption, I decided, if she so wished, she should accompany me on my trip. We thought it would take her mind off things for a bit. They all shook hands with her in turn and as they did so, Jemima felt unexpected warmth in the handshake, a strange warmth, emitting a feeling as if they were not meeting for the first time. Despite this, the newcomer felt an accord with her hostess. Having lost her shyness with that first handshake, Kate was the first to speak.

'How very pleased I am to make your acquaintance Mrs Paxton,' she said sincerely, with the same American drawl as her stepfather, adding, 'I feel we are going to get on just fine together.'

Jemima put Kate Dooley's forwardness, for want of a better explanation, down to the 'American way.'

'I am sure you are right, for I too feel the same way as you do Kate. It is as if we have met before,' she said, and she continued to look Kate up and down trying hard to link at least one of her guest's features or mannerisms with that of someone she already knew.

'Let us go through to the winter room and catch up on what has transpired since you were here last, Thomas. It will give my family I the opportunity to get to know your beautiful stepdaughter,' Chris Paxton suggested.

The party made their way to the winter room and Jemima continued to search her brain thinking who Kate Dooley reminded her of, but no one came to mind.

Chapter 13

The visitors from America had been at Shinwell Hall for almost a month and Miles Paxton had surprised everyone by announcing he and Kate Dooley were going on a trip to Newcastle for the day.

I'll show her the shops, mother. You know how you enjoy a day shopping in Newcastle. Especially the shops in Grainger Street, Grey Street and Clayton Street, which are particularly fine and Grey's Monument at the head of Grey Street, is of interest to the tourist.

Jemima shot both her husband and Thomas Mays a quick querying glance. She didn't approve of the sudden interest their son was showing the widow from America. For one thing, she didn't approve of the age difference of ten years between Kate Dooley and their son. This was rich coming from Jemima. Thankfully, from Jemima's point of view, the rest of the company seated at the table were not aware of her hypocrisy. In her opinion, what was good for Jemima was not good for Miles, she was uncomfortable with their plans for the day, and she hoped there was nothing more in it than an innocent day trip. But she still pondered over why they had not asked her to go with them when Miles knew how much she also enjoyed the Newcastle shops. She saw the usefulness in playing gooseberry, but the invitation to join them was not forthcoming.

'I'm sure Kate will enjoy her day in Newcastle, though it may struggle to compete with the grandeur of New York City,' his mother replied, trying to dampen his enthusiasm but for respectability added, 'have a pleasant time.'

Later in the day, Thomas Mays returned from Robert Stephenson's locomotive works and realised Kate and Miles had not returned from Newcastle. He was anxious about them becoming too familiar because he and his newly acquired wife were the only persons that knew the full story behind Kate Dooley and her mother Mary Crowley. Apart from the age difference, any romantic attraction between them needed nipping in the bud. On meeting Jemima and Chris in New York back in 1860, he had not told them the full story about Dan Swains' death. He had shown them where he was murdered and where he was buried. To save her embarrassment and in order not to tarnish the memory of her father, he had decided not to tell her of the other reason Michael Crowley had committed the murder. The theft of her father's life savings was opportunist but in truth it came secondary to the real reason Michael Crowley had murdered Dan Swain. Unbeknown to the rest of the residents of Shinwell Hall he was the sole person aware of the single act of transgression between Mary Crowley and Dan Swain that resulted in the birth of a baby girl nine months later. That girl was Kate Dooley, now his stepdaughter. Bringing her to England to recuperate after the sudden death of her husband now seemed a bad idea. If he revealed her identity, apart from being hurtful to Jemima, it would also reveal the fact that Jemima Paxton and Kate Dooley are indeed half-sisters and any sexual relationship between Kate and Miles would be unlawful.

The two day-trippers arrived back from Newcastle in gay mood, laughing and chattering as they made their entry bursting in on the other members of the family who were sitting down to dinner. Jemima cast a stern look in the direction of her husband; a look that told him she disapproved of their son's behaviour. Thomas Mays also noticed the serious frown narrowing her eyes. Chris Paxton, picking up on his wife's displeasure at their behaviour, addressed his son in an unusually stern manner.

'Please, Miles where are your manners? Offer us the decency of more appropriate behaviour while we are having our meal.'

Immediately Miles and Kate were stunned into silence. After a few heavily charged seconds, Miles was the first to speak.

'Sorry father, you are absolutely right. I do apologise for both of us; our behaviour is unforgiveable,' Kate said nothing thinking to do so was the more prudent course of action. Chris Paxton was not finished yet and continued reprimanding his son rather than Kate.

'You are late, you can either eat in the kitchen or wait until we are finished here and have vacated the table,' he said sternly.

'We have already eaten in Newcastle thank you father,' he replied and immediately hoped his father didn't think he was being flippant.

'I think you are forgetting that our guest is still in mourning for her lately departed husband,' and addressing Kate directly he added, 'I apologise for our son's over exuberant display of thoughtlessness.'

'I am sorry sir, but I can't let Miles take all the blame. You are perfectly correct to point out our lack of forethought, but we both got so carried away with our enjoyment of each other's company that we must have left our manners in Newcastle,' Kate stated in order to defuse the situation.

During the whole of the exchange, Thomas Mays said nothing, all the time squirming with embarrassment.

'Are you finished your admonishment of us father?' Miles asked bravely.

'I am, indeed, I have said all I have to say on the subject.'

'In that case we will apologise once again and take our leave of you all.'

Miles and Kate retired to the library. 'I need a drink after that,' Miles Paxton said, 'I never thought a day at Newcastle would cause so much commotion,' he added. He poured himself a large whisky. 'Can I get you anything Kate?'

'I don't suppose you have any bourbon Miles.'

'As a matter of fact, father got some in just in case it was your father's favourite tipple.'

Taking another glass, he poured Kate a similar amount of bourbon whiskey.

'That was not the best of receptions back there that I have ever received,' Kate said in her New York accent. 'Must have been something they ate at dinner,' she quipped, and they both laughed out loud again.

After they settled their laughter Miles said, 'I got the feeling mother doesn't approve of our sharing time together.'

'You may not be alone,' Kate opined.

'We must remember to invite her next time,' Miles said.

'Maybe just the once, I so enjoyed your company today, I am reluctant to share you with anyone. You were the perfect gentleman despite what your father thought of your behaviour on our return,' Kate said, and she kissed him on the cheek. 'What your father doesn't know is, while he is theoretically correct that I should be in mourning, in fact, I am not mourning my late husband at all. He was never the gentleman you are Miles. My life with Stephen was not easy. After our marriage, he was very possessive and left me no room in which to breathe. I felt stifled by his overbearing jealousy. On our return from a night out, he would accuse me of flirting with any man who looked in my direction and he would vent his anger by physically attacking me in the privacy of our bedroom. Even now, now that he is dead, I find it hard to talk about him. I have bottled it up inside me for too long and to you as a doctor I feel I can reveal things about our married life that at the time I couldn't even tell my family. Sex with Stephen followed a regular pattern; the accusations, followed by the beating, then the false apology, and finally the sex. He knew that after the beating, I would be in no fit state to fight him off and so it went on throughout our marriage. It seemed to me that he was unable to perform the sex act without the precursory violence. So, you see Miles, in truth, for me, my husband's death was more a release from his domination, than a bereavement. It saved me the trouble of having to flee from his tyranny. You are the first person I have come clean with about our relationship. Until now, I felt too ashamed to tell anyone what I had suffered at my husband's hands. With you, whether it's your doctor's qualities, I felt I could get it all off my chest. Even my mother hasn't heard what I have just told you. I must be honest with you, when Thomas asked me if I wanted to come to England with him to get over my husband's death as he thought, I said yes and came along just for the ride as we say. I wasn't exactly even with him,' she concluded.

Miles had listened intently to her every word but at the same time, he felt uncomfortable and embarrassed about being the confidant of Kate's tale. There followed a moment of contemplation between them. He felt rather shocked at her revelations but at the same time, he felt both pity for what she had had to endure and admiration for her honesty. She was even surprised at her own frankness in telling a relative stranger, details of her marriage that until now she felt unable to talk about even to those people closest to her.

'Did your mother or stepfather not notice any bruising about your person?'

'Oh, he was very selective in where his blows fell, and he never struck me where it would show.'

Miles Paxton pondered Kate's past predicament a moment longer, then opening his arms to her said, 'Come here Kate, you poor thing. How you must have suffered at the hands of that brute of a husband,' and she walked into his open arms. He closed his arms around her, and their bodies rocked gently in a very warm embrace. She rested her head on his shoulder feeling a sense of sanctuary from a man for the first time in a long, long time. They continued their embrace swaying as if they were dancing without moving from the spot. The static dance continued until the lock on the door clicked. They broke away quickly as the door opened and Jemima Paxton entered the library. They both tried to compose themselves quickly, hoping they did not appear too flustered.

'I'm sorry. I hope I am not interrupting anything,' she said knowingly.

'Err no, not at all. We were just about to leave, mother,' Miles replied, unconvincingly.

'Oh, that *is* a pity as I was just about to ask if one of you cared to make up a four for bridge.'

'I'm afraid I don't play that well. I would hate to create an imbalance in the game,' Kate offered. 'You take the place Miles; I think I shall retire to my room and have an early night. Thank you, Miles, for a most interesting excursion to Newcastle. It may be lacking in skyscrapers as such, but interesting, nonetheless. So, if you both excuse me I will leave you. Until tomorrow,' she said and left.

Left on their own, Jemima turned to her son. 'Tell me Miles, there is nothing developing between you two is there? You both appeared to be flustered when I entered the room.'

'I don't know what you mean mother. If there *is* anything developing, then I suggest it is in your mind.'

Before the conversation continued further, Chris Paxton and Thomas Mays entered the library for a game of bridge.

Chapter 14

Chris and Jemima Paxton sat in the library, he was reading, and she was brooding. He watched his wife over the top of his book and spotted her doleful countenance.

'Is everything all right Jemima? Something seems to be bothering you lately. You aren't sickening for something, about which you aren't telling me?'

'I'm fine health wise,' Jemima replied. 'But I am concerned about having our guests stay with us for so long.'

'In what way? Why do they make you feel so disconsolate?'

'It is just that I get the feeling that Kate Dooley is making a play for Miles and there is such an age difference. He is so naïve in these matters, and I don't want her, as a woman of experience, to exploit his innocence. She must be all of ten years older than he and the time spent away studying, has left him with little time in the company of available young women. I am sure I nearly walked in on something the day they came back from Newcastle.'

'But I am six years older than you remember Jemima. Does an age difference matter?'

'The answer to your question is no, I haven't forgotten you are six years older than I, and no, I don't think age difference matters,' she said with confidence. For some reason, which I can't explain, she makes me feel uncomfortable, especially when I see the two of them together. Call it a woman's intuition if you like. All I am saying is we must keep an eye on things and not let the situation get out of hand. There is something about her that leaves me irritatingly puzzled.'

'Come now Jemima, she is not that bad an influence on him and if I may say so, you may be forgetting that he is no longer a child and very intelligent to boot; he can take care of himself.'

'I hope you are right. All I am saying is, where affairs of the heart are concerned, he has much to learn.'

'I concede darling. You are right; we *must* keep an eye on things. From a selfish point of view, as sweet as she appears, I would not want her for a daughter-in-law.'

Although the conversation had gone Jemima's way, the subject content had raised in her mind her own hypocrisy.

*

Thomas Mays returned from the Stephenson locomotive factory with the news that his business in Newcastle was almost completed and he and his stepdaughter would be leaving for New York in two weeks. Allowing them to spend a little time travelling in England before returning home. Jemima's heart leapt at the prospect of their leaving. She was delighted that she would no longer have to worry about any involvement between Miles and Kate Dooley. At last, she had a date on which to concentrate, and her mood immediately improved. Chris Paxton noticed the uplifting effects this news had on Jemima, for he too found satisfaction in the thought that their son would be relieved of any temptation put his way by Kate Dooley.

'I have plans to make our way down country stopping off at a few places of interest en route for Southampton, where we will embark for New York and home. I hope Kate agrees with me on these plans. I haven't discussed them with her yet as work at Stephenson's was finalised quicker than I expected. One or two little problems in design which had been proving difficult to surmount, suddenly all fell into place and now my work here is done,' Thomas Mays explained, adding, 'where is Kate by the way?'

'After you left for Newcastle, she and Miles left for the hospital,'

Jemima revealed, with a degree of contempt.

'Miles wanted to show her the hospital to which you had so kindly made a most generous donation Thomas. A gesture, for which we will be ever grateful,' Chris Paxton added, with more enthusiasm than Jemima had shown.

'It is thanks to the man whose name it bears. But for him, I wouldn't be here,' Thomas Mays said. He paused briefly as he arranged his thoughts. 'I am finding what I am going to say next, very delicate and difficult to put into words without offending your hospitality.'

'What is it Thomas that bothers you so much?' Chris Paxton asked. 'Please, feel free, you can talk to us,' he added.

'I have noticed and I'm sure you have too, the association developing between Miles and my stepdaughter. With my business in Newcastle completed, I have decided to return home early. I have omitted to tell you hitherto something I now realise, I should have told you sooner, Jemima. Kate is not only my stepdaughter, but she is also your half-sister.'

Jemima was dumbfounded. She just could not take in this sudden revelation and to give her time to gather her thoughts, Chris cleverly diverted the conversation back to Thomas. 'Would you wish to elaborate more Thomas?' Chris challenged.

Thomas continued, 'What I did not tell you about my housekeeper, now my wife, is that she was the widow of Michael Crowley, your father's killer, Jemima.'

'Oh! No,' she cried and immediately swooned into Chris's arms. He steered her limp body into an armchair and immediately rang the bell by the side of the fireplace that summoned the maid. Alice Cogon soon appeared. 'Quickly Alice, fetch smelling salts,' Chris Paxton ordered.

On Alice's return, Chris Paxton placed the smelling salts under Jemima's nose and after a short while, she came around. The two men allowed her time to regain her senses. Her husband was the first to speak.

'Do you want to continue with this my dear?' he asked.

With bleary eyes and her mind struggling to make sense of her husband's words, she eventually answered her husband with a weak reply.

'Please, yes,' was all she could say.

'Please continue Thomas,' Chris Paxton said.

'Are you happy for me to continue Jemima?'

'Please, continue Thomas.

'I have remained silent until now to save you any unnecessary hurt. But when I saw Miles and Kate together on the landing two nights ago, kissing each other good night before retiring to their respective bedrooms, I knew I had to act quickly. They didn't see me further down the corridor as they both bid each other goodnight,' he said and looked at Jemima who was the next to speak.

'What I don't understand, from what you have told us, is how on earth your stepdaughter can be my half-sister?' Jemima asked, her mind still not functioning at full speed.

'Are you ready for this?' Thomas asked with a warning in his voice. He continued, 'When I met you in New York in 1860 I deliberately avoided telling you all the facts that led to your father's death. I thought it was prudent at the time to save you the hurt but now I realise my mistake and under the present circumstances, I need to reveal the truth to you. Apart from Michael Crowley killing your father for his money, Jemima, he also had a score to settle, following a single act of adultery between your father and Crowley's wife Mary. There was no affair between them other than that single act of infidelity, which resulted in the birth of Kate Crowley, her name before marrying her late husband Stephen Dooley. So, you see, you and Kate share the same father,' Thomas disclosed, reluctantly. 'My wife never disclosed the truth to Kate, as to who her real father was and as far as she was concerned her 'father' had died before she was born.

The three of them remained silent as they mulled over the gravity of Thomas's revelation. It was Thomas who started the conversation once again. 'So, you see any involvement between Miles and Kate is impossible and must be discouraged. Torn between two loyalties, the memory of your father, and the loyalty to my stepdaughter during her time of need, I now realise, with the benefit of hindsight, I may not have been as generous with the truth as I might have been. If by keeping my counsel I have still caused you distress, then I am deeply sorry. I hope you can find it in your hearts to forgive me for my deception. My secretive behaviour, conducted for the best of reasons, was not to capitalise on the situation to my own ends. I thought the decision I made was the best course to take in order not to upset you. If I could do anything differently, I would have left Kate at home and travelled alone. I thought the trip to England would be of benefit to her following her bereavement. I couldn't legislate beforehand for a romantic involvement between Kate and Miles. I thought the age difference would be a natural barrier between the two, but it lets you see, love knows no bounds,' Thomas Mays concluded.

'Please Thomas; I would be telling lies if I was to say to you, I am not shocked by what you have told me. The word disappointment is an understatement for what I feel on learning of my father's behaviour. But it is all a long time ago and everyone's circumstances have changed over the years. I am pleased you kept the truth from me all this time. I think had you told me all those years ago, the impact on me then would have been much greater. It can't have been easy for you, with all the weight of the truth resting on your shoulders all this time,' she said.

While sincere in her forgiveness of Thomas's deceit, her acceptance of her father's indiscretion was easier to take, with the memory of her own recent indiscretion with Bobby Anderson so fresh in her mind. She knew there and then that she had to do something about her own too intimate friendship with Bobby Anderson.

'We will have to decide how we go about informing Miles and Kate that any romance between them is out of the question,' Chris

Paxton stated.

'Leave Kate to me, I'll deal with her,' Thomas stated.

*

Thomas Mays' recent revelation convinced Jemima, that any future involvement between herself and Bobby Anderson was out of the question. It had brought her to her senses. It pleased Jemima and Chris Paxton that Thomas Mays's business in Newcastle was now completed, leaving him with no reason for further visits concerning the four locomotives. *Thank goodness for Robert Stephenson's efficiency,* Chris Paxton thought.

*

Thomas Mays and Kate Dooley left by train on the first part of their journey south, calling at York on the first part of their itinerary to Southampton. It was three days after Thomas Mays had disclosed the truth about Dan Swain's past. Chris Paxton had been correct in his assumption on how Miles and Kate would respond to the news that his grandfather and her father was the same person. Knowing the truth made them realise how close they had come to a serious dilemma from which they would have found it difficult to extricate themselves.

*

Following Thomas Mays's recent revelations Jemima had become very subdued. She constantly found her mind concentrating on what had been, and very few of her thoughts focused on the future. Thoughts of her stage career filled her with pleasure, her son filled her with joy and even now, as a man he gave her much reason to be proud. Since her retirement, life in general, had not brought her happiness. Her marriage had suffered since the end of her stage career. Now that she and her husband Chris were not working and touring together, her life once more felt empty. She hardly saw her husband these days, much of his time taken up with his horses. She had tried to involve herself in his world by buying the two colts, but she realised this was not enough. The horses had not brought her and her husband closer together in her retirement. If anything, it had brought her and Bobby Anderson together more and she knew the danger in that situation. Therefore, she had endeavoured to suppress the feelings which she felt for Bobby Anderson. She knew in her heart that this was not going to be easy, for she knew she had to work hard at this. It may be the sensible way for the future, and it would probably resolve the problem on the surface but within her, she knew she was going to feel hurt. Nevertheless, she had decided to sell the two colts; they provoked too many thoughts of remorse. What had happened between them should disgust her, but it did not. In her attempt to justify their actions, she told herself it had been an act of desperation when her world seemed to be collapsing about her. Thinking back, she must have been going through some sort of breakdown. I must have been out of my mind, she heard herself saying. Their dalliance had been nothing more than a brief distraction, but it was not the solution to her problems. To all around her, she had to make it appear there was nothing between them, it was getting increasingly difficult to uphold this charade, and she now regretted the whole episode. She thanked God quietly that he had sent their visitors from America, and it pleased her immensely that their stay had interrupted the visits of Bobby Anderson; a welcome break which had given her the breathing space that she had needed to regain her senses.

*

Following their guests return to America, Bobby Anderson resumed his Sunday visits to Shinwell Hall. On his first visit after the resumption, he noticed a change in Jemima's attitude towards him. She was cool and seemed reluctant to make any eye contact. He ached so much to spend time with her alone. She deliberately avoided him, making sure such a situation did not happen. What he did not know, she was feeling the same about him, but she vowed her moment of madness was in the past and that is where it would stay. In her mind she took all the blame for what had happened between them, realising she had made all the play. She had changed the route her walks in the park took. Now, she avoided strolling down the five-furlong gallop, being unable to bring herself to pass the glade in the woodland, where the incident between her and Bobby Anderson had taken place. She had tried all manner of things to cleanse her conscience of what had happened that day. Her abhorrent memories had intensified since learning of her own father's transgression.

She had now taken to attending church with Sally Binney every Sunday morning, knowing this would reduce the possibility of a meeting with Bobby Anderson. How could she discourage him from his regular visits? In the first instance, she thought her cold treatment might get through to him and discourage him from frequent visiting. She believed to over- react could have more dire consequences and she knew she had to deal with the situation with discretion, but only she knew the hurt inside that her present actions caused her. She realised it was impossible to discuss the subject of Bobby Anderson's visits with her husband. To ban his visits without reason would be difficult to explain away. Therefore, she decided to ignore him hoping he might get the message that he was no longer welcome and would therefore stop visiting of his own accord. Nevertheless, all her negative thoughts concerning Bobby Anderson was a deliberate effort on her part to suppress her real feelings. She knew, deep down in her heart, she still had strong feelings for him and during moments of solitude, her thoughts returned to that sole occasion in the grounds, and it made her feel good. She knew that was all she had, her memories of that one moment of madness, a moment they could never repeat.

*

It was not Jemima's approach to her dilemma that broke off his visits, it was a single action by Fraser Copeland that provided the solution. Bobby Anderson had just returned from the gallops and was leading the horse he had been working with, back into the yard when he saw Fraser Copeland talking to a couple. He instantly recognised Lord Fillingham, but he didn't recognise the beautiful young lady who accompanied him.

'Bobby, I have someone here who is itching to meet you,' Fraser Copeland called across. Bobby responded immediately and joined the party. He touched his cap and bowed, 'Your lordship,' he said. He smiled politely and removed his cap as he turned to face the young lady, bowing for the second time.

'Let me introduce you Bobby. You have already had the pleasure of meeting Lord Fillingham, on several occasions. Let me introduce you to his lordship's youngest daughter, Lady Isobel Percival.'

Bobby Anderson removed his riding gloves and quickly wiped his palm up and down his breeches before taking the young lady's proffered, gloved hand. Bobby Anderson was speechless for what must have been the first time in his life. He could not take his eyes off the beauty standing before him. Lady Isobel realising Bobby's awkwardness, was the first to speak. 'I have been looking forward to meeting you for so long Mr Anderson. Your fame on the racecourse has earned you legions of admirers,' she said.

'Thank you, Lady Isobel, you are too kind,' was all Bobby could muster in reply as he stared into her eyes, almost to the point of embarrassing the young beauty. He realised he was still holding her hand and immediately released his hold and closed his gaping mouth. Lady Isobel smiled at the fact he had gawped at her so blatantly. Bobby Anderson was tall for a jockey and Lady Isobel was of a similar height. Corn coloured hair tumbled in curls to her shoulders. Her complexion was as pale and as smooth as alabaster, which emphasised her beautifully defined neck. She held her head in an elegant manner, which some observers may have described as arrogant. Instantly smitten, he could see nothing but Lady Isobel's beauty.

*

Since starting up as a racehorse owner, Lord Fillingham had placed several good horses under Fraser Copeland's charge and Anderson being the stable jockey was now getting several successful rides from that source. The Lady Isobel, a competent horsewoman in her own right, had pestered her father to take her with him on a visit to Richmond Gill Stables ever since the great Bobby Anderson had risen to stardom.

*

Jemima heard of Bobby Anderson's courtship of Lady Isobel Percival from her husband.

'Have you wondered why we haven't seen much of Bobby Anderson these last few months Jemima? He was never away from here at weekends but recently we have seen neither hide nor hair of him off the racecourse.'

'I had wondered Chris, had we offended him in some way, and he wasn't telling us,' Jemima replied, without revealing how pleased she was that his visits had ceased.

'Let me explain. He has met the Lady Isobel Percival, the youngest daughter of Lord Fillingham. From what I have heard from Fraser Coleman, she besots him, and he is now a regular visitor to Fillingham Hall.'

The news that Anderson's visits had ended filled Jemima with relief. She felt a huge load lift from her shoulders and now she could return to some sort of normality, but she knew she could not let herself become too complacent and let the truth slip.

Chapter 15

1892

Bobby Anderson's career continued with great success. The young couple were in love and the conversation between them had ran to discussing marriage although Bobby had yet to pluck up courage to ask his Lordship for his daughter's hand. He was not convinced that his Lordship would be keen on giving his daughter away to the son of a coal miner, despite Bobby's success as one of the best jockeys in the country. The prospect of popping the question to one of the most prominent peers of the realm filled him with more fear than finding himself in the middle of a twenty-runner field coming around Tattenham Corner on Epsom Downs. He had promised Lady Isobel he would talk to her father next time he visited Fillingham Hall, but he didn't relish the prospect. This would be worse than facing Coroner Dean's interrogation at the West Fell Colliery disaster inquest, he thought. At least on that occasion he had managed to convince the coroner that he had not tampered with the regulator door.

Having grasped the nettle, he eventually confronted Lord Fillingham, and asked for Lady Isobel's hand in marriage. As it turned out, it was not the traumatic experience that Bobby had feared, and they were married in the little chapel on the Fillingham estate the following year, in June 1893, following the Epsom Downs

Derby meeting. Tommy Cogon was Bobby's best man and as they sat in the front pew awaiting the arrival of Lady Isobel and her father, they reminisced of their childhood.

'Who would have thought all those years ago that I would have ended up sitting here waiting to marry the daughter of one of the richest landowners in the North of England,' he whispered out of the corner of his mouth. Before Tommy could respond to Bobby's aside, the organ, mimicking a fanfare of trumpets with the opening bars of Mendelssohn's wedding march, brought the chatter of the congregation to an abrupt halt, heralding the entrance of the slow bridal procession. For a moment, the shuffling of feet as the congregation rose from their seats, muffled the music. The beautiful young bride accompanied by her father, followed by her bridal entourage, slowly made their way down the aisle. The less patient members of the congregation turned to view the bridal party as it serenely progressed down the aisle in time with the music. Bobby also chanced a quick backward glance and saw this vision of beauty dressed in white, on the arm of her father, slowly gliding towards him, like some heavenly apparition.

*

On retiring to their bed on the night of their daughter's wedding, Lord, and Lady Fillingham discussed what had gone before.

'Well, that's that over and done with,' her Ladyship commented adding, 'She did look beautiful darling, don't you think?'

'Of course, my dear, she is born of you. What else would you expect? But I will give the marriage one year; two at the most.'

'Why would you say such a thing? How can you be so sure of such an opinion so early in the marriage? The ink is hardly dry on the marriage certificate.'

'Believe me, I know our daughter. The best way to deal with her whims is to let her have her own way and once she gets what she wants, she will tire of him and cast him aside like one of her toy dolls when she was a child. She has always had a capricious streak in her. I love her implicitly. Nevertheless, I have come to realise, as she gets older, the best way to deal with Isobel, when she is on one of her sensationalist moods, is not to argue with her and let the episode die a natural death. Challenge her and she will dig her heels in and do the opposite of what you think is in her best interest. Agree and leave her to her own devises, she will gradually come around to my way of thinking. You mark my words darling, that little silk-clad husband of hers is on borrowed time.'

'How well you know her my darling. I must agree you are so right; you always are. But what of all that expense you have gone to?'

'My dear, when you are one of the wealthiest men in the country, one can indulge oneself in what today was a mere bagatelle; look on it as an investment. The return will outweigh the loss and hopefully she will learn from her experience. After all, she is still a child in her ways and still needs to improve her worldly wisdom. With that in mind, I have met with Robson Parkinson, and he has drawn up the necessary legal paperwork which will place Isobel's wealth in a trust fund out of reach of our horse-riding pit boy,' his lordship concluded.

'Darling, you are so clever; I am so lucky to have your wisdom to call upon when needed, and with that they retired to sleep.

*

The young couple honeymooned for two weeks in Paris and Bobby, not one to miss an opportunity of a winning ride, had accepted the offer to ride Baron P de Satendron's, Fontain Roi, in the Grand Prix de San Martin, at Longchamp racecourse, which he duly won.

On returning to the winner's enclosure, Bobby Anderson dismounted and faced the winning owner and his trainer and family and friends. They shook his hand repeatedly and as in France they kissed him on both cheeks, even the men in the company. Isobel, for a little while translated the congratulatory remarks directed at Bobby. Calls of *'bien fait Robert, vous êtes fantastique,'* rang out across the paddock. 'What are they shouting Isobel?' Bobby quickly asked.

'Well done Robert, you are fantastic,' Isobel translated into her husband's ear. But she was already disagreeing with the crowd. She deliberately let the pressing crowd overtake her, as the ecstatic throng swallowed up her husband, while she looked on in desperation. She realised at that point so early in their marriage that she would always have to share her husband with his adoring followers even on their honeymoon, but what she found strange about it all – she didn't care.

'What am I doing here?' she asked herself. She, the daughter of noble birth and daughter of a Lord of the realm felt totally out of place playing second fiddle to some minor French Baron and his sycophantic entourage. Considering her social position back in England, the shortcomings of marrying beneath oneself, suddenly struck her. His fame, despite her being the wife of a jockey rankled her. She watched with despair from the outer fringe of the congratulatory crowd, as her husband wallowed in his fame. It was what he had come to expect, and he loved it all. Probably more than he loved her, she thought. As only being the wife of the jockey in the eyes of some members of the French crowd, she felt totally ignored. Never in all her life, had she experienced such treatment. *After all, who are these people who dared to ignore her like a pauper in the street? Outside of Paris, nobody would probably have heard of them*, she thought. Suddenly racked with homesickness, she needed her mother's reassurance at this very moment.

On the coach journey back to their hotel and away from the Longchamp crowds, Isobel vented her anger on her husband who was still high on his success.

'What is wrong Isobel? You seem quiet; have I upset you? I thought you would have been pleased for me and my success,' he suggested.

'There you go! You! You! You! It is always you. Did you have to accept a race ride on our honeymoon? I would have preferred to take in some of the tremendous culture Paris has to offer but not you. Oh no! I felt very lonely at Longchamp, ignored by a bunch of nobodies who felt the wife of the winning jockey was beneath them. What their tiny minds were not aware of, was that my breeding traces back to Elizabeth, ruler of the greatest country in the world.' She was seething at the way the Baron and his entourage had treated her. 'After all, if the truth be known, he has probably bought some trumped up title and he is a 'baron' in name only, a charlatan of the first order.'

'Maybe they were just taken up by the euphoria of their horse's success,' Bobby suggested, as he tried to make excuses for them.

'That is no excuse for their abysmal manners. They were ignoring me totally even before their horse had left the paddock for the start of the race. Even though I was left in their company while you were busy riding their 'precious' horse. With you engaged out on the racecourse and despite my impeccable French, those shallow minded idiots excluded me completely from their conversation. I felt as if I too were in their employ, reducing my standing to that of a mere interpreter, my fee included in whatever pittance they paid you to ride their substandard animal in a substandard race,' Lady Isobel concluded furiously.

Her husband pondered for a while as his wife's admonishment filtered through his mind but after several moments contemplating her words, he was unable to offer even the weakest argument against her. They had had their first argument and it disappointed him to think it had come so soon in their marriage. It would prove to be the first of many between this young couple from such differing backgrounds.

*

In the April of 1894, two months before the first anniversary of their marriage, Lady Isobel left Bobby Anderson, and returned to the family home at Fillingham Hall. Her father's prediction on the night of her wedding was correct but for two months and she and Bobby Anderson were divorced within the year.

The divorce had been swift, following Lord Fillingham's influence. Divorce for a working-class woman in Victorian England was almost impossible once she married. In the eyes of the law, she became her husband's property, together with all she owned. Among the rich and famous, it could be 'arranged.' His lordship had consulted Tristan Emerson-Crags the family physician, who had devised a scheme whereby they could prove that Robert Anderson, while normally of sound mind could, during wasting that is, going for long periods without eating, to reduce his weight, could become capable of temporary madness. During these periods, he claimed Lady Isobel was in danger of serious harm at the hands of her husband and consequently, she had found it necessary on several occasions, to return home to find sanctuary and it was on these grounds, that the court granted her divorce from Robert Anderson.

Chapter 16

Two years after Lady Isobel Percival had gained her divorce from Bobby Anderson, fate dealt her ex-husband a cruel blow. Being tall for a jockey, he was always aware of his body weight and indeed, he had waged a running battle for most of his career. He had resorted to the usual 'treatments' that most jockeys with similar problems practiced, vis-à-vis, wasting, using Turkish baths, taking diuretic tablets, and purgatives. Some jockeys in desperation had tried spurious concoctions made from unknown ingredients with dire consequences and on a few occasions even death. Even the great Fred Archer, whom Bobby had marvelled at, on his visit to Thirsk, had shot himself in the head during a period of similar circumstance.

In the early days of his problem, Bobby had managed to keep his weight down by using any one of these treatments. Recently he was finding it increasingly difficult to make his riding weight. His continuing failure to make the weight had taxed the patience of the owners of the better horses and he now found himself having to accept rides which two years ago he wouldn't have given a moments consideration. To compound the problem further, he had taken to 'hitting the bottle' to drown his sorrows and he was gaining a reputation for unreliability amongst the owners and trainers. Even Fraser Copeland, who had launched his riding career, had lost patience with his former jockey, and no longer put good rides his way.

*

And so, in 1896, Chris Paxton, realising his former prodigy needed medical treatment, had brought him back to Shinwell Hall, where Miles Paxton diagnosed liver damage. He had him admitted to the Dan Swain cottage hospital, where he could be treated, starting with a better food regime to build up his strength. Once he was stronger, Miles would then tackle the problem of his liver – free of alcohol.

Jemima was not altogether happy about the arrangements put in place by her husband because she knew that with her involvement at the hospital, she and Bobby Anderson's paths would surely cross sometime. Although she had decided to avoid Bobby Anderson over the last three years or so, she wished him no harm and she hoped her son could get him back to a full recovery.

*

Away from the rigours and responsibilities of race riding, and benefiting from Dr Miles Paxton's ministration, Bobby Anderson made good progress along the road to recovery. He had decided, following advice from his former patron, Chris Paxton, that he should retire from race riding, a decision which would free him from the restraints and disciplines endured by a jockey; especially one riding on the 'flat' where the horses carried less weight and the lower weights brought greater demands on the jockeys. Chris Paxton had told Bobby that following a complete recovery, a job awaited him at Shinwell Hall where he would take over the dual role of coachman and odd job man on the retirement of Thompson, who would be seventy on his next birthday. Bobby seized this opportunity with both hands. He saw it as a way out of the situation into which he had allowed himself to sink. He blamed no one for his demise. He was non-judgmental towards either of the two women in his adult life; neither Lady Isobel Percival who was now deep in his past, nor Jemima Paxton who had also figured in his past but who could figure very much in his future if he took on the job at Shinwell Hall. Despite the strong yearning deep inside him for Jemima Paxton,

Bobby also looked forward to reuniting with his childhood friend Tommy Cogon. He knew he would hold the senior post but that would be in name only. They would work together as a team. It would be like old times, and he saw it acting as a spur towards his recovery and so, in 1898 Bobby began his new role at Shinwell Hall.

*

The little cottage hospital was flourishing. Since the opening, the infant mortality rate in the locality had decreased year after year and at the last assessment, the average for the hospital stood at less than one in ten. Jemima was enjoying life more now that the hospital was fully operational and her involvement as secretary was giving her a newfound interest in life for the first time since her retirement from the stage. She felt she had found a new niche as secretary to the hospital. She had taken to visiting the expectant mothers in their homes, accompanied by Mrs Collingwood who acted as her adviser in these matters. Although not a qualified midwife, Lily Collingwood had gained much of her knowledge through her own experience. The whole community deemed her the ideal person for the job. Every expectant mother in the village of West Fell, recognised Lily as the local 'midwife', an unofficial role she had held since the establishment of the pit village. In her time, she had given birth to seven children of her own without any fatalities and had 'officiated' at innumerable births of other peoples' babies born in the area. With her experience, the villagers of West Fell regarded her as a dependable aide at any childbirth. Together, the two women were a great asset to the pregnant women in preparing them for the pre-natal issues to ensure that everything was in place on the day of the baby's delivery in the hospital. Jemima enjoyed this work and she and Mrs Collingwood worked together as a successful team, Lily making the practical assessments and Jemima keeping the notes, which she entered up in the patients' files on her return to the hospital.

As the hospital flourished, Miles Paxton's workload increased. So much so, the hospital committee had called an extraordinary meeting and had decided that the funds were such that an assistant to Miles Paxton was within the compass of the funds. An advertisement placed in several appropriate medical journals and other local newspapers had the desired response.

Miles was aware of the struggle women were experiencing in their attempts to gain a place in the medical universities in the United Kingdom. He was also aware of the greater struggle they experienced in gaining recognition once they had qualified in their chosen profession. He instructed his mother as secretary, to place the same advertisement in the Edinburgh press, knowing that the work being done by the likes of Sophia Jex-Blake was gaining strength in that area of the country. Unlike his male contemporaries, he was keen to give a female the opportunity to enhance her career. It suited his socialist tendencies. In 1878, Jex-Blake had founded the Edinburgh Provident Dispensary for Women and Children offering medicine and advice to working class people and in 1883, she had accommodated a few patients in her own home, a Regency house named Bransfield Lodge. She had expanded the premises and in 1885, it had taken on the name of the Edinburgh Hospital for Women and Children. Miles believed any woman arriving from that environment with the right credentials should fit in well at the Dan Swain Hospital at West Fell.

Chapter 17

Jemima Paxton in her role as secretary to the Hospital Fund had taken the carriage to Newcastle Central station, with Bobby Anderson as driver, to meet Dr Jeanie Kilbride, the applicant from Fife, in Scotland, for the post as assistant to her son Miles. Somehow, they seemed to have missed her; the train from Edinburgh had arrived and left again to continue its journey south.

'Maybe she has chickened out,' Bobby Anderson suggested rather flippantly.

'I very much doubt that an enthusiastic female trying to progress her career in the medical profession, would be so careless. I would say we have either missed her or she is arriving on a later train,' Jemima Paxton countered brusquely. 'We will await the arrival of the next train from Edinburgh and if she doesn't show up after that then we give up on her and return to Shinwell,' Jemima declared, with an air of annoyance. 'In the meantime, we can partake of a coffee in the station café, not that I hold much hope of it being remotely palatable,' she added cynically.

*

Jeanie Kilbride MB, who had gained her degree from the Edinburgh Medical College for Women, arrived at West Fell cottage hospital on that gloomy Monday in November. She placed her suitcase on the floor and knocked timorously on the door. A plaque bearing in gold paint, Dr Miles Paxton, Medical Officer. When the door opened, she expected to see an aged doctor, moustachioed, smelling of pipe smoke and not very tolerant of the burgeoning ranks of female medical practitioners. She was pleasantly surprised when on the other side of the threshold stood a man, much younger than her imagination had conjured up for her. The man standing in front of her was clean-shaven and certainly not smelling of tobacco-smoke and her confidence soared.

'My mother found you alright on your arrival in Newcastle?' Miles Paxton asked mysteriously, of the young lady on the doorstep.

With Miles Paxton's mild interrogation completed and having provided all the right answers, she had impressed him tremendously. He saw Jeanie Kilbride as the epitome of the type of person he had in mind as his assistant. Another point on which she had scored strongly in the young doctor's favour, she was the daughter of a Fife coal miner. She had won a place at High School before going on to Edinburgh Medical College for Women.

As far as he was concerned, she was the perfect applicant, and she had a pleasant personality and pleasing on the eye. He looked forward to their collaboration in the running of the Dan Swain hospital. He could see her being popular with the women and children of West Fell.

'What arrangements have you made for your accommodation Dr Kilbride?' he asked.

'Oh, please Dr Paxton; if we are going to work together can I suggest we drop the formality. Please call me Jeanie at least when we are in our own company,' she suggested.

'In that case you can call me Miles,' he replied, readily.

'In answer to your question, I dared not pre-book any accommodation as I did not want to tempt fate by being so presumptuous,' she confessed.

'Well, you need not worry on that score there is sufficient space out at my family home at Shinwell Hall. If you are uncomfortable with that arrangement, being under the same roof as your boss, then we can find you alternative accommodation somewhere more suitable to your wishes,' Miles Paxton offered.

'I am prepared to give your idea a try for now. It is kind of you Miles,' she said, remembering her own previous suggestion of informality.

'In that case, I will fix you up with a white coat and we can go on a tour of the hospital as long as you don't mind starting right away. We will draw up your terms of employment in the morning if that is all right by you. I would like you to meet Ivy Turpin; she could present you with your first delivery, as she is due to give birth within the next couple of days.'

'Those arrangements are fine by me and oh, by the way, lest I forget. Please apologise to your mother for her wasted journey to Newcastle.'

'You can apologise to her yourself when we finish here later. I'm sure she won't hold that against you. She can be quite forgiving, when she wants to, he said reassuringly.'

During the tour of the hospital, Jeanie felt complete elation on gaining a place at the West Fell Hospital. It was just what she had hoped for on qualifying in medicine. Working with women and children was exactly what she had always wanted; and her boss was so amiable.

Chapter 18

Bobby Anderson was fit and well again, fitter than he had been for some time. Thanks to Chris Paxton's concern and Miles Paxton's expertise, he had put on weight; weight which he did not have to worry about, and he was now enjoying his new occupation at Shinwell Hall. In the early days, he had felt self-conscious dressed up in the finery of his official uniform. On reflection, it was no stranger than dressing up in multi-coloured silks as a jockey and he had come to terms with the coachman's livery. He had met Jemima several times in his new role and although their meetings were purely on an employer, employee basis, she was at least more amiable than he remembered her in the days and weeks after their indiscretion. While he still respected her as a woman, his sexual feelings for her over the years had waned; after all, she was now in her sixties. Until now, he felt she had allowed the incident to fade into the depths of time and she now seemed to have generously allowed it to stay there; lost forever. What Jemima had not revealed to her coachman was that she too was pleased with his progress, and it pleased her to see him looking so well once more.

*

Bobby Anderson had now been in his new role for two years and he and Tommy Cogon worked well together; something which Chris Paxton was confident of, when he offered Bobby the job at Shinwell Hall. The two pals worked well together sharing the work rather than

Bobby allocating it. Instead of a place of work, Shinwell Hall had become a place of fun. They worked together on the gallops when the horses needed exercising, vying with each other on the fast five-furlong straight gallop. A day at the races was their favourite pastime when they had free time to spend. The reunion with Tommy had been very cathartic and Bobby was enjoying life again. When at the races, all of Bobby's genuine acquaintances from his riding career were pleased to see him and wished him well. Some whom he had crossed in the past, were still smarting from the experience. It seemed to Tommy that once Bobby had crossed you, you stayed crossed.

*

With the passing of time, there was an indication of some sort of reconciliation between himself and Jemima Paxton, although neither of them had raised the subject of their one-off relationship. The fact that she was amiable towards him was enough for Bobby and he could live with that. He had been free of alcoholic drink for two years and he was happier than he had been for some time. He knew for certain, he had come to terms with the fact that he would never be able to have Jemima. Nevertheless, she was the only woman he would ever love.

*

After spending thirteen successful years in India employed as the retained jockey to the Gaekwad of Rajkarat, Jed Smyth had returned to England to escape an outbreak of the plague, which was ravaging the Princely State. On the final stage of his long journey 'home' from India, he had stopped off at a pub named 'The Fleece' near Newcastle Central Railway Station. The pub was busy, as it was the Saturday of the 'Hoppings Fair' on the Town Moor. He was killing time while he waited for the train to South Shields on the coast where his parents lived. He hadn't visited them since he left Richmond for India in 1885. Even the train journey from King's Cross to Newcastle had been long and tedious and he was looking forward to a pint of ale with which to slake his thirst. Taking a pint of ale from the barman, he looked around for a seat, having no fancy for standing at the bar. His eyes settled on a table in the far corner of the bar occupied by an old man seated on his own. Making for the vacant seat, he began to weave his way through the throng trying all the time to protect his pint from spillage. Dodging several threats from menacing elbows, he eventually reached his target.

'May I?' He asked the old man, politely.

'Make yourself at home son,' the old man said in a friendly manner adding, 'looks as if need that pint. Have y' travelled far?' he asked.

'I have come up from London today; the final leg of my journey from India.'

'India y' say. That's a journey and a half, and y' now find yourself in Newcastle of all places.'

'I'm on my way to South Shields, to my parents' place,' he replied immediately picking up on the local vernacular on hearing the old man's accent. He quickly snatched a long draught of his ale before his newfound companion had a chance to interrupt him with more interrogation. Sinking half of the beer down his throat in several thirsty gulps, the old man continued.

'By, you *are* dry man. That hardly touched the sides. I bet you could have downed that in one go,' the old man said, stating the obvious.

Jed Smyth reluctantly replaced his glass on the wooden topped table. The heavy table was made of cast iron with three legs. At the top of each leg was an image of a human head. On either side of each head was a pair of upturned hands creating the impression that they were supporting the wooden tabletop. He looked at his glass and thought the old man had the right idea, so he picked it up and quickly drained it of the contents in one quick gulp which still failed to slake his thirst. The old man spotted the chance of a free drink, had beaten Jed in emptying his glass. He sat with anticipation as he watched the thick froth slowly slide down the inside of Jed's glass.

Jed picked up his own empty glass and leaned over to collect the old man's.

'I tell y' what, make it a whisky, Scotch; medicinal-like, understand, too many long drinks and ah'll be up all night with the chamber pot,' the old man revealed.

Jed Smyth made his way once more to the bar. He eventually returned with two more drinks, and placed them on the table, the whisky in front of the old man.

'You were in India y' say. What were y' doin' over there, are y' in the military?'

'No, not at all, I'm a professional jockey to an Indian Prince.'

'What y' doin' back here then son? Sounds like you've left a damned good job to me, like.'

'Escaping the plague,' Jed said, deliberately withholding any explanation and trying to gain a reaction from the old man. He was not disappointed as the old man threw himself back in his chair.

'Not catching' here is it?'

'Don't worry yourself on that score. Even the plague can't travel that well,' Jed said, and the old man settled back to enjoy his free drink.

'I worked with horses until I retired; I was head groom and coachman at Shinwell Hall, on the fells above Standale, working for Chris and Jemima Paxton. Although, when she was on the stage she went by the name of 'Mimi Martin,' the Norfolk Lark. She's retired now, like.'

Jed's ears pricked up when he heard the old man mention Chris Paxton.

'Chris Paxton you say. I used to ride Chris Paxton's horses when I was with Fraser Copeland at Richmond Gill stables, before I left for India thirteen years ago. Do you know if Bobby Anderson is still riding for him?'

'He's still workin' for Paxton but he's not ridin' anymore. Well not his horses,' the old man said cryptically.

'What do you mean by that remark?'

'Put another whisky in there and make it a double and I'll tell you what I mean,' and he tapped the side of his nose with his forefinger conspiratorially.

Before Jed left once more for the bar he asked, 'What do you say your name is old man?'

'I didn't,' the old man said without any further elaboration.

Jed returned with another whisky for his newfound companion. He slid the glass containing the double measure, over to the old man.

'Now what was it you thought I might be interested in?' he enquired, keen to keep the conversation going.

'Ah never cared much for the young upstart from the day the master invited him and his mate to ride the horses. My horses, I'd had those horses from foals and there they were, a pair of young 'pit-yackers' with the master's permission mind, riding my horses. That young Anderson was full of himself; the other littlun wasn't so bad. That bairn lost his dad' in the pit, so I had a bit o' sympathy for that'n.'

'Howay old man, hurry it up a bit, I have another train to catch. You've told me nothing yet that is of use to me,' Jed said, getting anxious as he slipped into the local idiom, and he looked at his pocket watch.

'I said, Anderson was no longer riding Paxton's horses, but I know he has ridden his missus. I saw them wi' me own eyes. I watched them in the woods that form the park attached t' the grounds of the big house. They had no idea I was there watchin' every move they made.'

'Is that right?' Jed Smyth mouthed with immediate interest, and he moved to the edge of his seat. *Now this is getting interesting,* he thought to himself. 'Go on old man. I'm sure you are going to tell me more. How do I know you aren't making all this up? Why should I believe you?'

'Now why should I tell y' a pack of lies bonny lad? But I sense y' have a score to settle with the great Bobby Anderson yourself. Now what is it that yer after?'

'Proof for one thing, would be very nice otherwise it's my word against theirs.'

'Y' know those big white fivers that I don't see too often, but what I noticed are bulging y' wallet out a bit? Well, if you were to place one o' them under this 'ere empty whisky glass, I'll give y' the proof y' seek.'

Jed Smyth pondered for a little while as he considered the old man.' *Five quid, not a huge amount if it will get revenge on the man who ruined my career in this country*, he thought. Taking his leather wallet from his inside pocket, he slowly withdrew a five-pound note. Folding it twice, he creased it slowly between his finger and thumb and placed it under the whisky glass. 'Now old man, quickly, the proof I need to bring down Anderson once and for all.'

'The proof y' need son is this. Jemima Paxton, or Mimi Martin the world-famous soprano, has a big birthmark on the inside of her right leg, right at the top, I tell y.' Is that proof enough for y.' How would I know that if I hadn't seen it for meself?'

'Is that it? Is that your vital information? juicy as it might be. It does conjure up interesting thoughts of the lady of the manor, who always was a stunner, I'll admit. Well, I'll have to take your word for that. Your tale alone is worth a fiver and a couple of whiskies. I could have stayed and chatted longer if I weren't in a hurry for my train to Shields. So, I bid you goodbye,' and he left his new acquaintance slipping the newly earned fiver into his waistcoat pocket. Old Andrew Thompson tapped the pocket of his waistcoat now with the recently earned fiver safely ensconced and muttered in an undertone, 'not a bad day's work that, not bad at all,' and hopefully draining the last semblance of whisky from the already empty glass; he made for the door and home.

*

Jed Smyth completed his journey from Newcastle to South Shields and arrived at the door of a two storied, red bricked terraced house, with bay windows on the ground floor. Jed's father was a retired river pilot whose name was True British Smyth the son of a seagoing captain. He had been born at sea on his father's ship, the *'True British'* and Jed's grandfather had named his son after his ship. Throughout his life he was always known as Brit Smyth.

Jed knocked on the shiny blue door nervously even though it was his family home. It was almost fifteen years since he had seen his parents and he didn't know what sort of reception he might receive. The last time he had seen them was in 1885 when he had a ride in the Northumberland Plate on the new course at High Gosforth Park. The door opened and an old grey-haired woman, of round build and a friendly face greeted him. She wore a floral pinafore tied tightly, high around her waist, the tight strings emphasising her ample bosom. She studied him for what seemed an eternity before she threw her hands up to her face.

'Eeh our Jed! Where've you come from? You nearly frightened the life out o' your old Mam.' Come in bonny lad and tell us all about yourself and what you've been up to, and I'll put the kettle on the hob.' The old woman didn't know what thoughts were in her son's mind as to what use he could apply the nefarious knowledge he had gained from the old man in the pub.

'Hello Mam. How are you? You look well,' he said and stepped inside. He kissed her on the cheek.

'Have you been drinking, our Jed? Y' have, I can smell it on y' breath,' she said, as mothers do. 'But I still love y',' she added, giving him a big hug. He knew he was home.

Chapter 19

1900

The world was now in the new century and Jemima Paxton since her association with Lily Collingwood was learning at first-hand about the lives of the miners' wives. They were a proud lot who realised that their men worked extremely hard underground in the bowels of the earth. They knew that their men, down in the pit, were constantly in great danger of instant death or at best, they may survive but with the legacy of life-changing injuries or ill health. They revered their men and a miner's wife would have a zinc bath full of hot water ready for him on his return from the pit with the family's meal of simple fare but full of sustenance, cooking on the black leaded range. She kept the house clean, and the family's clothes washed and ironed without complaint, for she knew he worked hard down the pit, she worked hard in the home. The system worked in most households, and they were really proud to be 'working-class.'

In the mining villages, there was only one police constable. This was enough as a lot of the time they policed themselves. There was a self-imposed code of conduct, which all 'decent' families adhered to and any family that did not comply would be ostracised by the rest of the village. Most of the men gave their wage packets up to their wives each payday. They were paid every fortnight and the first week without pay was called 'baff week.' In most cases, the wife was the exchequer, and she paid all the bills and costed for their weekly needs including her husband's pocket money. When it was 'baff week,' and he had no pocket money left, he had to wait another week until pay day and he went without his beer and *'baccie.'* While this system, although not popular with everyone, did teach them thriftiness.

Jemima thought there was one area where there was room for improvement, were it not for ignorance. Rightly or wrongly, she thought the miners and their wives could reduce their responsibilities by reducing the size of their families, if they were aware of contraception. She also knew that this was a very delicate subject to enter into from several aspects. For one thing, the couples with large families appeared to shower great love and care on their children. Secondly, they resented interference from outsiders. She knew from her conversations with the villagers when doing her rounds with Lily Collingwood, some of the more enlightened women were already performing some form of contraception. Even with their limited knowledge, a few had limited their families to three, two, or in some cases one child. Some husbands of the Roman Catholic faith had even banned the local priest from their homes for filling their wives' heads with threats of damnation being cast upon them for practicing birth control which in the eyes of the Roman Catholic church, was a mortal sin. Now Jemima Paxton was walking amongst their women informing them of the virtues of the practice of birth control. Even those miners, who were secretly practicing some form of birth control and preferring to keep their own counsel on the subject, took umbrage at a well-to-do woman from the 'Hall' feeding their women with knowledge on the subject.

Jemima had discussed the subject with Dr Jeanie Kilbride and Lily Collingwood. Dr Jeanie Kilbride agreed with Jemima and thought the women should be made aware of contraception, so they could practice birth control if they so wished. Lily Collingwood, being more familiar of the ways of the village advised Jemima against her idea.

'At least they would be in control of their own bodies for the first time. Now they could decide whether they wanted more children or not. A position which hitherto they had had no control over whatsoever,' Jemima argued.

'We'll see,' was all Lily had to say on the subject.

*

Jemima was also taking an interest in 'Women's Suffrage' and movements that had been set up to get women enfranchised. She at last had found something which she thought would interest her sufficiently to replace her stage career. She was still trying after twenty years to fill the vacuum left since ending her stage career. She had read of the campaign of Millicent Fawcett who in 1897 had founded 'The National Union of Women's Suffrage,' as a vehicle for attaining enfranchisement for women; Fawcett believed in peaceful protest. Her approach to the problem was patience and argument. She believed acts of violence would make men think women could not be trusted with the vote. Her opinion being, if parliament made laws and women were subject to those laws, then women had a right to some say in the process of establishing those laws. Fawcett's views appealed to Jemima Paxton. Even so, she had not joined the movement. Moreover, she had not actively joined any of the lobbies campaigning for the 'Votes for Women;' instead, she decided to start her own local campaign to enlighten the women of West Fell on the use of contraceptives. Queen Victoria had done the struggle for Women's Suffrage no favours in 1870, when she had written *'Let women be what God intended, a helpmate for man, but with totally different duties and vocations.'* Over the past thirty years, this had become the public view on the subject. The male public had certainly embraced her majesty's opinion, as one would have expected; it suited them to do so. And now it had become, except for a small section of the female population, the accepted stance on women's suffrage. Despite Fawcett's passive approach, there was a group of women suffragists who were ready to fight physically for what they believed in.

In response to Jemima's own campaign to enlighten the women of West Fell on contraception, Miles Paxton commented, 'You are poking a hornets' nest Mother, if you go down that road. Certain members of society will come down on you like a ton of bricks if you pursue your idea, especially the church, both Anglican and Roman Catholic. They will see you as playing God and that is a dangerous pastime in their estimation. Not to mention some members of the local community who would see your activity as interference with their lives,' Miles argued.

'These are fine ideals that you foster Jemima, but I must agree with Miles that the whole concept is fraught with danger. I do not think the working class is ready for tampering with nature quite yet, even on as small a scale as using West Fell as a nucleus for your scheme,' Chris Paxton stated emphatically. 'I might add in conclusion, that the coal owners may see your campaign as a threat to their natural source of continued recruitment for strong coal hewers and that would not go down well in some quarters.'

'That is what this argument is all about. This is exactly how I would expect both of you to respond to my idea. Your attitudes are those of most men. Can't you see? I am not contemplating issuing contraceptives to all the women of Great Britain or indeed the world, but just to simply make literature available to the women of West Fell, which would inform them of the availability of such means of contraception if they so wished. It would at least let women see their destiny could be in their own hands. Partners would decide after discussion between them, whether they go for the male prophylactic or some form of the female contraceptive such as the 'Dutch' cap. The decision should be theirs,' Jemima countered.

'So be it Jemima. I know you by now and you will go ahead whatever I and Miles will say to the contrary. But, a word of warning, be ready for an angry counter reaction from some quarters,' her husband warned.

'I intend to go ahead with my plan and work on the content of a pamphlet explaining what is available and how to obtain such contraceptives. Once a suitable publication is designed, and printed, I intend to distribute a copy from house to house,' Jemima explained.

'My dear, I have always admired your determination but a cautionary note, please, for your own sake, do not act too zealously,' her husband implored her.

'Count me in Mrs Paxton,' Jeanie Kilbride said adding her support to Jemima's cause. 'I can certainly see the merit in your reasoning. It can do nothing but good for these women.'

Jeanie Kilbride had settled in well at the Dan Swain Hospital. She had been much more fortunate than some of her women contemporaries who had qualified in medicine. It was fortuitous that she was practicing her skills in an environment such as here at West Fell where she met with less opposition from her male counterparts.

Jemima Paxton went ahead with her scheme for women's enlightenment on birth control.

Each time she and Lily Collingwood visited an expectant mother; she discussed birth control with her and left a copy of her handbill for her perusal. Word got around the rest of the community and soon women who were not pregnant were making enquiries about the handbill. Those who were illiterate were asking other women to hold readings, so they too could gain knowledge on birth control. It had become the topic of the area. Several men, as Jemima expected, raised their objections. They looked upon it as interference in their private lives by an outsider and they burned her handbill. They ordered their wives to ignore the advice it contained. It also came as no surprise when Roman Catholic priests and Anglican vicars raised the subject from their pulpits, criticising Jemima's pamphlet and some had physically gone about retrieving the pamphlets and destroying them. To say it caused a furore was something of an understatement.

Things turned nasty when a group of irate men approached Shinwell Hall after dark with burning torches, hurling stones, and shattering many windows. Chris and Miles Paxton had faced the baying crowd with loaded shotguns and after addressing them with their promise of an end to Jemima Paxton's campaign, the miners had reluctantly dispersed back to their homes muttering words of victory as they left.

*

'Well, my boy, I think this calls for a brandy. We will retire to the library and celebrate our victory. We will deal with the broken glass in the morning.'

'Not exactly a 'Trafalgar' or a 'Waterloo'. Nevertheless, noteworthy as far as we are concerned father. Lead on sir.'

The following morning Chris Paxton confronted Jemima on the subject, expressing his concern for her safety.

'I know you are going to say "I told you so" and I know recent events have proved you and Miles were right in your predictions. Despite that, I stand by my actions and at least I have achieved what I set out to do; it was always going to be nothing more than an act of enlightenment. I have sown seeds in the minds of the women of West Fell. Even those among the female community who can't read, now know the content of my pamphlet and all the burning by the husbands and the confiscations by the holy men can't remove the information now installed indelibly in the minds of the women. I did not start this as a worldwide campaign, but to educate the local women on birth control. To this end, I think I *have* achieved what I set out to do.'

'You have put your case so eloquently my dear, I must agree with you that some good will come of this. But please, I beseech you, be careful.'

'Have no worries darling, I have put away my soapbox and my campaigning is over. I apologise for the cost of replacing the broken windows. I am firmly of the opinion that the end has justified the means.'

*

The news of Jemima's campaign had reached the local newspapers and three of them, namely, the *Newcastle Gazette*, the *Gateshead Herald* and the *Shields Tribune* all carried the story. Jed Smyth picked up a copy of the *Tribune* and was about to turn directly to the racing page when the headlines on the front page caught his eye. 'Lady of the Manor advises on Family Planning', the banner headline shouted out. Jed Smyth delayed his perusal of the day's runners at Ripon and concentrated on the front-page story. Interesting, he thought as he read the article.

Jed Smyth read no more as his mind was working overtime as to how he could capitalise on the intimate information he had gained from old Andy Thompson. Wonder if she made Bobby Anderson wear a rubber during their little session in the woods. Shouldn't think so, considering how much older she is than he. How convenient I met the old lad in the pub that day in Newcastle. I will have to work out a plan for how best to use my information and make it work to my best advantage. I want them both to suffer by blackmailing them into coughing up some decent cash, he thought, as he plotted to bring down Jemima Paxton and Bobby Anderson.

Chapter 20

Jed Smyth sat on a bar stool in 'The Infantryman'. He had come to the village to glean information on the old man whom he had met in the pub near Newcastle Central Station on his homeward journey from India six months ago.

'Do you know of an old chap who used to work as coachman to the Paxtons' up at Shinwell Hall?' he asked of Sam Bailes, the pub landlord.

'Now why do y'ask that bonny lad?' Sam Bailes asked, immediately becoming suspicious of the nosey stranger sat on the other side of his bar. Sam had travelled the world in his military days and had met all manner of people during his time spent in the army. He prided himself in his ability to judge people on first appearance.

'A' can quickly weigh people up; got it from me old mother,' was the way he described his skill, adding 'and I'm rarely wrong.'

Jed Smyth continued the conversation, 'I met this old man in a pub in Newcastle about six months since and he said he had worked as coachman at the Manor. He just seemed a decent old fella' to me and gave me advice on how to get to South Shields.'

'Shields y' say, I'd buy him a pint for gettin' me out of Shields,' Sam said, adding, 'who got you out?' Jed Smyth laughed at the landlord's quip. 'I think you have had the misfortune to make the acquaintance of old Andy Thompson. But I don't know about him bein' a decent old man, I think you must 'ave met his brother or somebody posin' as him from what y' say. I've always found 'im a miserable old bugger who tended to be a bit of a loner who nobody had much time for.'

'Y'say his name's Andy Thompson; any idea where I might find 'im?' Jed Smyth probed.

'I take it you've been back to where y' met him? That's where I would start lookin.' When he left the Manor, he went to live in a flat in Newcastle close to 'The Fleece Inn.' I would say that's y' best bet, not that I would bother about the old bugger. The only pint ah'd buy 'im would be a pint of poison.'

'What do y' know about the lady of the manor, Jemima Paxton? How is she these days, I used to ride her husband's horses at one time before I moved abroad,' Jed Smyth revealed.

'By y're askin' a lot of questions. Y' say y're a jockey, are y'sure y're not a detective, or a reporter. Let's just say first, she's not one of me regulars, nor is her husband, mores the pity. I suppose y' heard of all the commotion she caused over that birth control business. It was in all the local papers.'

'I'm neither detective nor newspaperman, but I understand she was quite friendly with the failed jockey Bobby Anderson.'

'Here, let me tell y' somethin' now. Ah'm beginnin' to take a bit of a dislike' to y'son. That's not like me. Ah'm usually a tolerant man but ah'm gettin' a bit fed up with y' questions, and before ah finish with y', let me give y' a final bit of advice, don't let any of these big miners here abouts, hear y' call Bobby Anderson a failed jockey, or y're in real bother. Ah'll 'ave y' know, around here he's a legend in his own lifetime. Now, finish that pint in front of y' and continue y' search for that miserable Andy Thompson. I reckon the two of y'll make a right pair,' Sam Bailes said with utter contempt.

Jed Smyth finished his pint in one gulp and jumping off the bar stool he left with his tail between his legs.

'That buggers a good for nowt and he's up to no good.'

*

A couple of nights later, Bobby Anderson and Tommy Cogon, having bedded the horses down for the night, took a stroll down the fell to 'The Infantryman.' On arriving, Bobby Anderson ordered two pints of Sam Bailes's best ale straight from the wood.

Sam put the first pint of copper coloured ale in front of Bobby and said, 'A bloke was in here a couple of days back enquiring after y' Bobby.'

'Who might that be I wonder?' Bobby replied.

Sam turned from pouring the second pint from the barrel set up on the rack behind the bar and placed it in front of the awaiting Tommy.

'I might be able to shed some light on that one Bobby son. He said he had met old Andy Thompson in 'The Fleece,' opposite Newcastle Station. He knew Chris Paxton and his missus and said he had ridden Chris Paxton's horses in the past. He looked to me as if he had lived out of the area for some time. He had a bit of the local lingo, but he struck me as if he was putting it on for my benefit. He certainly had the build of a jockey, but his complexion was darker than yours which made me think he had spent time abroad; somewhere in a hot climate, like when I was in India all those years ago.'

'Reminded you of India you say Sam, and he rode for the Paxtons at one time? That's got to be Jed Smyth,' Bobby said with conviction, adding, 'I've had a run in with him in the past. Early in my career, he was stable jockey to Fraser Copeland when I arrived at Richmond Gill stables. I 'jocked him off' Chris Paxton's horses following his terrible handling of Indian Empress in the Epsom Oaks in 1885 and eventually replaced him as Fraser Copeland's first jockey. It was shortly after that; he got a chance to ride in India for the Gaekwad of Rajkarat. As far as I knew, he was still out there. He *was* from South Shields before he left to be a jockey,' Bobby concluded.

'Remember the followin' year Bobby, y' did us all a favour when you rode Black Gold to victory in the Oaks. The biggest part of the village was on her that day,' and Sam's eyes looked up towards the ceiling as if to be in a reverie as he thought back to that memorable day when Bobby rode his first classic winner. Returning from his thoughts of the past, Sam continued.

'Well, that's the first lie he's told us. He told me old Thompson told him how to get to South Shields,' adding, 'I'd watch me back with that'n if I were you Bobby me lad. I thought him a bit of a rum 'un the first time I clapped eyes on 'im.'

Bobby felt a warm mix of pride and nostalgia when Sam had referred to his past glory.

'Don't worry Bobby, if he turns up here again shapin' for a fight, he'll have half the village to contend with,' Tommy said in support of his lifelong mate.

'I'll second that Tommy, now you two forget about that'n and enjoy y' beer,' the landlord said.

*

On the way home, Tommy Cogon was still thinking about Sam Bailes's account of his meeting with Jed Smyth. 'What did you make of the business of Jed Smyth asking questions of you, and he also seemed to be interested in the lady of the manor?' Tommy asked. The reference to Jemima Paxton had raised trepidation in the mind of Bobby. So much so, he had found it difficult to concentrate on little else for the rest of the evening.

Chapter 21

Chris Paxton thumbed through the post, which had arrived at Shinwell Hall earlier that morning. Some of the handwriting on the envelopes he recognised readily and others he filed in his mind as official. Although one letter, the envelope of which had come from a cheap form of stationery and addressed in a childlike scrawl, caught his eye. 'From whom could this be? Probably one of the village girls applying for a place in my employ at the Hall,' he thought.

Taking his place at the large desk, he slit open the envelope with his engraved silver paper knife and removed the note from within. He opened the single page of cheap blue paper which matched the colour of the envelope. The ruled notepaper was to aid the inexperienced scribe, to keep the writing straight across the page. Chris Paxton straightened the page from its single mid-page crease and cast his eye across the scrawled note. He noticed it bore neither address nor signature. He commenced reading the short missive.

'I have information on your wife which could be of interest to you. Bobby Anderson doesn't get off Scot-free either. But it will cost you money. I will be in touch again soon. Keep an eye on your wife Chris and that Bobby Anderson.'

Chris Paxton stared at the few words the note contained. There seemed neither rhyme nor reason in what he read. He folded the page and replaced it in the envelope. Turning the envelope over, he scanned it with an investigative eye for a giveaway postmark indicating its place of origin. The postmark clearly read Newcastle upon Tyne, but he knew the perpetrator could have posted it anywhere so as not to leave a true lead. He pondered over the meaning. The letter threatened future extortion and it suggested a compromising situation between his wife and Bobby Anderson but little else. Surely, it was someone out to cause mischief between himself and his wife. Any sexual involvement between the two did not add up in Chris Paxton's mind, considering the wide age gap between them, he decided to take no action. His initial instinct as to why the author of the note had acted in such a malicious way was because of his wife's campaign on birth control. After a little thought, he decided not to contact either Jemima or Bobby Anderson on the subject. I will let sleeping dogs lie for now, he thought.

A month elapsed before the blackmailer got in touch again. Using the same notepaper as before he was more forthcoming with his second letter which Chris Paxton noticed was much more sizable. He wrote in the same scrawl; still there was no indication of the author other than it was by the same hand on the same cheap paper.

Hello Chris.

As I promised, it is time I enlightened you a bit more on what your wife and Bobby Anderson have been up to behind your back. But I am keeping the best bits for the newspapers. She made the local newspapers with her campaign on birth control. Considering her international fame, what I might reveal would sell well to the newspapers anywhere in the world. So, it is up to you, cough up the cash yourself or I go to the papers. I know they would be very forthcoming with the cash for what I have to offer concerning the national treasure, 'Mimi Martin.' The figure I have in mind for you to settle is £500. If you decline the offer, then be it on your head. It is up to you. I am giving you the opportunity to keep it out of the papers or I sell to the international press for twice the price. So, you see I am being very lenient with you. There you have it. £500 and it's all hushed up, or you refuse, and it's all made public knowledge. Your wife's credibility and reputation are gone forever along with that of your little 'pit pony rider.' Mind you Chris, I think you will agree he destroyed his own career some years ago which had nothing to do with me. You can't keep coming to his rescue. He had this coming. I will be in touch later to explain to you how you can contact me with your decision.

P.S. Don't think of going to the police, as I know your wife has a large brown birthmark inside the top of her right thigh. Now you wouldn't want that to be 'out in the open', would you? Although it has been already, if you catch my meaning. I'll be in touch again soon.

Ever since the night in the pub, Bobby had agonised over Jed Smyth's motives for asking questions about himself and Jemima Paxton. How much does he know about them, if anything, or was it all in his own guilty mind? He would like to raise the subject with both Jemima and Chris Paxton although not at the same time, but he knew that was impossible and too indelicate. After much deliberation, he decided he would at least mention it to Jemima at the earliest opportunity. At least he would learn from her if her husband had said anything on the subject.

*

Over the next few days, he had prepared in his mind how the conversation with Jemima might go. Before he had a chance to put it into practice Chris Paxton confronted him when he came into the yard to take out his hunter on a hack round the Grand Drive. Tommy and Bobby were in conversation when Chris Paxton approached them.

'Tommy, could I have a word with Bobby on a private matter please.'

Tommy left the other two and made himself scarce by checking the hay nets and salt blocks within the stalls of the stable block. As he progressed along the stalls, the louvre vents to the stable were open and Tommy could not avoid hearing the conversation between his friend and their master who stood just below the open vent.

'I am in receipt of two anonymous letters demanding money if I do not comply with the author's demands. There are further letters threatened, until I come up with the money the perpetrator is demanding. He has based his claim on his knowledge of a sexual nature; knowledge which he purports, concerns yourself and my wife. Before I make a payment of any proportion, I would like you to confirm or refute any such scandal. I would like to give you the opportunity to make your contribution on the sordid subject. What do you know if anything Bobby?'

Tommy inadvertently had heard what his master had said to his friend and waited anxiously on Bobby's reply. Bobby's reply was not immediate as he studied how much he could reveal. 'I can't say how any stories have gotten around concerning your good wife and me master, but I can say they have no truth. It is just someone being mischievous and trying at the same time to make big money for him or her.' His skin crawled as he deceived for the second time the man who had helped him so much in the past.

'Well, I will leave it with you to mull over. If anything comes to mind let me know immediately. I am sorry to bring this up with you Bobby, but it needed saying. I can't just blindly meet this villain's demands without making enquiries of my own.'

'Can I ask you master, have you brought this up with Mrs Paxton?'

'I'm glad to say I have not Bobby, nor will I, now I have your side of things.'

*

Tommy mulled over what he had heard. He did not know whether Bobby was implicated or not, but his thoughts were on the conversation with Sam Bailes in 'The Infantryman' at West Fell. He soon reached the conclusion that Jed Smyth had something to do with these serious allegations that threatened his lifelong friend's future and his livelihood. He decided there and then that he would pledge himself to do whatever he could to track Jed Smyth down and confront him on the subject. Whether Bobby was guilty or not, he had earned Tommy's loyalty over the years.

*

The following Sunday Bobby asked Tommy if he fancied a pint at 'The Infantryman.'

'Sorry Bobby, I hate to turn me best mate down on our only day off especially when there is no coachin' to do for the Paxtons. But I must go over to my Aunt Gracie's in Ravensgarth. She's fallen, leaving her with pneumonia. Me mam's workin' this weekend and can't make it, so ah'll have to go in her place.'

'We'll go together and have a pint on the way,' Bobby suggested.

'That's a good idea Bobby but I can't take you to me Aunty Gracie's place. You know how it is; she's never been like our mam's are. It would embarrass me to death if you could see the place. She never bottomed the place when she was well, so God only knows what it's like now she's laid up,' Tommy lied.

'Alright please yourself mate,' Bobby said dejectedly. Tommy wasn't happy that he could not go for a pint with Bobby, as he liked to keep an eye on his drinking. The last thing he wanted was for Bobby to lapse into his old ways. What Tommy was really planning was to track down his old boss Andy Thompson. Sam Bailes had said he could be found at the 'Fleece Inn' near to Newcastle Central station.

*

Tommy scanned the public bar of the 'Fleece Inn' for his old boss and sure enough, there he was, seated in the far corner on his own, which came as no surprise to Tommy. Tommy got a pint from the barman and made his way over to Thompson's table. He still thought of him as Thompson, but he thought better of calling him Thompson to his face as he hoped to humour him. Something he didn't relish but needs must, he thought.

'Hello Mr Thompson, how are you?' Tommy asked sheepishly.

Old Andy Thompson stared at Tommy for a moment. 'Oh, it's you? What brings y' round these parts?' Thompson asked. In keeping with his reputation, old Thompson's reception of Tommy came as no surprise. What Tommy didn't know; he could be unusually friendly when he thought a free drink was a possibility.

'I'm in Newcastle to see me sick aunt,' Tommy explained trying to be as convincing a liar as possible. 'I met a bloke in 'The Infantryman' in West Fell, by the name of Jed Smyth and he said you'd been talking to him about Bobby. But he had quite a bit to drink on him and he wasn't making much sense. I thought you would be able to tell us what you told him.'

'Now how did you know it was me he was talkin' to? Whatever gave y' that idea? I never talked to anybody about Bobby and Mrs Paxton.'

'Now who mentioned Mrs Paxton, Mr Thompson? I think you've tripped yourself up there. You must be careful when you're telling lies, you know,' Tommy countered smartly.

'Look son, I have no axe to grind with you. So, if you can find it in you to get an old man a drop of scotch, we might be able to have a similar crack as I had with that Jed fella,' and he slid his empty glass across the table as he had done with Jed Smyth. Tommy went to the bar and returned with a double whisky for his old boss...

*

On the journey back to West Fell, Tommy thought over what Old Thompson had revealed. If what he had learned from Old Thompson was all true, it disappointed him deeply. Never had he thought that Bobby could do something so stupid, especially with the wife of the man who had given him his best chance in life. It didn't make sense to him at all. How could he have stooped so low and what of Jemima Paxton? What about her part in this? She didn't come out of this whiter than white. To see her going around the village with Lily Collingwood, you would think butter wouldn't melt in her mouth. But he now knew differently, and he tried hard not to be too judgmental of them.

*

The omnibus pulled up with a squeal of breaks outside 'The

Infantryman.' Tommy pulled his pocket watch from his waistcoat pocket as he alighted from the vehicle. *Ten o'clock, I might still catch Bobby if I'm lucky*, he thought.

He entered the pub, made straight to the bar, and ordered a pint. 'Y' late tonight Tommy. Have y' been somewhere nice? Y' mate's over there. He hasn't said much all night. He's either got somethin' on his mind or he's missed y'company,' Sam suggested.

'I've been to Newcastle to see me sick Aunt Gracie,' Tommy lied once more.

'Bobby looks as if he needs another to cheer him up,' Sam Bailes suggested.

'Oh no Sam he looks as if he's had more than enough already. I haven't been here to keep a watchful eye on 'im,' Tommy stated as he noticed the three empty glasses lined up in front of his friend. 'I tell you what Sam forget the pint; have it on me,' Tommy said as he slid the money over the bar, adding, I need to get Bobby home; he's had enough,' and he made his way over to his friend.

'Hello Tommy, by I'm glad t' see you?'

Tommy noticed Bobby's glass was almost empty. Bobby drained his glass and held it up to Tommy indicating a replacement.

'Good timing Tommy. Just what I need,' Bobby said in a slurred manner.

Sam mustn't have a pot-lad tonight, Tommy thought noticing once again the empty glasses gathered in front of his friend.

'We're going, Bobby. I need to talk to you.'

'We can squeeze another in before chuckin' out time, Tommy,' Bobby protested.

'Not tonight Bobby you've had enough. Finish that and we're off home,' Tommy insisted. Had he been with Bobby all night he would have paced his drinking better. He worried about him reverting to his old ways with his drinking. Their usual practice was to make two pints last all night. But tonight, Bobby had not had a monitor to keep a watchful eye on his intake.

Sam Bailes rang his bell and called, 'Time me bonny lads lets have y' home now. Y're all welcome back the morn,' he shouted. There was a clattering of glasses and a shuffling of feet and as burly as these men were, they knew better than to quibble with big Sam Bailes and they obediently made their way out of the pub door.

'See y' the morn Sam,' several shouted as they filed past Sam's bar.

'I hope so lads, God willin,' Sam replied jovially.

*

Tommy and Bobby made their way back up the fell to Shinwell Hall. Once Bobby got out in the night air, he became more unsteady on his feet and Tommy had to grab him to stop him losing his balance and staggering off the path. With Bobby in this state, he decided to postpone discussing his meeting with Andy Thompson, and revealing what he had learnt of Jed Smyth's knowledge of Bobby's liaison with Mrs Paxton. He would wait for a more appropriate time to broach the subject.

Chapter 22

The following day, Tommy, having allowed enough time for Bobby's head to clear from the previous night's drinking session at 'The Infantryman' brought up the subject of Jed Smyth's attempt at blackmailing Chris Paxton and the incident that brought it about.

Tommy remonstrated with his friend, 'Whatever were you thinking about Bobby? You must have known it was dangerous to get involved with Mrs Paxton. I thought you had more sense. I have always looked up to you.'

Bobby said nothing throughout. After a silence that seemed like an eternity to Tommy, his friend eventually responded.

'I have no idea what brought it on. I was surprised at Jemima Paxton's response. I have always found her to be an attractive woman and I have fancied her ever since I first saw her. I was making a play for her, and she was returning my advances. First, I thought she was just stringing me along, simply a bit of flirtin' on her part, but I soon realised she was being serious. I was becoming excited at the prospect of having sex with her. I had always fancied having sex with her but that was as far as it went. On that day when we strolled on the five-furlong gallop, things started to move at a pace and we were both becoming sexually aroused,' Bobby Anderson confessed.

Tommy listened intently without interruption to his friend's description of the events leading up to the transgression between his friend and Jemima Paxton. He found it strange, that on listening to

Bobby Anderson's account of what had taken place between Bobby and Jemima Paxton, instead of spicing up his imagination as it might some men, on the contrary, he found the thought of Jemima Paxton having taken Bobby, angered him immensely. For he too had feelings for his friend. Feelings which he knew could never be encouraged. He realised many years ago that Bobby had no such feelings. Society and the law prohibited it, and Tommy had come to terms with the situation many years ago. 'What are we to do now Bobby? Now that there is the threat of exposure by this damned Jed Smyth. Exposure that we both know would ruin the pair of you, not to mention the shame it would bring on you, and the Paxtons.'

'I know what I'd like to do to Jed Smyth,' Bobby said with venom in his voice.

'That be as it may. But we both know that's not the answer. A good beltin' is not goin' to make it go away Bobby. We must think more cleverly than that. At this stage we have to rule out violence,' Tommy suggested, quickly adding, 'for now anyway.'

'What happens if Chris Paxton takes it up with Jemima? Until now she knows nothing of Jed Smyth's scheming and the longer she doesn't know, the better for all concerned.'

'It's a bit late for that now. You should have thought about that when the two of you did what you did Bobby.'

'I've got to talk to Jemima. She's got to be aware of what's afoot with that schemin' bugger Smyth.'

'What will you do if she lets it slip out to her husband that she knows all about Jed Smyth's plot; the fat'll really be in the fire.'

'We'll do nothing for now. Paxton's bound to get another letter from Smyth instructin' him on the payment of the money. Until we hear from Chris Paxton again, we'll sit tight. It'll give us time to plan our course of action,' Bobby concluded.

'Right, that's what we do then,' Tommy agreed but without any conviction, for he had his own plans for dealing with the situation.

*

Chris Paxton received the next letter two weeks after the second in what had become the now familiar cheap blue envelope. He tore it open with anger and began to read. He quickly realised the contents of the letter contained instructions for dropping the blackmail payment.

Hello again Chris.

Here's what I want you to do. This coming Thursday night at midnight, take the sum of £500 wrapped in a watertight bag, to the dropping point which I will describe to you. On the road across The Leas between South Shields and Marsden above Frenchman's Bay, you will find two large boulders. Under the one nearest the cliff edge, you will find a hollow on the side next to the sea. In this hollow is where I want you to hide the package. Remember, no informing the police and no other monkey business. Make the drop successfully and, this will be the last you hear from me. I'm sure Chris, you are a sensible man who will meet my demands without any trouble. I hope to see the package and nothing more on Thursday night. If I do, you won't see or hear from me again as I plan to return to India where I will set myself up as a trainer and 'The Norfolk Lark' will sing without harm or hindrance.'

The following day Chris Paxton once more confided in Bobby Anderson about the latest correspondence from Jed Smyth, containing the instructions for dropping the blackmail money.

Armed with the knowledge of Smyth's latest demands, Bobby Anderson, and Tommy Cogon sat in 'The Infantryman' talking in undertones as they discussed Jed Smyth's plan for the collection of the pay-off money.

'Has Chris Paxton said anything to you Bobby as to who's going to plant the money?'

'He hasn't mentioned it. I imagined he plans to do it himself,' Bobby said.

'Ah wouldn't mind doin' it for him,' Tommy stated. 'If ah did ah'd see Chris Paxton wasn't out of pocket.'

'What do you mean by that daft offer?' Bobby replied.

'Well, if you tell him ah'm prepared to be the messenger boy, suggesting I needn't know anything about the package containing money, then you would find out,' Tommy schemed.

'I tell y' what we'll do Tommy lad; you've given me an idea. We'll both go but as far as Chris Paxton's concerned, I'm going alone. We'll take his hunter Duke, and you can jump up behind me. There's safety in numbers at that time of night,' Bobby suggested.'

That's it then Bobby; we go together, say no more on the subject.' Tommy was perfectly happy with these plans. Inadvertently he had got what he wanted, and he would be in on the action.

*

Thursday night arrived, and Chris Paxton handed a package wrapped in oilskin and tied in twine. Duke stood patiently as Bobby received his orders for Jed Smyth's pay off.

'I don't want any heroics over this final act in this sordid business. You give this villain his money and you return unharmed. I don't want you confronting Smyth at all. You drop the money as Smyth demands and you return here immediately.'

'I will master, have no fear.'

'One more thing Bobby,' Chris Paxton lowered his voice and said in a rather menacing tone, 'I know Jed Smyth was telling the truth about you and my wife. He has undeniable proof that you and my wife lay together in the woods, and you lied to me. So, you see Bobby, it is for both you and Jemima's sakes that his demands are met. As yet my wife knows nothing of this and that's the way I want it for now. Go now; take care and return safely, there has been enough drama already,' Chris Paxton concluded.

*

Later, Bobby met Tommy Cogon outside of The Infantryman. 'Have we time for a quick whisky Tommy. Call it, 'Dutch courage,' he said quietly.

'Better not, you've been doing well, and I don't want to encourage you into your old ways. You had enough the other night, remember? Now you have found me, we'll be on our way. We can't hang about here. It's best nobody sees us together on one horse or they'll start asking questions.'

Bobby reached behind him and gave Tommy a lift up and the two friends set off for South Sheilds.

They reached South Shields and headed for The Leas, a grassy expanse above the sea.

Everything around them was quiet except for the sound of the waves, crashing against the foot of the cliffs, followed by an ominous snake like hiss as the sea receded through the shingle, at regular intervals, Tommy looked at his watch; *eleven thirty, half an hour to go*, he thought. By the light of the full moon, they could clearly see the shape of the two boulders, the outlines of which were vaguely reminiscent of two sleeping cows.

Tommy slid off the horse's back and crouched close to the ground as he concealed himself behind the boulder closest to the sea, under which the ransom money would be hidden. He positioned himself facing up the coast in the direction of South Shields, from which he knew Jed Smyth would make his approach. With Tommy concealed behind the boulder Bobby dismounted from Duke and removing the package from inside his coat he quickly tucked it into the hollow under the boulder nearest the cliff edge. He remounted Duke and walked the horse away until he was at a distance far enough back to conceal them in the darkness. Tommy strained his ears knowing the time must be midnight. His left leg was almost dead with cramp, when he heard hasty feet scuffing through the grass and coming towards him. He soon forgot the pain from the cramped left leg as the scuffing was upon him. The figure of a man, whom in the moonlight, he assumed was Jed Smyth, came closer. The shadowy figure made for the boulder closest to the sea, unaware that someone was watching him. His hand fumbled beneath the large stone. He hesitated briefly before squatting down and pulled the package out from under the boulder.

'Got it,' he said quietly and immediately stood up and puffed out his chest in an expression of triumph. He started to open the package with too much haste for his own good. He was so keen to see that the package contained money and not cut up newspaper, that he became careless. With the blackmailer, preoccupied with greed, Tommy made his move. He dashed from behind the boulder and rushed headfirst into Smyth's midriff. The two of them careered across the grass. Jed Smyth dropped the package and Tommy quickly grabbed it from the ground and threw it far behind him into the safety of the darkness. As he did so, Jed Smyth caught him with a kick to the side of the head. It was only a glancing blow and Tommy shook it off. Recovering his stance, he grabbed Jed Smyth by the shoulders and they both wrestled each other. The angry roar of the waves smashing violently against the base of the cliffs orchestrated the action on the cliff top. The two antagonists were now close to the cliff edge. With Smyth's back to the sea, Tommy held the advantage. They were now a yard from the edge and Tommy realising they were both in danger of going over, released his grip on Jed Smyth's shoulders. Jed Smyth pushed hard with his feet to propel his body forward to take advantage of Tommy Cogon's relaxed grip. At that very moment, a large section of the overhanging cliff edge, on which Jed Smyth was standing, broke away and he disappeared over the edge. Tommy stood listening into the darkness. He heard a dull thud, barely audible over the roar of the sea, which he assumed was Jed Smyth's body hitting the rocks below the cliff. A few more loose stones cascaded down the cliff face. Tommy listened intently. For a moment, there was nothing but the noise of the waves. A mixed 'choir' of sea birds disturbed from their nocturnal roosting took to the air. They soared above the cliff face squawking a noisy, tuneless dirge over the body of Jed Smyth, which Tommy imagined lay sprawled on the rocks fifty feet or so down, for the moonlight did not illuminate the beach below. *Within the next two hours, the angry incoming sea would float Jed Smyth's mangled body from among the rocks and claim it as its own,* Tommy thought.

Bobby Anderson sensing something was amiss, rode up at speed to see what had caused all the commotion. He found his friend scrambling around in the dark in his attempt to retrieve the package containing Chris Paxton's cash.

'What the hell has gone wrong Tommy? Bobby shouted.

Tommy having grabbed the package from the ground hugged it to his body and leapt up onto the back of Duke as Bobby pulled up alongside him.

'Quick Bobby ride like the devil let's get to hell out of here. 'Why! What's up like Tommy?' Bobby shouted breathlessly.

'Keep your voice down, there's nothing up Bobby. It's all over with Jed Smyth though,' Tommy murmured in his friend's ear.

'What do you mean?'

'He's gone; over the edge. He's gone for good. You and Jemima are safe from him now. Do you hear? Safe, Bobby. No more worries and Chris Paxton still has his cash. Now let's get out of here.'

*

Once back at Shinwell Hall, the two friends hurried to give Duke a quick rub down and bedded him down for the night which would have to serve until morning. As they went about their late duties, they talked in whispers. The two friends knew it was imperative that they we're not seen together this late.

'I didn't exactly mean to push him over the edge; I just wanted to scare him, so he would see sense and keep quiet. The cliff edge gave way and if I hadn't let go, we'd have both gone over.'

'So, y' not a murderer, Tommy. It can only be manslaughter,' Bobby Anderson said, hoping to console his friend.

'Hang on Bobby, whose side are you on? Are you accusing me already?' Tommy said with contempt. 'Remember, if I'm guilty of anything, then we're both in this together and don't you forget that' adding, 'even manslaughter carries a penalty of twenty-five years,' Tommy said solemnly.

Bobby's attempt to make Tommy feel better about what had

happened, although well meant, was misconstrued.

*

The following day Chris Paxton arrived in the stable yard to debrief Bobby on what had happened in South Shields and if the blackmailer's demands were met.

'Well, how did it go last night Bobby?' Chris Paxton asked anxiously.

'Believe it or not master, he never turned up,' and he quickly produced the oilskin package from the manger in an empty stall behind him. 'It's all here untouched. I waited, and he never took the money from its hidin' place. It was gettin' extremely late, and I didn't want to leave all that money there all night, so I recovered it, and we came home. Duke was becoming restless, ah should have bedded him down for the night, hours before. I thought Smyth would get in touch with you again if something had cropped up causing him to change his plans,' and he handed the now distressed package back to its rightful owner.

Chris Paxton remained silent but pensive. He continued to look at the package and he bounced it up and down on the palm of his open hand as if to judge whether it was all there. He finally spoke, 'It looks as though someone has attempted to open the package Bobby. What would you say to that?'

Bobby Anderson was on his guard, and he was ultra-careful in his reply. 'I hope you don't think I had a go at openin' it, boss?' he asked guardedly. Bobby noticed Chris Paxton ponder on his reply and quickly added, 'The hollow under the boulder Smyth had chosen was ragged and when I tried to pull it back out, it got stuck and in the dark I had a struggle to get it back.'

He waited, watching Chris Paxton's face for any response to the explanation. He gave nothing away and finally spoke. 'Well Bobby, we will just have to wait and see, will we not?' was all he said, much to Bobby's relief.

*

A month later the *Shields Tribune* carried the front-page headlines; 'Body found on Roker Beach.' It is believed, although not yet confirmed, that a body found on the waterline at Roker beach, Sunderland, early yesterday, to be that of Jed Smyth the famous jockey, who was born in South Shields. A member of the public found the body while walking his dog. The constable who was on the scene told our reporter that foul play was not suspected, even though the body bore much injury. This, he thought, was due to the body having been in the water for some time.

If the body is that of Jed Smyth, a family member of the dead man has said he had been missing from home for the past month. They thought he had not returned to India where, until recently, he was the first jockey to an Indian prince.

All his belongings were still in their place, at his parents' home. On the night of his disappearance, he had left home for a drink in 'The Compass Inn,' but the landlord said Smyth had not been in on the night in question. He never returned home, and the next day, his family reported him missing.

The constable believed the body entered the water further up the coast, nearer to his hometown of South Shields and the prevailing currents carried his body down the coast. We must emphasise, this is an unofficial report and our man in Sunderland is keen to add it is as yet, unsubstantiated, and may change following the outcome of the official postmortem.

*

Jed Smyth's father had the gruesome task of identifying the body found washed up on Roker beach. The body, or what remained of it, had suffered much tidal damage by impaction against the rocks. Extensive consumption of the body, by crabs and seabirds, had also made formal identification impossible. Most of the face including the eyes was missing and all that remained of the head was the skull, which surprisingly had suffered little damage. On a small section of the skull, there remained an area of skin and hair, which made it possible to establish that the deceased had blond hair. The few strips of clothing still on the body bore no revealing markings. The length of the body indicated that the deceased had been five feet four inches tall, the same stature as Jed Smyth. This fact alone was inconclusive and as a result, Brit Smyth was unable to identify the body as that of his missing son.

*

The inquest returned an open verdict. The coroner, Mr Cecil Armitage had stated that he could not be certain whether the victim had killed himself, had died accidently, or indeed had died at the hands of another person. A post-mortem conducted on the body had indicated that the victim had died from drowning. Indications of a recently occurred landslip near Frenchman's Bay would suggest it was possibly the point from which the deceased had fallen from the cliffs. It was possible that the deceased met his death when he walked too close to the edge and his body weight caused the edge of the cliff at that spot to collapse, taking the deceased's body with it. Too much time had elapsed since that day to establish whether the deceased was alone or in the company of others.

The cause of death was drowning. The pathologist found it surprising that there was no skull damage, considering the body had fallen from the cliffs. If someone had fallen onto rocks below the cliffs at Marsden, one would expect more skeletal damage. The prevailing currents had carried the body southwards before depositing it on the beach at Roker. Further deterioration to the body had been the result of the time the body had been in the water, and it had suffered further damage from the waves, buffeting it against the rocks on successive tides. Too much time had elapsed since that day to establish whether the deceased was alone or in the company of others. Much pedestrian traffic had passed along the cliff tops since the discovery of the body, destroying any forensic evidence. 'So, it is difficult for me to say whether or not foul play was a contributing factor to the death.

A local man, Jed Smyth, a professional jockey went missing from his home four weeks before a member of the public found the body washed up on the beach at Roker but without any positive identification, it is not possible to state categorically that the remains found were that of Mr Smyth. Another fact that compounds my findings is that it has come to my attention that a Norwegian sailor fell overboard from a ship, which had left Newcastle bound for Bergen after discharging its cargo of pit props. It could have been the body of this man, found washed-up on Roker beach, Mr Armitage concluded.

Having considered all the evidence before me, I have no alternative but to return an open verdict as a result of this inquest.

*

'Have you seen the papers Tommy?' Bobby Anderson asked his friend the following day.

'It seems we got away with it,' Tommy replied.

'Shut up Tommy, not so loud, you'll get us hung shoutin' like that,' Bobby warned.

'Hold on, Bobby. I thought you said it could only be manslaughter anyway, twenty-five years at the most, remember?'

'As long as you keep your mouth shut it'll be nothing.' The coroner returned an open verdict. It could not be said, with any certainty, that the body was that of Jed Smyth; the body had received so much damage by the sea.

'That's it. Say no more Bobby,' Tommy agreed.

Chapter 23

1902

Doctors Jeanie Kilbride and Miles Paxton made a good team working and running the 'Dan Swain Hospital.' Jeanie soon proved to Miles Paxton that he had made the right decision when he had offered the job as his assistant to the young doctor from Scotland, two years ago. She was popular with the locals and the women and children simply adored her. Her manner was something special; she was considerate and sympathetic, and she had a special affinity with the whole of the mining community. This was understandable, coming as she did from a mining background herself. She knew at first hand the problems and ailments miners and their families had to confront. She had seen the traumas miners endured through her own father. The periods of sickness and dizziness which were the symptoms of Nystagmus brought on through long periods of working in inadequate light. Nystagmus, Jeanie knew was involuntary eye movements which brought on sickness, dizziness, and headaches. She knew from discussions with her father about working conditions at the coal face that the involuntary eye movements which brought on the sickness etcetera were not solely due to lack of light. She had given the condition a great deal of thought and had formed her own theory on the cause. She believed the position the miners adopted when they were wielding their picks meant they were quite often looking upwards for long periods with their heads tilted backwards and quite often lying on one shoulder as they hewed out an 'undercut' at the base of the coal seam to create what the hewers called a 'loose end' to weaken the coal and make it easier to hew. Over the years, she had watched her father's health deteriorate. Like many other miners in her community, he had fallen victim to a disease commonly described as 'black lung,' a form of chronic bronchitis, until it claimed his life at the age of forty years when she was eighteen.

Once established at the hospital Jeanie Kilbride put no time off in suggesting to the committee that a large store area could easily convert into a small laboratory for pathological testing. With the finances worked out, and the space partitioned off, it was fitted out with analytical equipment. Jeanie now had her small laboratory for pathological testing of samples taken from the seriously ill patients.

Miles Paxton found Jeanie Kilbride's medical skills most admirable, but he also found himself physically attracted to her. He had not given any woman a second glance since Kate Dooley had returned to New York. At first, he had missed her. While they were ignorant of their strange relationship to his grandfather, they had briefly been very fond of each other. With the passing of time, he had come to realise what attracted him to Kate, was nothing more than infatuation and not true love. With this still fresh in his mind, it had left him very wary of starting a new relationship with anyone and he had thrown himself whole-heartedly into his work. This was different. Jeanie Kilbride was different. In fact, he found her the most fascinating woman he had ever had the pleasure of meeting. They shared the same interests, and she had a fine intellectual mind. She had the ability to get into the minds of the people of the village in a way that he, coming from his background, could not. He felt himself becoming more attracted to her and he had said as much to his mother who was relieved that he had got Kate Dooley, her own half-sister, out of his system. The very thought of her son's brief relationship with Kate Dooley still embarrassed her. To think how disastrous such a relationship could have been beyond her imagination. That apart, she too liked Dr Jeanie Kilbride and the idea of her being her daughter-in-law was a pleasing prospect.

In her little laboratory, Jeanie Kilbride had studied sputum samples taken from patients suffering from tuberculosis, commonly known as consumption. Her sampling showed evidence of blood in the sputum, indicating at an early stage, the presence of affected lungs. The victims often showed evidence of weight loss. Other symptoms were a chronic cough, fever, and night sweats. Jeanie's early investigations indicated the possibility of consumption before the sputum showed signs of blood. This had led to early detection of the condition. She had also suggested opening the wall running down the rear side of the ward and building a long terrace open to the fresh air from the fells. Her plan was to have folding doors fitted, which would allow the movement of the beds out onto the terrace during the daytime and brought back in at night. The principle behind her thinking was to expose the patients to an environment of maximum fresh air. Once her diagnostic tests confirmed the presence of the disease, she had the patients transferred to the terrace to begin their fresh air treatment. She had learnt that the findings of one Hermann Brehmer, a German physician who had opened an open-air sanatorium in Germany, which produced results surpassing any other treatment of the disease.

Dr Kilbride's treatments were proving successful; her consumptive patients were benefiting from her open-air treatment at the 'Dan Swain Hospital' located high on the fells above the smoke and contamination from the industrialised valley below. The prevailing winds coming off the Pennines tended to carry any pollution towards the North Sea to the east. The strides Jeanie Kilbride was making in treating this killer disease, which hitherto had been almost incurable using older methods, impressed Miles Paxton. She advocated good food and exercise to bolster the patient's constitution and so she introduced good dietary practices. He admired her enterprise and her enthusiasm, factors that attracted her to him and day by day, he found himself falling more in love with her.

Chapter 24

Bobby Anderson sat at the kitchen table in the lodge house, which was his home at Shinwell Hall. In front of him stood a half empty bottle of whisky, he had already consumed the other half and it already was influencing Bobby's senses. As he sat staring across the room, he caught his reflection in the mirror hanging on the opposite wall. He began soliloquising about his feelings for Jemima Paxton. 'I still love her you know, I always will. She will always be the only woman for me,' he confessed to his reflection. He took a further swig from the bottle and wiped his lips on the back of his hand before he replaced the bottle on the table and continued his conversation with his own image. 'That blue blood Isobel was nothing more than a cockteaser. She cared nothing for my success and soon ran back to Daddy. Could be he was shagging her. Ah've' heard it said they're all interbred,' he mumbled in a drunken slur. 'She had a lot to learn, that one,' he continued. 'No good at all to me, not as good as some o' the lasses down on the quayside at Gateshead,' he confessed, drifting back into his local dialect. 'Too hoity toity, that one. Not my style at all.' Yet again he caught his image in the mirror, and he smiled for no apparent reason like drunks do. 'Here, y' not laughin' at me are y' bonny lad? 'Cos ah'll soon knock that smile off y' face,' and he hurled the empty glass at the mirror on the wall. It shattered against the wall to the left of the mirror. He looked at the mirror once more, 'That's took the smile off your face; nobody laughs at Bobby Anderson, and don't you forget that,' he continued. 'Ah bet you, y' one of them that thought ah closed that regulator panel in the door the day of the explosion at West Fell pit, all those years ago. Well, ah'm goin' to tell you now, and ah'm tellin' nobody but you, so keep this to yoursel' – it was me. The cold wind whistlin' through the gap in the door was freezin' me to the core, so ah' shut it. There now, y' know as much as me now. It's good to get that cleared up.' He took another swig from the bottle. 'Here, while ah'm getting things off my chest, you know that business with the jockey Jed Smyth. Well, that was Tommy Cogon and me. Ah notice y' not smilin' now. That's come as a shock to y' hasn't it? It's got y' thinkin' more seriously now. What ah've told you has come as a real shock to y' ah can see that,' he said repeating himself. His mind went back to the pit disaster. 'Ah know what you're thinkin', and you're right; y' believin' us now aren't y'. It was me that was responsible for the deaths of those twelve men in the North Winnin.' Now we both know the truth.' He took one last long swig from his bottle and swallowed it slowly, smacked his lips and slumped over the table in a drunken stupor.

*

Tommy Cogon was becoming more concerned about his friend. Try as he may, he could not stop Bobby Anderson from reverting to his old drinking habit. It appeared to Tommy that Bobby was rapidly losing his control over the bottle, and it had worsened since the incident at South Shields which culminated in Jed Smyth's death. Apart from Bobby's health, Tommy was worried about his job prospects. Tommy knew Bobby was on 'borrowed time' where Chris Paxton was concerned; he knew Chris Paxton was only tolerating him following his affair with his wife Jemima. He did not want Jemima to know he was aware of her dalliance with Bobby Anderson. Tommy knew any further deterioration in Bobby's lifestyle would lead to his dismissal and not only would he be out of work, but out of a home. He was aware that Bobby was becoming more scruffy. He was losing his self-esteem and he constantly smelt of drink. Until now, he had not made any serious mistakes, more by good luck than good management. Tommy was finding it more difficult each day to cover up his friend's mistakes and it was only a matter of time before Bobby's luck ran out.

He often turned up late, but his timekeeping was getting worse. Yet again Tommy had to take one of the horses and ride down to the lodge house to see where Bobby was. As usual he found him unkempt and slumped over the kitchen table with an almost empty whisky bottle in front of him. He quickly got him outside and putting his head under the water pump he sluiced him down with cold water. Bobby spluttered to his senses and shook the water from his hair like a dog returning from a swim in the river.

'Come on man Bobby what can I do to make you see sense. You are wearing my patience thin with your behaviour. You must start getting your life together again. You did it once, you can do it again.'

'What life? I haven't got a life these days. Not that you can talk of, anyway. I have too much on my conscience,' Bobby moaned.

'Quick jump up behind me and let us get back before they miss us up at the Manor,' Tommy said with concern.

As they made their way back, Bobby remained silent as he tried to remember anything from the events of the previous evening, but as always, his mind was a blur. Any recollection of his conversation with the mirror had disappeared with his image. Tommy ran over in his mind what Bobby had just told him and he tried to assess what was on his friend's conscience that had driven him to hit the bottle again.

There was the affair with Jemima, for he had told him of his undying love for the woman he could never have. Then there was the death of Jed Smyth. Tommy knew nothing of the truth about Bobby's involvement in the West Fell explosion.

Chapter 25

Bobby Anderson's dismissal came as no surprise to anyone at Shinwell Hall. They had all seen his decline and had all tried in their own way to bring him to his senses. He had received good advice from every quarter including Chris Paxton. Bobby's recent bad behaviour had forced Chris Paxton to saturation point, and he could no longer tolerate the behaviour of someone who appeared to be hell bent on self-destruction. Letting his head rule his heart and with much regret, he paid Bobby a month's wages and sent him on his way. Jemima Paxton made no attempt to contact Bobby before he left.

It was a sad sight to see the great jockey from the past, close the door to the lodge house behind him and head up onto the fells. He knew there was a derelict stone-built shepherd's shelter, which at least had four walls standing, and although the roof had suffered damage over the years, he thought he could repair it with makeshift materials. He knew he could make his money go further if he wasn't paying for accommodation down in the village.

He also knew nobody would want to take in someone like him and over recent times, he had come to prefer his own company and he had left without saying goodbye even to Tommy Cogon.

*

Bobby Anderson had spent his first year up on the fells. He squatted in his makeshift shelter drinking from his stone bottle. 'The only time I am happy is when I am drunk and then I don't know much about it.

I feel as if I am in a spiral, sinking deeper and deeper into a dark place and I can't stop myself. I'm finished – my life's over. I have had it, he thought. It eases the aching I feel, by not being able to share my life with Jemima Paxton. My life ended when Jemima shunned me. Why did she lead me on the way she did? When Isobel Percival left me and ran back to her family, although I never loved Isobel, I needed Jemima to love me and fill the void that Isobel left. I needed Jemima to reassure me and tell me my life was not over. Jemima was unavailable and on my return to Shinwell Hall, she made it obvious to me that she would never leave her husband for me. For her it had been a one-off moment of madness; for me it was unrequited love which left me unfulfilled and more desperate than ever for her,' he thought.

*

Bobby had cobbled up the derelict shepherd's shelter with bits and pieces of wood and old tarpaulin. Anything that would cover a hole in the roof had been utilised. He had become more reclusive and had stopped going into the village some time ago – except to replenish his stone bottle. He had tumbled from local hero to local nuisance. Long gone was the slaps on the back and calls of, 'What fettle Bobby?' Now most people when they saw him staggering down the street towards them would change their route to avoid him. Woman quickly ushered their children indoors and some children did not even need ushering, as they were terrified of this man who had long shaggy hair and wearing ragged clothes that stank. The braver ones among them shouted insults and even threw stones at him. Each week he called in The Infantryman and got his stone bottle filled from the slop trays that caught the drips from the pumps and Sam Bailes would pull him a pint 'on the house' out of pity, remembering Bobby for what he had once been. He had instructed Bobby to get there early after opening time, before his regular customers started arriving, for some of them had threatened to stay away if he continued to allow Bobby Anderson to frequent his premises. No one could dictate to Sam Bailes, but he knew from where his business came, and he had come up with a compromise. *Some people have short memories*, he thought, and he ran some of Bobby's great successes on the turf through his mind.

On his weekly trip into West Fell, Sam Bailes would let Bobby have his free pint with Tommy Cogon who would come down specially to meet his old friend. 'Things are gettin' bad Tommy. I think I'm goin' to have to stop comin' into the village; even the bairns are throwin' stones at me.'

Even though Tommy still didn't approve of Bobby's drinking, he realised long ago that he was fighting a lost cause and it was too late now to try to reform him. 'I tell you what Bobby; I'll bring a drink and one or two other things up the fell for you each week and we can natter as long as we like. Save you coming down here and risking injury,' Tommy offered.

I wonder if Tommy would be so generous if he knew the whole truth about me, Bobby wondered, his thoughts going back to the West Fell pit disaster.

'Come on Bobby, on y' way now,' Sam Bailes ordered. Bobby obediently gulped his drink down, rose to his feet and made for the door, head bowed like the lost soul he was.

'See y' next week Bobby,' Tommy promised.

Bobby neither looked behind him nor replied to the men but shuffled through the pub door, which he let slam loudly behind him not having the strength to control it. Without batting an eyelid, he stepped out into the street. Hoping he would not meet any irate villagers, he made his way up the street leaving a strong odour in his wake.

Back in the pub Sam Bailes was propping the door back and he had removed his apron and was whirling it like a windmill. 'Bloody hell; ah don't know how you put up with that Tommy,' the landlord said before putting his hankie to his nose.

'It makes my heart ache to see him like he is Sam. When you think how much success he enjoyed before his life all began to collapse about him.'

'Aye ah know what y' mean bonny lad. He's a sad case right enough. But ah'm goin' to have to tell 'im he cannot come here anymore. Doesn't he ever wash, Tommy? He's bad for business, man.'

'I know how y' feel Sam and I don't blame y'. Leave Bobby to me. I'll deal with him. He's foragin' for food off the fells; fruits such as the wild bilberries and wild strawberries, which he eats as he picks them. He's like an animal grazin' off the land. He's made friends with Ben Turnbull, the fells man, when I say friends, I mean Ben has taken pity on him and drops him the occasional rabbit. Who'd 'ave thought Bobby would come to this Sam? Each week ah'm takin' him a few provisions up, otherwise he's a goner the way he's shapin'.'

'That's really good of y' son. Nobody could have a more loyal friend Tommy. I tell y' what, I'll give you a couple of pints of ale from me each week.'

'I used to try and keep it from him Sam, but I know now he's a lost cause.'

*

A couple of weeks after Tommy's conversation with Sam Bailes, Jemima Paxton confronted Tommy Cogon as to Bobby Anderson's well-being.

'I've heard from some of the villagers that he is living in a makeshift shelter up on the fells. Is that the case Tommy?' she asked with concern in her voice.

'That is true Ma'am.'

'What state is he in both mentally and physically?' Jemima Paxton asked.

'Mentally, he is quite alert. He needs to be, as he is living off his wits. The truth is he's a physical wreck. He no longer washes regularly, and he is unshaven and totally unkempt,' Tommy replied.

'Do you think he would see me, Tommy?'

'He's not a pretty sight these days, Ma'am.'

'That be as it may, but both my husband and I have fond

memories of Bobby as he was before his sad demise.'

This remark led Tommy to recall the truth of Jemima's 'affair' with Bobby and he wondered how much this had contributed to his friends decline. *Did she think, seeing Bobby again would give her an opportunity to reform him, thereby saving her own soul of what had occurred between them in the past. Did she think that one final act of charity, on her part, would right the wrong and everything would be fine again? Could she be so condescending as to think such a thing?* Tommy thought.

'Where exactly is the hovel that serves as his shelter?' Jemima Paxton asked.

'It is high on the fell Ma'am, in the lee of Tolson's Scar. I can take you up there if you insist on going. It would be better if we travelled up there on horseback. The horses would be more surefooted than we would. How soon would you plan to go?'

'Whatever time suits you Tommy.'

'Give me a couple of days and I will try to tidy him up before you meet him Ma'am. I will let you know when I am ready to go. But I make no promises for you know how stubborn he can be.'

*

Before the end of the week, Tommy had visited Bobby with the news that Jemima Paxton wanted to see him. 'Bloody hell man Tommy, y' told her what a state ah'm in didn't y.' How can ah face her like this?'

'We'll get y' cleaned up down at the millpond that drives the dynamo for Shinwell Hall and Bobby when we do, could you get into the habit of goin' down there each day and clean up. You could even bathe in there. I know how well it will be for you two to meet again. She could give you yet another chance Bobby. The Paxtons have been good to you in the past and ah'm sure they would be in the future.'

'Ah'm not sure about this Tommy. Ah loved that woman in the past and ah still do; ah know she will always be out of my reach. You know the truth Tommy of what happened between her and me. Do you think she ever felt anything for me?'

'Ah won't lie to you Bobby; ah think she used y'. She was bored with her life after her great stage career, and she saw y' as a way of spicin' up her life. She was annoyed with Chris Paxton for the time he spent with his horses. Maybe he wasn't satisfyin' her in bed, and she saw y' as a way of gettin' what she was missin' from her husband. She tried it once with y' and after doin' so,' she was full of remorse.'

'Ah can't face her Tommy.'

'Of course, y'can Bobby, y' know she is not a bad person. You know that – look she has helped you in the past, and she will help you in the future, believe me,' Tommy reasoned. However, he was not convinced Bobby was happy with his plan.

'Alright, ah'll see her the day after tomorrow,' Bobby replied with an air of reluctance.

'That's good Bobby and don't forget to clean up and try to wash your clothes while you're down at the millpond,' Tommy reminded him before he set off back down the fell.

Chapter 26

Jemima Paxton entered the stables of Shinwell Hall to find Tommy Cogon had saddled up two horses in readiness for their visit to Bobby Anderson at his shelter on the fell.

As the two horses picked their way upwards towards Bobby's 'abode.' The two riders talked as they went along. Jemima Paxton was the first to speak. 'You said the other day Tommy that Bobby appeared to be a physical wreck. Do you mean he is showing evidence of illness or just his general demeanour which a good clean up would put right?'

'A good clean up would help Ma'am but without a doctor's examination God only knows what's goin' on inside him. He is drinking anything that is available to him. and he has been at it for some time now. Anything and everything, even the beer from Sam Bailes's slop trays.'

The two horses continued strenuously upwards until they had almost reached Tolson's Scar and within a fold in the scree-strewn slope, they spotted Bobby's hovel. They dismounted, and Tommy pulled back the flap of canvas covering the entrance and peered inside. To save Jemima Paxton from the embarrassing stench of the place he quickly withdrew.

'It's not that Ma'am; it's just that he is ashamed for you to see him in such a low state.'

'In that case, tomorrow you can return alone just to see if he is all right. In the meantime, we will have a scout around here and see if there is any sign of him. I would hate to think he is out on the fell in a state of collapse,' Jemima Paxton suggested.

They searched the fell near Tolson's Scar calling his name but without a trace of Bobby.

'We'll have to be gettin' back Ma'am, the light will be going soon,' Tommy reminded Jemima Paxton.

*

Jemima and Chris Paxton were enjoying an after-dinner drink in the withdrawing room when the lights guttered several times and then finally went out altogether. Momentarily, they sat in complete darkness before they heard footsteps outside the door. The door opened, and Alice Cogon entered the room carrying a large candelabrum, which immediately illuminated the room.

'Thank you, Alice, it appears we have a malfunction with the dynamo. We will have to make do with the old candles until we can conduct a full investigation in daylight tomorrow.' Jeremy Paxton suggested.

'So much for modern technology,' Jemima Paxton retorted sarcastically.

'I have a candelabrum outside on the hall table and I will place one in your bedroom before you retire sir,' Alice Cogon said.

*

The following morning Chris Paxton and Tommy set off with two more labourers to check out the Siemens dynamo installed in the old mill house. On reaching the scene, foreboding struck Tommy. Strewn along the far bank of the millpond were articles of ragged clothing, which Tommy readily recognised as those belonging to his lifelong friend, Bobby Anderson.

'I hate to say this Tommy, but I think Bobby's body has fouled the water wheel.'

'Oh! Bobby! What have you done?' He began sobbing unashamedly.

'I will dive in and investigate sir,' Tommy offered.

'Are you sure. You have had a tremendous shock. I think I should do it Tommy. I am a strong underwater swimmer, and I have made my mind up,' Chris Paxton said, and immediately began shedding his clothing down to his underpants and he dived into the millpond. He swam over to where the waterwheel was nearest to the sluice gate. Rising high in the water, he filled his lungs with air; he arched his body before disappearing below the murky water. He was missing for quite a while before a series of bubbles indicated to the watchers on the bank, that he was coming to the surface. Chris Paxton broke through the surface and shaking the water from his eyes and mouth, he revealed the news none of the onlookers wanted to hear.

'I'm afraid Bobby is dead. His body is wedged between the wheel and the sluice gate, stopping the wheel from turning. We will have to open the sluice to reduce the water level and gain access to Bobby's body. It will take at least two of us to open the sluice. We will have to do it gradually so as not to affect the water supply to West Fell village. We must not alert the village to the fact that Bobby's body is in the sluice, they may think it might be contaminating their water supply; better, they find out later.'

Chris Paxton and Tommy Cogon operated the sluice before the two labourers took over. After enough time for recovery, Chris and Tommy took over again, by which time the water level had fallen to the base of the wheel. With two of them standing precariously on the top of the sluice, they were able to drag Bobby's forlorn body upwards and out of the waterwheel. They laid Bobby's body on the side of the millpond in such a way as to let the water drain away from him. While Chris and Tommy dealt with Bobby's body, the other two brought the sluice back to its original position. Once enough water accumulated behind the sluice, the large wheel began to turn; slowly at first and then gradually turning to its working speed.

From the dynamo house came a whirring hum as the dynamo once more began to function.

Their attention returned to Bobby Anderson's lifeless body. To give his corpse what little dignity his meagre clothing could provide, they dressed him, before carrying his dead body back down the fell to the hospital morgue.

As Tommy sorted through the clothes, he noticed they were in two piles one of which was dry, and one was wet. Tommy glanced at Chris Paxton, and he realised he had also noticed the wet and dry piles of clothes. Tommy was the first to speak.

'This was an accident,' he said to Chris Paxton, with a sense of relief. 'Did Mrs Paxton tell you of our visit to Bobby Anderson yesterday?'

'Yes, she did, and she aired her concern at the fact that you had failed to meet him.'

'When I arranged the meeting at Mrs Paxton's request, I had asked him to clean himself up and wash his clothes.'

'Please do not assume responsibility for the death of your friend Tommy, it would appear Bobby had been busy washing his clothes and for some reason which we will never know, he unbalanced and fell in the mill pool where the turbulence from the wheel carried his body towards the sluice. Once in the water even the strongest swimmer would have struggled to survive. Please Tommy, do not admonish yourself over what has happened here. Nobody could have been a more sincere friend than you were.'

*

The inquest on Bobby Anderson returned a verdict of accidental death. Bobby had fallen into the water while washing his clothes was the consensus. Shortly after, Tommy decided to go to the old shepherd's shelter. He wanted to rid it of any evidence of Bobby's occupation. While clearing the detritus, he found a letter concealed under his makeshift bed. He unfolded the letter and began to read.

This letter is for the two most important people in my life. A life, which I intend to bring to an end very soon. The two people in my life who have meant so much to me are Tommy Cogon and Jemima Paxton. I love you both for different reasons and in different ways. Tommy, as dear a friend as you have been, there is something I have kept from you all these years. I closed that regulator panel on the door on that day in 1884, causing the firedamp explosion in West Fell colliery, which killed your father and eleven other souls. I am sorry Tommy but being the coward that I am, I couldn't tell you to your face. The incoming air was icy cold that day and I closed the regulator to be warmer. So, you see I lied at the inquest, even under oath.

The other person I have loved, as you well know, is Jemima Paxton. Even though I knew from the start, she was always going to be out of my reach, but we did have one moment of passion, which I will take with me to my grave. The other thing I have hidden is the business with Jed Smyth's fall from the cliffs. I have wanted to get all these secrets out in the open for years and now it's as good a time as any, while I am in this mood. Maybe the water will cleanse my soul. At least I'll smell sweeter than I have lately. I hope you can forgive me, Tommy. If you find this and I know you well enough, to think you will, please cover for me and save Jemima from any shame. This is my goodbye to you both. I am tired, and I can't go on anymore.

Tommy folded the letter and stuffed it in the waistband of his trousers. He continued to dismantle the crude fabrication that had served as Bobby's shelter in the last period of his life. Little by little he removed every stick until it was back to the bare stones of the original structure. Once everything was back to as it was before Bobby's occupancy, he gathered brushwood from the fells to use as kindling and he set fire to the pile of debris. As the fire roared, Tommy took the letter from the waistband of his trousers and pondered over his next move. He slapped the letter anxiously, two or three times into the palm of his hand as he pondered the question, *should I, or shouldn't I?* He considered for a moment how Bobby had contrived the arrangement of his clothes to create the impression that he had been in the process of washing them when he 'fell' in. Without further hesitation, he threw Bobby's confession into the middle of the fire and watched the words turn to ash. He subconsciously read random words as the flames devoured the incriminating text. Ironically, the combustion slowed at the words *'save Jemima from any shame…'* and then it was gone.

Chapter 27

The next day Chris Paxton asked Tommy about the fire up on Tolson's Scar. 'I thought it was someone lighting a beacon to celebrate the end of the second Boer War, it could be seen from the village.

'Oh, ah was gettin' rid of any evidence of Bobby havin' lived in that hovel up on the fells. That was not a good period in his life and ah didn't want others fishin' around up there. Ah wanted it to be back to as it was before he moved in. So, ah burnt everything that would burn; all that's left is the stones that once was the shepherd's shelter, or what's left of it,' Tommy said with an air of relief.

'Good for you Tommy, I would have done the same if I were in your shoes.'

'Ah miss Bobby a hell of a lot and ah still cannot come to terms with what has happened. Ah keep thinkin' he's has just gone away on a trip and he'll be back soon. But, ah soon come back to reality and then ah know what the truth is,' Tommy confessed, and tears ran down his cheeks. Taking a handkerchief from his pocket, he wiped his eyes and blew his nose. 'Just look at me now, actin' like a little girl.'

'Don't worry Tommy; I know how you feel. There is no shame in grieving, especially when you lose someone close to you.'

Should ah tell the boss about Bobby's letter? Tommy pondered, quickly dispelling the thought. He knew he needed to tell someone, as fostering the truth was proving more difficult than he had thought it would be at the time he burnt Bobby's confession.

*

Two months later, Tommy was busy grooming the hunters in readiness for the hunt. Jemima and Chris Paxton were riding to hounds with the Derwent Hunt at their meet at Shotley Bridge the next day, an activity they both enjoyed. As Tommy worked, his thoughts once again, were on his deceased friend, Bobby Anderson. Several lives had been lost which could be associated with Bobby Anderson. In his mind, he listed the deaths. The twelve miners at West Fell pit, including Tommy's father, the death of Jed Smyth, although an accident, Bobby *had* been involved. Most importantly of all, there was the truth of Bobby's own death, which was not an accident. Bobby was a man of many secrets and he had left Tommy with the legacy of secrecy in the letter he had found under Bobby's bed. Finally, there was the secrecy of Bobby's involvement with Jemima Paxton. He felt more uncomfortable with the burden Bobby had bestowed upon him and he knew that eventually the truth would have to come out. He could not live with this much longer. Daily, it ate away inside of him.

Bobby Anderson had touched several people's lives during his time on this earth and in doing so, he had bestowed on each of them an element of secrecy, each unaware of the other's involvement. Jemima Paxton fostered the truth in her illicit assignation with the deceased, the truth to which only she, or so she thought, was privy. She was unaware of her husband's knowledge of the truth, for he had never discussed it with her. Chris Paxton in turn was unaware that Tommy Cogon knew the truth about his wife and Bobby Anderson. He was now of the opinion that his wife's secret had gone to the grave with the deaths of Bobby Anderson and Jed Smyth.

Tommy Cogon, on the other hand, bore the burden of truth more than anyone did, for he had read Bobby Anderson's suicide note in which his friend confessed to being instrumental in the death of the twelve miners in 1884 including Tommy's father. He was also aware of his friend's involvement with Jemima Paxton, and he knew the truth concerning the death of Jed Smyth. All of this was preying on Tommy's mind, and he was finding it difficult to sleep at night. He knew he had to speak to someone soon or he felt he would go out of his mind.

*

Initially, the death of Bobby Anderson had brought peace of mind to Chris Paxton, but lately he too found himself pondering over the past. He had hoped that the death of Bobby Anderson was the end of the matter of his wife's indiscretion. The more he thought about it, the more it ate away at him. Did anyone else have knowledge of the truth? How had Jed Smyth known about the birthmark on the inside of his wife's thigh? He realised for Jed Smyth to have knowledge of something so intimate about his wife, he must have seen it for himself or someone else had told him of the fact. Smyth could not have seen it for he had sacked Smyth before that incident had occurred and another thing, he had left England to ride in India before the incident took place. *So, who could have informed Jed Smyth?* Chris Paxton wondered. If the answer to that question was no one, that raised the imponderable, had Smyth also had a sexual relationship with his wife Jemima at some time? He was sure Bobby Anderson would not have told Jed Smyth of his relationship with Jemima. Bobby Anderson would not confide in Jed Smyth anything of such a personal nature, for he could not stand Jed Smyth. Chris Paxton consoled himself in the fact that Smyth was now dead, and his secret had died with him if he had not told anyone else. He could not be sure and that was his present dilemma. Unbeknown to Chris Paxton this question was resolved when he received notice of the death of his former groom and coachman Andrew Thompson who had died in his sleep after a short illness. So, in fact, all the people who knew of his wife's transgression were now dead, except for his wife and himself, or so he thought.

But there was one other person ... Tommy Cogon.

Chapter 28

Miles Paxton and his assistant Jeanie Kilbride arrived at Gateshead Register Office in April 1903. They tentatively loitered outside the entrance to the building in Swinburne Street as they discussed between them the legal requirements for their marriage. Jeanie had the necessary residency qualification having lived at Shinwell Hall since her arrival from Scotland. The rings were in Miles's pocket. The only missing element that would complete the scene was the two witnesses. Their wedding was to be so quiet they had told no one of their plans, and they were even about to ask two complete strangers off the street to stand witness to the ceremony.

Several people passed them, whom on approach, they dismissed by a silent shake of the head from either of them or on one instance from both with grins as wide as the Tyne. The arranged time for the marriage was eleven a.m. Almost at the point of despair, along the street came a couple who looked to be in their thirties, tidily dressed and linking arms as if they too were in love. 'Pray that these are our witnesses,' Miles Paxton said to his future wife in a whispered aside.

Stepping out in front of the couple, Miles Paxton confronted them.

'Excuse me, but may I ask a favour of you both; would you be prepared to stand as witnesses to our marriage?' in a manner that sounded more like a plea from the heart than a simple request. The couple looked at each other in amazement. The man was the first to speak.

'What do y' think lass? Should we give it a go?' he asked his partner.

'Ah'm for it, if you are,' she said readily.

'That is splendid. We are most obliged to you both. Let me introduce ourselves. I am Dr Miles Paxton of Shinwell Hall and this is my fiancée Dr Jeanie Kilbride. Jeanie and I are working partners at the Daniel Swain Hospital at West Fell, and you are?'

'I am Walter Chandler, a draughtsman down at Palmer's Jarrow shipyard and this is me wife Elsie.'

They shook hands and Walter started the conversation again. 'Shinwell Hall you say, why man what are you doin' gettin' married at Gateshead Register Office of all places?'

'I'll explain everything after the ceremony,' Miles Paxton promised, rather hurriedly as he looked at his gold Hunter. 'It is time we were going in,' he added as he anxiously shepherded the others into the building.

*

After the ceremony, Miles Paxton thanked their witnesses for their services rendered at such short notice. As he shook the hand of Elsie Chandler, she asked him what the young couple planned to do with the rest of their wedding day. 'We have no real plans, but I think it would be only right and proper for you to join us for a glass of wine with which to toast our future happiness,' Miles Paxton replied.

'Well, ah wasn't lookin' for a free drink, but been as yer offerin,' it would be bad manners to say no, what do *you* think Walter?'

'Couldn't agree more lass,' he replied, himself contemplating a drink much grander than his usual glass of ale. Elsie started the conversation once more.

'That's it then, lead on kind Sir,' she said.

'Not being from Gateshead, and you living within its environs, we will let you choose the venue for our wedding breakfast,' Miles Paxton replied.

During these exchanges Jeanie Kilbride, now the newly declared

Mrs Jeanie Paxton listened with amusement as these two local people, with so much natural amiability, were unwittingly fashioning her wedding day. This she found pleasing to her; herself being the daughter of a humble Scottish coal miner. *This could not have gone better had we pre-arranged it*, she thought.

'There's a nice hotel, 'The New Bridge,'' only a street away, we could go there,' Walter Chandler suggested. 'It's not top notch, but it's decent,' he added, realising he had witnessed the wedding of a young couple who were used to a better standard of living than he and Elsie was used to. He wanted to make the most of the situation, knowing an excellent opportunity like this may never happen again.

"The New Bridge' it is then,' Miles Paxton concurred. The hotel of choice, as Walter Chandler had predicted, *was* a respectable establishment, which Miles Paxton thought suitable. On arrival, the small party had been ushered to a table for four, placed to one side of an attractive Louis style fireplace in which a coal fire burned cheeringly. The wine waiter approached them, and Miles suggested to his little wedding party that the occasion called for Champagne. 'Unless of course you may prefer some alternative drink,' he added. Walter and Elsie hesitated and looked at each other questioningly. After a brief pause, they both replied almost as one and with a smile on their faces, 'that'll be very nice.'

The waiter who had ushered them to the table returned. 'Excuse me sir, would you be liking a drink?' he asked Miles.

'Do you have vintage Champagne, waiter?'

'We do indeed Sir,' adding quickly, 'this is but a humble hotel and we only stock wine from one house, that of Möet. I can offer you a bottle of the 1895 brut for your approval, which I have heard on good authority, was quite a good year.'

'Well let us not stand on ceremony; the 1895 it is then,' Miles agreed.

The waiter returned with the Champagne, uncorked the bottle with the minimum of effort and poured half a glass, and offered it to

Miles Paxton.

Miles held the glass up to the light, sniffed it and then rolled a sip on his tongue before stating to everyone's delight, 'This is fine,' much to the waiter's relief who proceeded to fill their glasses.

'I have brought menus for you and your guests' perusal Sir. I will leave them with you,' and he quickly withdrew.

Raising his glass Walter Chandler said, 'May ah propose a toast to the groom Miles, and his beautiful bride, Jeanie.' Chinking their glasses together, Walter and his wife Elsie, toasted the future happiness of the newlyweds.

Over the meal, Miles explained why they had chosen Gateshead Register Office for their marriage. The newly acquainted couple listened intently at Miles's every word.

'You say you are a draughtsman in the shipyard, Walter.'

'I am that... workin' on a destroyer. She was laid down last January at Palmer's yard.'

'If you like, after we have finished here, we can have a walk over the Swing Bridge to Newcastle and we'll probably see Tommy 'on the bridge' Ferens,' Elsie suggested, excitedly.

'Who is Tommy 'on the bridge' Ferens?' Jeanie asked with great interest.

'Tommy's a blind man who stands in the very middle of the swing bridge where he begs from 11 a.m. to 4 p.m. every day except Sunday and holy days. He was born Thomas Ferens, the blind son of an Oakenwell miner, here in Gateshead and by the age of five, he was orphaned. He is a small man, and he is normally peaceful but can pour out obscenities if someone drops a button in his hand instead of money. He is quite a character and over the years has become something of a tourist attraction,' Elsie concluded.

'I am quite intrigued. How about you Jeanie, what do you say? Should we take Elsie at her word?'

'I am all for it, if the rest are,' Jeanie replied.

'Newcastle and Tommy 'on the bridge' it is then.'

After the meal, Miles settled the bill and the four left the hotel for Newcastle.

They reached the Swing Bridge and as Elsie predicted, they did indeed meet Tommy Ferens.

*

Without saying anything to Tommy, Miles dropped a gold half sovereign into Tommy's hand. Immediately Tommy responded with, 'Not often ah get one o' these sir. What brings a toff like ye to the Swing Bridge? Ah naa, a man like yoursel' won't be tryin' t' dodge the toll levied on the High Level so ah take it y' not from these parts are y'?'

'My wife and I have just married this morning and these two good people stood as our witnesses.'

'Is that a fact, now?' Well let's be the first to wish y' both, aall the best for the future and God bless y'.'

They bid Tommy goodbye and continued over the bridge to Newcastle. On their tour of the sights, they passed the Theatre Royal in Grey Street. 'My mother has appeared here. She is the world-famous soprano whose stage name was Mimi Martin. Now retired from the stage, she has reverted to her real name, Jemima Paxton,' he revealed, hoping he had not come across boastful, for that was not his intention.

'Well, ah never. Ah saw her here when she gave the charity concert for the victims of the West Fell pit disaster, back in '84. Ah was only fourteen at the time. Ah went with me Mam and Dad. She was brilliant,' Elsie said.

Miles was tempted to reveal that he was the son of one of the partners who owned the mine, but quickly dispelled the idea. Before they left their newfound friends, Miles gave Walter his card, saying, 'We should at least, meet up each anniversary of our wedding and have a meal together. I see no reason why our friendship should not be ongoing Walter. Please keep in touch.'

*

On returning to Shinwell Hall, the newlyweds announced to Jemima and Chris Paxton the news of their wedding.

'Is this your idea of a joke Miles, if so, I do not think you have considered poor Jeanie if you are using her as the butt of such a joke,' Jemima Paxton stated, openly showing her disappointment.

Miles attempted to placate his mother by trying to explain as convincingly as possible how they had not wanted a big formal church wedding, much to Jemima Paxton's dismay. He knew she would have preferred a big formal wedding in Durham Cathedral or some other venue in the area impressive enough for the wedding of her only son, a register office ceremony did not sit comfortably with her. She would have tried vehemently to persuade them to change their minds had she been privy to their plan. This they knew, and this was the main reason for their subterfuge.

Chris Paxton intervened and asked Jemima if she was pleased for their son, and new daughter-in-law and did she wish them well for the future.

'Of course, I am overjoyed at our son's choice of bride. You know I love Jeanie like the daughter we never had. I was looking forward to a big wedding and most importantly I am extremely disappointed that your father and I were not there.' The latter part of the sentence she delivered between deep sobs and implying that it was entirely the fault of her son.

*

After a short while, Jemima came to terms with the idea of Miles' and Jeanie's wedding and soon she forgot all about it. The Daniel Swain Hospital had continued to flourish thanks to their combined efforts. The young couple were so dedicated to their work that they had not even taken a honeymoon. Instead, they decided to concentrate their time on the work they were both engrossed in at the centre. The health fund was flourishing so much that the committee decided they could afford to appoint a qualified surgeon as a stipendiary member. Miles Paxton and his new wife would assist the surgeon during surgical operations.

Miles Paxton was keen to relate to his father the news of the appointment of the new surgeon at the hospital. 'He is a newly qualified surgeon from London.

'Is he indeed? He is no slouch then, and his name?' his father asked.

'Sydney Brotherton. He is from a long line of surgeons and physicians whose roots are in the Northeast. His parents sent him to London for his schooling and he qualified last year. We are lucky to get him. I think the social qualities on which our hospital was founded, is what attracted him to us. Our enterprise thus far also impresses him and as a result, he prefers to serve the community of West Fell rather than the wealthy of London, possibly to his own financial detriment. It was this quality that endeared him to the whole committee.'

'Sometimes a man's principals can affect his career,' Chris Paxton declared somewhat patronisingly,' continuing with, 'while I admire his public spiritedness, I hope it does not prove to be his undoing. I wish him well.' Chris Paxton said rather cynically.

*

Two years later, Frances Jeanette Paxton was born making a grandmother of Jemima Paxton and for all time, any lingering semblance of resentment for her son and daughter-in-law's secretive wedding she cast from her mind.

Miles and Jeannie Paxton had become firm friends with Elsie and Walter Chambers, and they invited the couple to stand as Godparents of their new-born baby at her baptism, which they accepted without question.

Chapter 29

1906

The burden of the truth of his friend's suicide was becoming almost unbearable for Tommy Cogan. During each idle moment, Bobby Anderson's suicide note seemed to occupy his mind. Alice Cogon was getting more concerned about her son's demeanour. Lately, he seemed to be withdrawing within himself. Mother's instinct told her; her son's present state of mind had come about following his friend's death. It had hit her son badly. Tommy, now thirty-two years old, had never had a real girlfriend; indeed, girls had never appealed to him.

'What's up with y' our Tommy? Y' seem to have no interest in anything lately. I wish you'd get yourself a girlfriend or a hobby or something. Anything, to bring you out of yourself. I'm gettin' worried about y.' What is it son? Come and talk to your Mam about it. See if we can sort you out between us.'

For the briefest of moments, Tommy almost began to tell his mother about Bobby Anderson's suicide note he had found in the shepherd's refuge. Suddenly realising his mental promise to Bobby on reading his friend's suicide note, he managed to refrain from revealing any of the truth.

'There's nowt wrong Mam,' he lied. 'It's just that I'm missing Bobby somethin' rotten, believe me,' he said rather angrily.

'Alright, alright, don't bite me head off.'

He realised how close he had come to revealing all to his mother. He was aware that the burden placed upon him by his friend's actions was becoming unbearable. 'It's just that everybody seems to have taken Bobby's death so calmly. They all seem to have forgotten the days when he was at the peak of his career, and they were all backin' his winners. I'd give anything to be on me way to Newcastle races again, to see him ride the winner of the Northumberland Plate. That would bring me straight out of me gloom, Mam. Alas, that's all in the past and it would take more than a girlfriend to change all that.'

Alice stood listening to Tommy confess his problems to her without giving her the full facts of what was at the root of his problem. He knew that for the moment, that part of the truth must remain a secret.

'Why don't you have a day at the races Tommy? It would do y' good, take y' out of yourself a bit,' Alice suggested. Her son remained silent for a while before replying.

'It's not the same on my own Mam, not without Bobby. It was all so different then. Everyone knew Bobby and the banter was always great. On the few times I've gone on me own since Bobby...' He hesitated and then continued, 'Since Bobby died, it's not the same. Ah miss him so much Mam.'

As Alice listened to her son's problems, she spotted as mothers do, the glint of a tear in the corner of his eye.

'Come here son,' she said as she cuddled him into her, placing his head on her shoulder, the way she had done when he was a boy and he wept openly. 'I know y' miss y' friend Tommy and that's not easy to deal with. Some people deal with their grief more easily than others do. Look how we both felt in '84 when we lost y' Dad; we were both devastated. Through time, things began to get better and here we are now, livin' at Shinwell Hall. So, y' see son, there is truth in the old sayin' *every dark cloud has a silver lining*,' she said as she slowly ran her fingers through her son's hair, 'combing' it out of his tear-laden eyes.

*

A week or so later, Alice Cogon had a chance meeting with Miles Paxton when he had gone to the kitchen to tell Davison they were having extra guests for dinner. He and Jeannie were now firm friends with Elsie and Walter Chambers, who now were frequent visitors to Shinwell Hall since the couple had stood as Godparents at the baptism of their daughter.

'May I have a quick word with you Dr Paxton?'

'What is it Alice?'

'Could I have a word with you somewhere a little more private, away from Davison's flapping ears?' she said quietly.

'Come up into the hall. We can talk there,' he suggested.

They climbed the stairs from the kitchen and arrived in the sumptuous entrance hall to the large country house. Miles Paxton led Alice to a place on the far side of the hall, where a quality carved gilt wood console table shared the space with a fine pair of eighteenth century, gilded chairs with curved backs and upholstered arms, all supported on tapering fluted legs. The chairs, placed either side of the table, set it off to great effect. Miles Paxton gestured Alice into the chair to the left of the table and waited while she made herself comfortable. With Alice settled in her seat, he occupied the remaining chair.

'Now Alice, tell me what it is you want to discuss with me,' the young doctor asked.

Alice's mental rehearsals of what she wanted to ask Doctor Miles, she still struggled to put her thoughts into words. 'Erm, it's not me... em... I want to talk to you about doctor... no, it's not me I'm worried about at all,' she said stalling to think.

'Who is it then Alice?' the doctor asked, his patience strained by the maid's delaying tactics.

'I don't know if *you* have noticed sir, but it's our Tommy. He hasn't been the same since they found Bobby Anderson's body fastened in the millwheel and he's becoming more and more melancholy.'

'I have to admit Alice; I have noticed how withdrawn he has become since the passing of his friend. I will have a chat with him at the first opportunity, without him having to make an official appointment to see me. That way he may be more forthcoming as to his present state of mind. Leave it with me for now and I will discreetly have a word with the other family members to keep an eye on him so that his depression does not worsen.'

'Ee, thank y' so much Doctor Miles; ah feel much better already having shared me concern with somebody like your good self,' Alice said, slipping back into her local idiom in her elation.

Chapter 30

Tommy Cogon was on his way to Gateshead to collect a new saddle for Miles Paxton's wife, Jeannie. On the journey, and in his own company, Tommy's thoughts once again centred on Bobby's state of mind as he sank into the deep ominous water of the millpond.

Is there any sane reason for the action of someone choosing to end his or her life? Is there any reason other than a deliberate self-act of defiance against the prejudiced view that life itself is a God given thing, which only He can take away? Because of this human premise on life, they deemed Bobby, and all others who decided to end their lives, to be criminals in the eyes of society; a society, which through their Christian upbringing, had grown up with an irrational fear of death. This is the cause of my dilemma, he thought.

How he wished the law that stated that society should embrace life and leave death to God, was not the case. *Bobby, in recent times, had had no life at all and it would be much easier now,* he thought. *Who are these arrogant people who say Bobby was a criminal for ending his life?* He asked himself. *A life which, in Bobby's opinion, had become less than worthless and as such, unbearable.*

He felt his own life becoming unbearable but unlike Bobby, he was not brave enough to carry out such an act, despite people saying, '*suicide was the coward's way out.*' The burden of truth was crushing him day by day.

*

Tommy drew the cart to a halt in the yard of Jopling's saddlery in

Gateshead where an assistant wearing a green linen apron round his waist greeted him. 'What can I do for *you*, sir?' the assistant asked politely.

'Ah'm here to collect a saddle for Mrs Jeannie Paxton of Shinwell Hall; here's the order slip,' Tommy said.

The assistant took the receipt, and as he did, he felt he had seen Tommy somewhere before but couldn't remember where. Still pondering the thought, he disappeared inside the workshop. He quickly returned with the saddle and placed it reverently in the cart and came around to the front and said, 'If it's not to Mrs Paxton's liking, bring it back and we'll sort it out. But I doubt she'll have any problems; like all good saddles supplied from here, they are bespoke. By the way, do ah know you? Ah feel we've met before.'

'No, not me mate, never seen you afore in my life. Ah must have a double. They say everybody has a double somewhere on this earth,' Tommy replied.

'You certainly have. The saddle is for Shinwell Hall you say. That was a sad business about Bobby Anderson's suicide,' the Jopling's man said.

'Who said it was suicide?' Tommy challenged. 'I think you might find that's incorrect,' he added quickly.

'Well, ah know that was not determined at the inquest but y' know what people are sayin' and can y' blame them?'

'People can be wrong, can't they? Quite often, they are like you for instance. Ah would advise y' to keep your thoughts to yourself if ah were you. Especially in West Fell,' Tommy said.

Tommy Cogon shook the reins and started back to Shinwell Hall. All the way back, he racked his brain as to why the assistant should think they had met before. At least it freed his mind of the torturous memories of his departed friend, Bobby Anderson.

*

Left alone with his thoughts, the assistant at Jopling's remembered the day four years ago when he had gone to the shepherd's shelter, high on the fells. On arriving at the shelter, he found no sign of Bobby Anderson. He scanned the desolate moor below him, from the high vantage point at Tolson's Scar. Further down the fell, to his right, he saw a solitary soul, moving around at an old mill. *'That must be him. Who the hell else would be up here?* he thought.

The reason for his visit to Bobby Anderson's hovel that day in 1902 was twofold. One, he had gone to gloat over Bobby's fall from grace and two; he had sworn he would wreak revenge on his long-time rival. It was a bit of luck for him when the head horse keeper from West Fell pit pitched up at Jopling's to buy replacement tack for the pit ponies. On hearing, he was from West Fell he had quizzed the horse keeper concerning Bobby Anderson, and the horse keeper had been forthcoming with many answers. He had revealed how Bobby had become an alcoholic; how he had fallen from grace at the big hall, and he now lived in the hovel up on the fells at Tolson's Scar.

Now it was payback time, he thought. At first opportunity he would head to Tolson's Scar and confront his adversary of many years.

*

He had stealthily made his way down to the mill house without alerting Bobby Anderson. Lying prone amongst the heather, he watched like a lioness surveying her prey as Bobby went about doing his laundry, unaware that cruel eyes watched his every move. *This is not like you these days Bobby. According to the locals, you're a real scruffy bastard. Gettin' fussy, are y'? You must have changed,* he thought.

Bobby Anderson squatted down on the edge of the millpond as he wrung the excess water from his ragged shirt, now much cleaner than it had been of late. He spread the newly laundered shirt on the bank, his tormented mind was contemplating the next move in the devised suicide plan; he was totally unaware that someone was observing his every move.

Bobby stealthily slid into the water fully clothed except for his shirt, a washing exercise conducted to create the illusion of an accident rather than a suicide, and he sunk below the surface of the millpond. He sunk below the surface and instinctively held his breath. A white disc of light above him was gradually shrinking. He inhaled frantically and swallowed a huge mouthful of water. With his senses numbing, he realised he was now fighting for his life. *Is this what drowning is like?* he thought, and with what little strength his malnourished body could muster he reached upwards in the direction of the disc of light now reduced almost to the point of extinguishment. In the desperate time, it took him to break the surface; he decided his life was not going to end in this futile fashion.

From his concealed viewpoint the so-called Jed Smyth, realising he was witnessing a suicide attempt, jumped up. *He's doing the bloody job for me; this will never do. This is not what I wanted at all.* He knew he had to act quickly. His long-time rival was denying him his revenge before his very eyes. He dived in and swam underwater until the bleary outline of Bobby's body came into view. The force from the water wheel was quickly pulling Bobby towards the millrace. They both broke the surface of the water together. Jed Smyth swam alongside Bobby, who by now was flailing his arms and thrashing the water in a frantic fight to save his own life which a short while ago he was prepared to give up. The coldness of the water had suddenly shocked him back into reality and he was kicking for the bank side.

'No, you don't Bobby, you had your chance to do it your way but this time you've cocked it up. Let me give y' a hand,' and with his hand firmly on Bobby's head, he pushed down and held him under. Ominous bubbles floated to the surface as the air escaped from Bobby's saturated lungs. Soon, the bubbles ceased to break the surface, indicating that Bobby had given up his struggle to survive. Jed Smyth's alias Harry Appleton's last act of treachery was to release his hand from his victim's head and propel the body in the direction of the millrace.

The assassin climbed out of the water and looking around to see if anyone was in the vicinity, he stripped off his clothes and spread them out on the heather to dry. With the heather on the fells, now coming to the end of the flowering season, large patches had turned brown. Only the strongest blooms still survived. Jed Smyth lay in a patch of the dead heather as he watched the water for any signs of Bobby's body. As he watched, Bobby's supine body floating on the surface just where the water from the millpond entered the millrace. Here the flow of the water increased rapidly before rushing to feed the big wheel, taking Bobby's body swiftly with it. Smyth felt a moment of elation as he watched the churning paddle wheel devour Bobby's body. He rolled onto his back, the smell of dead heather in his nostrils as he contemplated his next move; he felt no remorse for his actions. As he lay there, he realised that the high-pitched whirring sound coming from the mill house had ceased; the wheel had come to a halt. An eerie silence came over the scene as the big wheel ceased to churn the water. Realising this would affect the power to the big house and fearing someone would be coming to investigate the problem, he decided to beat a rapid retreat from the scene of his crime. *One down, one to go,* he thought as he hurried down the fell, taking care to give Shinwell Hall and West Fell a wide berth.

*

Back in the present, it dawned on Jed Smyth where he had met the groom from Shinwell Hall. *You are that young bugger who turned up at Thirsk races with Bobby Anderson and Chris Paxton and it was you that rushed me on the cliff top at Shields, the night I supposedly met my death. Good right to think I should know y.' That's where I knew y' from. Fancy not spottin' y' first off. Mind you, there was only the moonlight and Souter's lighthouse beam that night,* he thought.

Jed Smyth was back with more malice than ever, and he was already scheming Tommy's death. This was the second half of his revenge. He may have planned a third death, but he needed Chris Paxton alive to pay the overdue blackmail money.

Chapter 31

The following day, Tommy Cogon was busy polishing the new saddle ready for Miles Paxton's inspection. He had painstakingly worked neatsfoot oil into the new saddle and all that was required now was for the owner to do plenty of riding, to break it in. He was giving it a final polish when Miles Paxton joined him in the tack room. Despite all the other equestrian paraphernalia occupying the tack room, there was a distinct smell of new leather in the air.

'It's ready for Mrs Paxton sir,' Tommy said proudly as Miles Paxton circled the saddle stand scrutinizing the Jopling's saddle, stopping every now and then to examine more closely the fine craftsmanship they had painstakingly put into their product. He stopped and caressed the leather in admiration.

'A veritable work of art Tommy, don't you think?'

'It is indeed sir,' Tommy concurred.

'Nevertheless, Thomas, I do detect an oversight. Despite their fine craftsmanship, they have omitted to embellish the saddle with my wife's monogram. A detail I distinctly specified. Not to worry, you can pop back with it today and no doubt, they shall rectify the problem while you wait,' he said confidently.

'Ah'll see to it right away sir.'

*

Tommy returned to Jopling's with the new saddle. The same assistant, whom he had met the day before, was there to receive him again. He was not to know the assistant was Jed Smyth and that he was back and planning Tommy's death. Tommy explained why he was returning the saddle and the assistant assured him it would be done while he waited.

'It's not like us to do a trick like that,' he said, and he apologised for the oversight before heading back to the workshop with the saddle.

He returned and said, 'They gettin' on to it straight away. Ah'm Harry Appleton by the way. Nice t' see yer again,' and he offered Tommy his hand.

'Tommy Cogon,' Tommy replied, 'pleased to meet *you* again.'

'Do you like goin' to the races Tommy?' he asked.

'I like nothing better, but I've hardly been since my friend Bobby Anderson died; it's not the same on my own,' Tommy admitted.

'How would y' fancy goin' to the races with me on Saturday, Tommy? I have two free tickets to High Gosforth Park this Saturday. The Jopling's always get complimentary tickets but seldom use them all, so I can easily get an extra one for you, so you're welcome to come along.'

'Are y' sure there's no other person that y' might want to take instead of me? A girlfriend perhaps?' Tommy suggested.

'No such luck in that respect Tommy, as appealin' as you make it sound. I am married, and the wife has no interest in the races so it's either me and you, or me on my own. What do y' say man? Apart from that, the fact that I have some good information about a horse runnin' in the mile handicap might sway y.' He needs the goin' to be on the soft side, to see him at his best. He doesn't like to hear his hooves rattlin.' Flying Ensign is his name, and his connections expect him to fly-in.'

'It's a yes then Harry,' Tommy said enthusiastically, being swayed at the prospect of some easy cash.

'We'll set off early, and we can walk the mile course before racin' and see what the goin' is like on the day, before committing our money. Ah'll meet you in 'The Fleece' near Newcastle Central station, about Twelve o'clock,' Jed Smyth, alias Harry Appleton, suggested.

'Twelve o'clock it is then,' Tommy agreed, adding, 'Ah'll look forward to the day out.'

'Good! That saddle should be ready by now. Ah'd better show me face or Old Percy'll be thinkin' ah'm skiving.'

After a short absence, the so-called Harry Appleton returned carrying the amended saddle. He held the saddle out to Tommy for his approval, giving a final smoothing of the surface of leather that now bore the newly applied monogram – **JP**.

*

Tommy arrived at 'The Fleece' at ten minutes to noon. He bought two pints of ale and took up a space at the bar near to the door where he could see Harry enter. Five minutes later, his *'friend'* arrived. 'Hi Harry. Got y' a pint of ale in, ah hope that's what y' drink.'

'Perfect,' said Harry Appleton. 'When we finish these, we'll get the charabanc up to the course.' After a bone-shaking journey of six or so miles, the charabanc pulled up at the racecourse. The racecourse at this time was sparsely populated but it would soon build in numbers, closer to the time of the first race on the card. This was the very reason Harry Appleton or Jed Smyth, had planned his early arrival at the course and his plan to 'walk the course' would take him and the unsuspecting Tommy Cogon a mile away from the winning post and the grandstands. There was a straight mile course at Gosforth Park and the area around the mile start, was heavily wooded. The geography of the course fitted into Jed Smyth's plans, and he gloated at the thought of the devious scheme which he was about to implement. They both ducked under the running rail in front of the grandstand, and they began the walk down the course to the mile start. Every two hundred or so yards, Tommy's companion for the day would hack his heel into the racecourse turf and declared his opinion of the 'going.' This is perfect for our fella, there's enough cut in the ground to keep him happy and with the luck in running that all winners need, he should run up to his best form.

Tommy said nothing, for he was impressed at the command of the racing lingo Harry Appleton used. It made him wonder had he at one time been in the profession. It could quite easily have been Bobby Anderson talking to him.

Suddenly, as they reached the straight mile start, that comparison rapidly evaporated from Tommy's mind as Harry Appleton suddenly drew a Colt revolver from inside his jacket.

'Over there Cogan,' the gunman ordered, menacingly. 'I knew I'd seen y' before, the moment I saw y' but I couldn't put a name to the face and then ah remembered that day all those years ago when that idiot Chris Paxton brought you and your mate, that bloody Anderson, to Thirsk races. What an embarrassing episode that turned out to be. Hurry up, into the woods with y', or I'll finish y' here and now.' He menacingly, pushed the revolver into Tommy's back. Tommy could not believe how the scene had changed from a day out at the races into a life-threatening situation a mile away from the grandstand. From leisurely walking the course at Gosforth Park, Tommy now found himself menaced by a desperate gunman, hell-bent on destroying him.

'You had no idea who I was, did y' Cogon? Ah fooled you, good and proper. You pit yackers are all the same, all brawn, no brain. You thought you had seen me off when the cliff edge gave way didn't y', that night up on the Leas above Marsden. Just before ah went over the edge, the beam from Souter's lighthouse, completed another revolution, lightin' your face and that was the last thing I remembered when I recovered consciousness,' he said, with venom in his voice. He was now standing directly in front of Tommy. Tommy fixed his gaze on the barrel of the revolver.

'Before you get rid of me,' Tommy said, 'tell me, how you weren't killed when you went off the cliff at Marsden?' he asked, deliberately wanting to prolong the moment when Smyth would pull the trigger.

'Well now Tommy, I'll tell you, seein' as this will probably be your last request. When that large section of cliff edge of soil and turf broke away, I embraced it tightly as I fell to the rocks below. This broke my fall as I plummeted to the beach below. When I regained consciousness, the tide was ebbing, and I lay still for what I thought was almost an hour as the lapping waves slowly eroded the soil and turf from under me until eventually, I was lying on a rock. I counted the number of seconds it took for each revolution of Souter's light as it reflected off the water to get an idea of time and how long I had lain there. Using my crude calculation, I estimated when an hour had passed and cautiously flexed my muscles. I needed to make a move before daybreak; I needed to get off the beach before anyone came and found me, for I had no idea what your story might be as to the happenings on the cliff top.'

'What about the body on Roker beach. Who was that?' Tommy queried, still unable to take his eyes off the embellished barrel of the gun pointed right at him.

'Well, it wasn't me,' he laughed. 'It could have been anyone who fell into the sea around the mouth of the Tyne. The currents would carry the body in the same direction as mine, had the sea claimed my body. So that's it Tommy, call me lucky bastard if you like, because that's what I was that night. Once I got to the cliff top, I headed in the direction of Durham. I broke into a house near Chester-le-Street, stole ten pounds, and kitted myself out with fresh clothes from the owner's wardrobe. Thank God, a widow didn't occupy it, for I was in no mood for wearing a dress.' At this point Tommy was surprised at Smyth's callous humour at such a time. He continued, 'Once I got to Durham, I bought a rail ticket to Kings Cross, and I spent the next few years re-establishing myself while the dust settled. I came back last year after all; I had some old scores to settle, so here I am. I must sort out Chris Paxton now, as he owes me £500, I might make it £600 with lost interest,' he said and laughed at the idea. 'You like the gun Tommy, do y'?' he continued. He was telling his story to Tommy in detail, knowing it was prolonging Tommy's anxiety. 'Nice gun isn't it Tommy? The Gaekwad gave it to me when I was ridin' for him in India. He was one of the richest Princes in India; said I needed it to protect myself from the brigands when travelling through the countryside. Strange, I never needed to use it until now. Never thought I'd have any need for it, back here in the northeast, few brigands round here, although from your point of view Tommy you might think otherwise. You're goin' to get it when I am finished with y.' Do y' know anything about guns? Well now, it is a Colt double action revolver. You'll get it when I am finished with y.' You're not sayin' much. Cheer up Tommy, I know you will not be here to appreciate it, but you'll be a record holder; you'll be the first person killed by my grand, gold-plated gun. Just think of that Tommy, in the bit time you have left. A record holder,' Jed Smyth taunted. The gun was extravagantly gold plated, and the handle grips were made of ivory. Just when Tommy thought the madman's ranting was over, he struck up again. 'Am I frightenin' y' bonny lad? I always thought you pit yackers were hard men.'

Tommy noticed a section of a sawn-off tree branch, lying on the ground behind Jed Smyth, as if someone had been collecting firewood and had dropped a short log. *If only ah could reach that,* he thought. Into view, behind Jed Smyth, came a couple of boys. A twig snapped underfoot, and Jed Smyth instinctively swung round taking his eye off Tommy for the briefest of moments. Quickly stooping down, Tommy grabbed the short club-like length of wood from the ground. Raising it above his head, he brought it down vigorously onto his assailant's forearm, which was holding the gun, causing him to release his grip. In a split second of the gun hitting the ground, Tommy darted down, and the over ornamented weapon was now in his hand and the roles were reversed. Now, he was the tormentor. Tommy pondered over what to do about the two young lads. Even though Jed Smyth had lost the balance of power, he continued to question them. 'What the hell are you two buggers doin' here anyway?' he asked brusquely.

'We were only bird nesting mister. Gettin' eggs, to add to our collections. Somebody told us there were jays nestin' in here. We wish we hadn't come here, now,' said the taller of the two, trembling at the sight of the gun. 'Shut up Smyth. You might frighten the bairns, but you are not frightenin' me. Get goin' lads and never come back here again and what you have seen here today you keep to yourselves for your own sakes. Take heed of what I say,' Tommy said, not knowing how this episode might end if Jed Smyth regained the initiative; they too could be in peril.

'We won't mister. Don't worry; it's as if we were never here. I promise. We'll be back in Gosforth before you can say Jack Robinson,' the taller lad, who had adopted the role of spokesperson for the two of them, said with terrified conviction and the two lads disappeared back through the trees, from where they came.

During that short moment when Tommy talked to the lads, Jed Smyth lunged at him to regain possession of the gun. The two rolled on the coppice floor but Tommy was determined not to relinquish his hold on the gun. He knew he had to silence Jed Smyth for the last time. He might have survived the sea, but again Smyth was fighting for his own survival. Gradually, after a fierce struggle, Tommy forced the gun up to Jed Smyth's right temple. Whispering in Jed Smyth's ear, he said, 'This is for Bobby,' and he quickly pulled the trigger. Jed Smyth's head shot convulsively to the left and then his body slumped to the ground. Tommy sat on the ground for several minutes. At that moment, he thought of running for his life in case someone had heard the report from the powerful firearm. Instead, he sat nonplussed watching Smyth's twitching body as a gooey liquid oozed from the side of his head and then he was still. He sat a moment longer and then quickly regained his senses. Picking up the gun with his handkerchief he carefully cleaned the handle and placed it in Smyth's right hand making it appear that Smyth had shot himself. Having completed the illusion of suicide, he quickly left the scene. Not wanting anyone see him leave the racecourse following Smyth's death, he chose not to return to the grandstand area. Instead, he walked the six miles or so, back to Newcastle station. As he walked, he thought of the train of events leading to Jed Smyth's death. Smyth had faked Bobby Anderson's suicide, and ironically Tommy Cogon had avenged his friend's death by fabricating Jed Smyth's suicide, and he realised how close he had come to death himself. He noticed a patch on his own jacket where Smyth's blood had splattered him and in the centre of this area, the burnt gunpowder had scorched the fabric. He stopped at a small stream where he attempted to remove some of the stain. It was here that Tommy realised that the jacket had to go. Two miles on, he came across a water-filled, disused quarry. He gathered a few sizable stones and filled the jacket pockets. With one last larger stone in the inside of the jacket, he drew together the arms of the jacket tightly across the front. With the bundle completed, he launched it as far out into the space above the water that had accumulated since the quarry had become non-operational. Tommy watched as the discarded jacket plummeted down through space. It billowed slightly despite the stones used as ballast, before hitting the water. It seemed to Tommy, it took an age to saturate, before sinking to the bottom of the quarry.

Once back in Newcastle, he bought an *Evening Chronicle* as he waited for a charabanc back to West Fell. He quickly scanned the paper for any news of the discovery of Jed Smyth's body; but there was nothing. He was about to fold the paper before dumping it in the litter bin when his eyes caught sight of the racing results in the stop press column on the back page of the *Chronicle*. 3.00 Gosforth Park - 1st: Flying Ensign 8-1.

Chapter 32

On the day after the horse race meeting at High Gosforth Park, a young couple walking in the area near the mile start decided to take their *'courting,'* into the wooded area that skirted the starting gate. As they ducked and weaved their way between the trees, looking for a suitable spot to do what they had come for, they were shocked to the core when they stumbled on a dead body of a man. A large gunshot wound had violated his right temple and at first glance, it appeared that he had committed suicide. A trail of blood stained his face and a copious amount of blood, now congealed, saturated his jacket and shirt. The young woman screamed shrilly, causing the birds to take flight in raucous alarm. Her male companion squatted down beside the body and was about to go for the gun lying on the ground close to the body.

'Don't do that!' The girl shouted, having quickly recovered her senses after her initial shock. 'The police will want to see things as we found them. We will have to contact the police and report what we have found,' she advised.

*

The staff at the office of the Newcastle Constabulary had christened the case as 'death at the races.' Many puns were doing the rounds among the members of the force, such as 'this one should be a dead cert.' and the 'clues to this one, should be visible a mile away.' In addition, the *pièce de résistance* was 'this case will give you a run for your money.' All this leg pulling directed at Detective Inspector Ian Bruce, a burly Scotsman and his working partner, Detective Sergeant Cyril Hepplewhite, was like water off a duck's back. They had enough experience to take all this leg pulling in their stride; amongst the plain-clothes division, this was normal banter. DI Bruce and his assistant DS Hepplewhite had a job to do, and they were keen to get on with it.

'Quite easy to say suicide, boss,' Hepplewhite said, as they viewed the scene before them.

'Let's not jump to conclusions at this stage, Cyril,' his boss reminded him. 'My gut feelings are telling me there is more to this than meets the eye. We must not disturb anything here until forensics put in *their* two-penn'orth.'

'What about that gun though boss? That *is* something special. I have never seen one as grand as that before. He certainly died in style, this fella.'

*

The forensics people had released their initial report on articles found at the scene. A few days later, Bruce and Hepplewhite, were in their office, mulling over the facts established so far in the report. Two fingerprints experts, brought up from Durham for the case reported that human fingerprints found on a short length of timber, were from several different people none of which matched the fingerprints found on the handle of the gun. This suggested the possibility that if the piece of wood had played any part in the man's death, then it was possible that two people had been present at the death. The scientists had stripped the gun down completely in the hope that it would give up its secrets and shed some light on who might own such an unusual weapon. The serial number indicated it was an M1889 double action revolver. The model designed in 1889 by the Colt Company for the US navy. Research had established the fact that a small order, specifically for the Gaekwad of Rajkarat placed in 1890, included the weapon bearing the same serial number as the weapon found at the death scene. This order was for the use of his personal bodyguards. Moreover, the gold plating, which was of Indian gold, suggested that this process was carried out in India. Following further scrutiny, under the right-side ivory grip, the scientists found an inscription, which read – *To Jed Smyth on riding your 300th winner in India,* 1890.

Bruce and Hepplewhite discussed further; the progress made so far. They also had the early report of the police pathologist, which they were studying with deep concentration. In the mind's eye, the report painted a vivid picture of the pathologist's version of what he thought had occurred on the day the victim met his death. On examining the body, he noticed the right wrist had suffered blunt force trauma, the result of a massive blow from a blunt instrument and it was his opinion that the short length of timber, used in a clubbing action by a second person, had caused the injury. The blow had smashed the radius bone on the right arm. This being the case, it was his professional opinion that this blow would render a person incapable of holding a Colt revolver to his temple let alone pull the trigger. As a result, the police were dealing with an act of murder and not suicide.

His final deduction was that the second person had initially been under threat by the victim, and he had used the piece of timber to club the victim's wrist to obtain the gun for his own advantage. It was his opinion that a struggle for the gun had ensued between the two. During the struggle, the victim's assailant, now grappling with a man who had an injured wrist had forced the gun upwards until level with the temple and shot his victim in the temple at close quarters. The angle of entry of the missile also suggests that the victim did not hold the gun himself at the moment of discharge. For one thing, his right wrist was injured rendering that action impossible and secondly, his right hand showed no evidence of gunpowder burn which it would have, had the gun been discharged at such close quarters. The area around the entry wound in the right temple showed the distinct pattern of the barrel of the revolver. Indicating that the perpetrator had discharged the gun while holding it pressed against the head of the victim.

'Let us run over what we know so far,' Bruce said. 'Some fella is found shot through the head in what at first glance is shouting out to us, suicide. Our friend down at the morgue tells us it is his opinion that he was murdered. Now it is our job to either prove him wrong or prove the dead man did indeed kill himself. If we agree with him then we have a killer to find. If not, it is a case of who he was and informing his next of kin that he has taken his own life; case closed. What's your view of things Cyril?'

'I don't want to jump to the wrong conclusion, boss, but my gut instinct is saying the pathologist is thinking along the right lines. It seems to me that he has made a strong case for murder.'

'Right then who is the victim? If the gun was his, then it's the ex-jockey, Jed Smyth who rode for several years in India for the Gaekwad of Rajkarat. Well done the pathologist.'

'Hang on guv, what is wrong with that is, our 'friends' over the river in Gateshead, thought he had met his death when falling from the cliffs above Marsden, several years ago. The body was unrecognisable, and an open verdict was recorded,' DS Hepplewhite reminded his boss.

'Right, you are then, let us assume Jed Smyth, because of the gun, is the victim. Then who pulled the trigger? Get somebody onto missing persons and draw up a list of all persons reported missing in the area and people in boarding houses or workplaces, not seen since last Saturday morning. That will give us something to go on as to who the victim is. Finding out who pulled the trigger is another matter altogether. I cannot help but think somebody must have heard or seen something. You cannot fire a gun outdoors without making a loud noise,' the DI said.

'What about the staff at the racecourse? We could question the people who operated the turnstiles. See if any of them saw anything strange. It is a long shot, but someone might have seen something,' DS Hepplewhite suggested.

'We will have to get someone to consult with Durham Constabulary on this. Find out what they know about the disappearance of Jed Smyth, also, get some of their men asking questions down on the Gateshead side of the river,' DI Bruce ordered.

*

The tedious job of knocking on doors, visiting workplaces, boarding houses, and questioning staff at the racecourse fell to a team of PC's, from both the Newcastle Force and Gateshead to establish the identity of the dead person. Although this seemed to be a forlorn hope, it did produce an interesting comment from the person operating the entrance for holders of complimentary tickets. He claimed he had seen the ex-jockey Jed Smyth enter with another male companion.

'Let us get onto this fella and see what he has to say for himself. Where can we find him?'

'He works part time but according to PC Stockton, who interviewed him, he will be there all this week working with the team of cleaners who collect the debris left behind by the crowds,' Hepplewhite replied.

'Let's get out to High Gosforth Park right away and ask him a few more questions,' DI Bruce said, with an air of urgency.

*

They arrived at the racecourse and soon they were in conversation with Eddie Stone, who operated the complimentary gate on the day of the races. 'Ah was sure it was Smyth. Ah used to ride professionally me self a long time ago now like,' he said. 'The minute ah saw him ah thought, *Bugger me, if that's not Jed Smyth, ah'm a Dutchman.* Ah nearly spoke to him, and then ah thought, *Ah never spoke much to the bugger when ah was race-ridin', why bother now?* He had another bloke with him who looked a few years younger and swarthy lookin' as if he worked out of doors; certainly not a pitman. He was short enough to be an ex-jockey and certainly had the build. About in his thirties I would say, at a guess, but his face rang no bells with me. Ah've seen jockeys come and go for years.'

'What happens to the stubs torn from the complimentary tickets when you close the turnstile?' DI Bruce asked.

'They go on a spike until someone comes over from the office and collects them at the end of the meetin',' Eddie Stone said.

'Will they still have them, do you think?' DS Hepplewhite asked.

'Ah've no idea how long they keep them for. If y're interested in *their* tickets, look at the stubs at the bottom of the spike. Those two blokes were some of the earliest to arrive at the course and ah remember there weren't many stubs on the spike at that time. If ah had to make a guess ah'd say they were here about twelve-thirty, two hours before the first race.'

'Will anyone be in the office now?' Hepplewhite added.

'Oh, aye the lasses are there most of the time after each meetin', seein' to prize monies, trophies and things like that. There's always plenty of work for them, you'll find somebody in the office,' Stone explained.

'Thanks for your help Eddie. Your information has been most helpful.'

'Good luck with your enquiries. Ah can't wait to see if that *was* Jed Smyth.'

*

The administration office occupied part of the impressive stone-built building, which had formerly been the seat of the Brandling family, rich Northeast coal owners. Also situated within the old house, were the jockeys' changing rooms, the weighing room and the stewards' room. The two detectives found a girl seated at a desk and another girl fingering through a tall wooden filing cabinet.

'Good morning ladies, I'm Detective Inspector Bruce and this is my assistant, Detective Sergeant Hepplewhite.' They both showed their warrant cards and DI Bruce continued, 'We are sure you must have heard by now, of the body found in the woods by the straight mile start.'

'Yes, it was a good thing the body wasn't found until the next day, or we would have had a helluva job sorting things out, if the meeting had been interrupted,' the girl said, without much thought for the deceased.

'We are interested in the stubs from the complimentary tickets which were used for admission at the last meeting. Do you still have them?'

'Yes, we have as it happens. You are lucky, we have just finished them this morning. We usually dump them once we have recorded which recipients used them. If we find they are not being used, we will renew the allocation list,' she said officiously.

While this conversation was going on the other girl who looked as if she might hold the lower position within the office, continued idly thumbing through the files as she listened-in to what was going on across the office. Ian Bruce glanced her way, and she quickly pulled a file from the cabinet and returned to her desk.

'Can you possibly give me a copy of the posting list of the recipients of the complimentary tickets, and we will take the ticket stubs as well. Do we need to return them to you?'

'I can do that right away as we just compiled the new list this morning. The old list should be still in the file; can you get that for Detective Bruce, Jenny, please?"

Jenny quickly returned and passed the file and the stubs to her colleague, who glanced at the date and passed them to Ian Bruce.

'You can take the old one with you as that is the one pertaining to the last meeting. Can we be of further help to you?' she concluded.

'Yes, there is one last thing, have you got an inkpad?'

'Of course, why do you ask?'

'I would like you both to give us your fingerprints. Not that we think for one moment you had anything to do with what happened down at the mile start. It is just to eliminate your prints from our findings. They will be destroyed just as soon as we eliminate them.'

'That's no trouble,' the senior girl said.

'Oh, I've never had my fingerprints taken,' Jenny said, as she strutted across the office in short, quick steps, in an excited fashion, stopping to collect the inkpad and paper on the way.

'I should hope not,' said her colleague. Cyril Hepplewhite took the pad and paper from Jenny and took the other girl's prints first.

'Your name miss?' he asked, after she had pressed her fingers to the paper.

'Sandra Prentice,' she stated. He repeated the procedure with Jenny and asked her the same question.

'Jenny Singleton,' she replied, with a doe-eyed look and a flutter of her eye lashes.

The two detectives thanked the girls again and left them franticly rubbing at their inky hands.

Chapter 33

'Morning Tommy, how are you today?' Miles Paxton asked.

'Ah am not too bad... I suppose sir,' Tommy replied, unconvincingly.

'You don't sound too sure Tommy. Is there anything wrong? I have just been talking to your mother and she tells me you had a day at Newcastle races on Saturday. I thought that would have cheered you up. I hope you did not gamble away all your money.'

'No nothin' like that sir,' Tommy replied. He knew he needed to talk to someone and offload all his problems. After Saturday's events, his problems had multiplied. However good a listener he knew Miles Paxton to be, he knew to disclose all his troubles to him would mean exposing Jemima Paxton's involvement with Bobby Anderson all those years ago. This would not only be unfaithful to the memory of his friend, but it would cause terrible distress within the Paxton family, a family who had been so good to him and his mother over several years.

'Your mother tells me you have been somewhat melancholy of late and your demeanour has deteriorated gradually over recent times. I must agree with her because I too have noticed a change in you, which in my professional capacity gives me reason to be concerned. Tell me Tommy did you enjoy your day at the races. Your mother said you had gone in the company of a person whom she led me to believe is an employee at Jopling's Saddlery.'

'That's correct sir. It was Harry Appleton. He said he had a couple of complimentary tickets for the meetin' through Joplin's,' Tommy replied, without disclosing the whole truth. He thought for a moment, and soon realised how essential it was becoming, to tell someone the whole story and he knew that time was now.

'That was fortuitous Tommy, as Father and I were both preoccupied on Saturday, and as such, we were unable to attend. Otherwise, had we been going, you could have gone along with us. What do you say to a trip to the races soon? Only if you feel it would please you,' Miles Paxton suggested.

He thought before replying, remembering the last time, as a boy he and Bobby had gone to Thirsk with Chris Paxton. 'That sounds like a generous offer sir, you and your father are very kind to me mam and me, but ah don't think you would want me tagging along,' Tommy replied. Almost in the same breath he blurted out, 'With respect to y' good self, ah would like to talk to your father, if y' could arrange that for me sir, ah feel, that would be a great help to me.' He knew, now was the time to get all his troubles off his shoulders.

'As you wish Tommy, I will set up an appointment for you to see father at a time when it is suitable to him. He will probably let your mother know a suitable time and date.'

'Ah'd rather nobody else knows about our meetin',' sir. It's something of a delicate nature ah wanted to discuss with him, if you know what I mean.'

'I shall be as discreet as possible, Tommy.'

*

Two days later Tommy waited in the library for his meeting with Chris Paxton. His eyes nervously scanned the books stacked around the walls, the symmetry interrupted here and there, by family portraits, some recent ones he could recognise, others meant nothing to him. Above the fireplace was a portrait of Jemima Paxton looking down at him. In all his time at Shinwell Hall, it was his first visit to the library. He stood waiting; his mind rehearsing what he wanted to say. As he stood there, the fine portrait in oils of Jemima Paxton stared down at him. The artist had caught her in a sort of half smile, which Tommy thought was rather contemptuous, and who could blame him. He stood staring at the portrait, and it seemed Jemima Paxton was returning his stare. *You have no idea do y', the problems you've brought into my life, woman,* he thought.

Just then, the door behind him opened. 'Now then Tommy, what is it that you want to see me about? I hope you are not here to resign, for you are irreplaceable. Come and sit down and tell me what is so important that it warrants such a formal meeting. First let me pour us both a small drink, the sun is high enough in the sky to make it respectable. Whisky is it?' he asked, for he could see Tommy was tense.

He handed Tommy the whisky and sat down opposite him. 'Take your time Tommy. Have your drink first,' he suggested hoping the whisky would relax the tension showing on his groom's face.

Tommy sipped at the whisky and began, 'Well sir, ah've much on my mind now and things only got worse when ah went to the races last week. One thing and another it's all gettin' on top of me, to the point where it's gettin' unbearable. Ah feel if ah don't tell somebody soon, ah'll lose my mind.'

'What has happened Tommy to get you in such a state? Come now; get it all off your chest. Tell me, it will make you feel better. You know what they say, *'open confession is good for the soul,'* trying to take a lighter approach to whatever was troubling Tommy.

Tommy related the happenings of the day at High Gosforth Park. How it came about that, he was at the races with Harry Appleton of Jopling's Saddlery. He described everything to the attentive Chris Paxton, even the point where he pulled the trigger and the moment, he spent watching the ruined body of Harry Appleton, twitching on the ground alongside him. Then he shocked Chris Paxton with the words, 'Only it wasn't Harry Appleton at all that ah killed, it was no other than Jed Smyth.'

'Are you sure Tommy?' That cannot be, Jed Smyth died when he fell from the cliffs some years ago. You remember it was in all the local papers. I grant you, his father could not identify the body and the coroner returned an open verdict at the inquest.'

'That's not all,' Tommy continued. 'Ah was with Bobby Anderson when Smyth tried to collect the blackmail money the night he met, what Bobby and me, thought was his death.

'That night, on The Leas at South Shields, we waited for Smyth to turn up to collect your money from under the boulder. As he removed the parcel of money from under the boulder, ah rushed him. Ah didn't deliberately go to push him over. We were grapplin' with each other when a stretch of the cliff edge gave way and that was the last we saw of him. Jed Smyth explained to me, how he survived the fall.'

Tommy went on to relate to Chris Paxton the account of Jed Smyth's survival.

'How much did you know of the facts behind Smyth blackmailing me?' Chris Paxton asked, realising for the first time that Tommy also knew of his wife's dalliance with Bobby Anderson.

'Ah overheard you discussing it with Bobby in the stable block. It would be shortly after Smyth had threatened to blackmail you. When you arranged to go along with his instructions for the money drop, I offered to accompany Bobby to South Shields. We thought it would be safer to go together. The next day Bobby returned your money and told you that Smyth never turned up.' Tommy waited a moment, contemplating Chris Paxton's reaction to the truth of what had happened that night on The Leas.

Chris Paxton's reaction, or more to the point, lack of it, was not what Tommy had expected. He thought his boss would have shown more surprise. After allowing for some reaction, Tommy continued his confessions. 'That's exactly what happened sir, ah promise you.'

There followed an awkward silence while Chris Paxton collected his thoughts, after which he said, 'Well Tommy, with regards to the happenings that night at South Shields, you and Bobby's involvement, in my eyes is commendable. However, the police may not share my view. The question is what we do in the meantime?'

Paxton once more paused for thought before continuing. 'Recent events at the races, involving you and the recently resurrected Jed Smyth, have opened a whole new complex issue. I think the best thing to do, is for you to confess to the killing of Jed Smyth, alias Harry Appleton.'

'That's not the full story,' Tommy Cogon said, despondently.

'What, there is more?' Chris Paxton asked, his mood changing rapidly. Now Tommy was getting worried again because he knew that what Chris Paxton was about to hear would not please him at all. He waited to pluck up the courage to reveal the truth about Bobby's suicide letter. He knew that to stand up in court under oath and relate the truth about Bobby's suicide letter meant disclosing to all and sundry Jemima Paxton's moment of madness with Bobby Anderson all those years ago. An incident that Chris Paxton thought he had laid to rest long ago with the 'death' of Jed Smyth and latterly, the death of Bobby Anderson. Now he was about to hear more details of which Tommy knew would deeply upset Chris Paxton, or indeed anger him. Nevertheless, he was aware that to salve his own conscience, the truth had to be out.

Again, there was silence between the two as Tommy teetered on the brink of further confession. Dare he reveal the full truth of what happened at Tolson's Scar four years ago? Taking a deep breath, he continued with great trepidation. 'What ah haven't told you yet, is that Smyth confessed to me before ah killed him, that he drowned Bobby in the mill pond,' and Tommy went on to describe the events leading to Bobby's death and Jed Smyth's part in that, including the details of Bobby Anderson's would-be suicide note. 'He genuinely loved your wife. He said he never loved another woman in his life. He knew she would always be your woman and she would never be available to him and that's what drove Bobby to distraction,'

'What did you do with Bobby's letter?

'After ah read it, ah burnt it when ah got rid of all that rubbish up at Tolson's Scar. I did it to protect Bobby's memory and to prevent the public from dragging Mrs Paxton's name through the mud.

'The question is, what are we to do Tommy?' He studied for a while; he was becoming anxious of the effect all this scandal would have on the Paxton name. Then he continued, 'I am sure if you confess to the murder of Harry Appleton and not mention anything of Bobby's would-be suicide letter when questioned by the police, it will stand you in good stead. The worst action you can take is to go on the run. Once you become a fugitive, you will be constantly looking over your shoulder and eventually you will be caught. The police are likely to show you leniency if you are honest with them concerning the death at the racecourse. Best come clean; yes, best come clean,' he said repeating the last phrase, more to convince himself than to convince Tommy that this course of action would work for himself more than Tommy. He was now thinking aloud, *best not mention anything about Bobby's suicide note,* he suggested, repeating himself once again. 'That would only compound things further. The fact that you burnt the letter would throw doubt as to its very existence and by the same measure, throw doubt on your integrity. Best you do not confess too much, it would not serve any useful purpose to your case Tommy. Keep things as simple as possible. The killing of Jed Smyth is enough for the police to know about in this. From what you have told me, there was too much in the content to rake up now, far better to let it stay in the past.' Paxton knew, by saying nothing about the letter Tommy had found, his wife's infidelity would remain a secret. He was not only scheming to save his wife's reputation but also that of himself and their family. Furthermore, the only person alive who knew the truth other than himself, and his wife was Tommy Cogon and even his wife was ignorant that he knew the truth of her act of adultery with his former jockey. His mind was working quickly; it needed to, for he was becoming more anxious than Tommy Cogon on what the outcome of all this would be. He could not have been more concerned about the ramifications, had *he* pulled the trigger. He had not had time to rehearse this conversation. If Tommy followed his advice, he had calculated, as he talked and schemed, that the best outcome for the Paxton family would find Tommy hanging by his neck in Durham jail. In his naivety, Tommy was not to know that there was an ulterior motive in Chris Paxton's advice. His advice would 'take care' of the only person other than his own wife, who knew that Bobby Anderson had cuckolded him. Until now, he had not even let his wife know that he too, knew of her brief affair with Bobby Anderson. He loved her enough to suffer in silence, the fact that Bobby Anderson had taken his wife under his very nose.

Although Chris Paxton's advice filled Tommy with fear, by confessing everything, he had shed the burden he had carried all these years and the relief was immeasurable. Tommy, in the relief this unburdening had brought him, felt confident he had an ally in Chris Paxton and followed his advice without question. Despite Paxton's advice and support for Tommy Cogon, his wife's reputation was at stake, and he would refute any information passed on to the police concerning Jemima Paxton. He would claim that it was an act of self-preservation on the part of a desperate killer. Tommy Cogon's blind dedication to his master would prove to be his own undoing.

*

While the conversation between Tommy Cogon and Chris Paxton was taking place, back at Gosforth Police Station, Bruce and Hepplewhite had made further progress. The fingerprints experts from Durham had discovered that 'prints found on the piece of timber, matched those found on one of the complimentary ticket stubs issued to the Jopling's Saddlery and the prints on the gun matched the prints on a second ticket from the same batch issue.

'This looks as if our victim had access to the tickets issued to Jopling's. Let us get out there Cyril and ask a few questions; see if we can find out anything from the staff of Jopling's Saddlery. They should know who received those two complimentary tickets,' Ian Bruce stated with urgency.

*

The two officers arrived at Jopling's Saddlery and Old Percy showed them through to the manager's office.

'Good afternoon, sir.'

'Carling, Timothy Carling,' the manager said as he came around his desk to greet the two detectives and he offered his hand.

They shook hands, 'Detective Inspector Bruce, sir and this is my assistant Detective Sergeant Hepplewhite.' he said as both men showed their warrant cards.

Carling gave the cards a cursory glance and then addressed Bruce. 'Please, take a seat. Tell me, what is this all about? What brings two detectives from Newcastle over the water to Gateshead? It must be serious,' he said jokingly.

'It is serious sir,' Hepplewhite stated, continuing, 'a man was shot and killed at High Gosforth Park racecourse last Saturday. Our investigations so far lead us to believe that the victim gained entry to the racecourse using one of a batch of six tickets issued to your company.'

Carling's manner changed on realising the gravity of the situation.

'If that is the case then your time here should be brief, as the only person here who avails himself of the complimentary tickets, is Harry Appleton, our assistant. On that Saturday, he had company. He asked for two tickets.'

'Do you know who was with him on that fateful trip, Mr Carling,' Ian Bruce asked eagerly.

'I am indeed inspector, for I teased him about taking his wife with him, a thing he never does, and his habits were not about to change, as he said he was going alone. Furthermore, he said the groom from Shinwell Hall, who was here to collect an expensive bespoke saddle, might be interested in one of the remaining ones. He suggested to me that it was a nice way of showing our appreciation, at no outlay, to ourselves. *It'll keep them sweet up at Shinwell Hall,* was the way he had put it and from a business point of view, I could not agree more.'

'Are you sure they did not go to the race meeting together,' Bruce asked.

'I suppose it is always possible, but I think it would be very unlikely, as Harry Appleton preferred to attend the races alone, saying other people's company proved to be serious distraction when trying to find winners.'

'Have you seen Harry Appleton since, sir?'

'I'm afraid he has not turned up for work since.'

'That tallies,' Hepplewhite muttered under his breath, earning a quick glare from Bruce.

'We had better get up to Shinwell Hall right away before the groom goes on the run. Do you have his name Mr Carling?'

'I should have it, as he should have signed the receipt for the saddle. Give me a moment.' He crossed to a filing cabinet, pulled out a drawer, fingered through the contents and extracted a file. Shuffling through the papers, he stopped and read out the name, Thomas Cogon.

'One more thing before we take our leave of you, how long have you employed Harry Appleton?' asked Bruce.

'He came to us at the turn of the century. He said at his interview, he had spent twelve years in India as an overseer on a tea plantation. I fired one or two questions at him on India, which he played with a straight bat. One thing I found strange at the time, was his knowledge of horse tack and saddlery and his command of the terminology in the trade. It was not what you might expect from someone with a background in tea growing. In fact, I was impressed, and I had him earmarked for a move within the company when the right opening came along in sales, or buying, say. Although I did not ask him the question, I thought he might have at some time, been involved with horses.'

'Thank you for your co-operation, sir. You have been a

tremendous help to us. We will show ourselves out.' Detective Inspector Bruce stated, and with a final shake of the manager's hand, they took their leave.

'We need to get someone from the South Shields force to contact Jed Smyth's father again. I know it is raking up the past for the old boy, but it needs doing. He was unable to identify the body washed up on the beach at Roker, as that of his son, so we have to see if he can identify the body found at Gosforth Park.' D I Bruce stated.

'Will do boss,' his colleague affirmed.

*

Two members of the South Shields force accompanied old Brit Smyth to the morgue in Newcastle. The morgue attendant withdrew the trolley on which the cadaver lay, from its housing in the wall. He drew back the shroud exposing the face and turned to old Brit Smyth with an enquiring look. Brit Smyth studied the corpse for only a brief time and with tears in his eyes, he turned to DI Bruce, nodded and said, 'yes Inspector that is my son Jed.'

Chapter 34

Alice Cogon knocked on the door of the summer room. The voice of Chris Paxton called from within, 'Come,' and she entered.

'Excuse me sir, there are two detectives in the entrance hall, wishing to see you.'

'Did they say why they wanted to see me, Alice?'

'No sir, they just said it was of a very serious nature.'

'Show them in Alice, I will receive them in my study.'

Alice returned to the two detectives, waiting in the entrance hall.

'Mr Paxton will see you in his study, gentleman. Follow me,' and they followed Alice Cogon along the oak panelled corridor. She knocked, before opening. Stepping aside, she allowed the two officers to pass through and announced, 'Detective Inspector Bruce and Detective Sergeant Hepplewhite, sir.'

'Thank you, Alice; please gentlemen, come in and sit down and tell me, how I can help you.'

DI Bruce was the first to speak. 'I understand you have a groom here, by the name of Thomas Cogon. Is that correct sir?'

'It is indeed inspector; he and his mother, whom you have just met, have worked at the hall since about 1885 and most dependable workers they both have proved to be. I have a good notion of why you are so interested in my groom. He has told me all about his involvement in the death of the man found dead in the woods at High Gosforth racecourse.'

'You are correct sir. That is our reason for being here today. So, he has confessed his crime to you has he sir; is he available? We would like to take him in for questioning.'

'Well, Inspector, basing my assumption on my recent discussion with Tommy Cogon yesterday, you will find him most eager to answer all your questions with a minimum of interrogation. When we talked yesterday, he was full of remorse and gave me the impression that he would be pleased to get this business off his chest.'

'Could we see him right away, sir?'

'Certainly,' Chris Paxton said. He walked over to the brocade bellpull in the corner of his study. He tugged it twice and shortly after, Alice returned.

'Could you ask Davidson to go to the stable block and ask Tommy to drop what he is doing and come to my study immediately please Alice?' Chris Paxton asked rather gravely.

'May I ask what this is about? Is he in trouble?' his mother asked.

'All will be revealed at the proper time, Alice. In the meantime, I suggest you return to the kitchen and make yourself a cup of tea. I will summon you later and explain to you, the meaning of all this.'

Alice Cogon left the study. Her face bore a look which was a mix of motherly concern and utter perplexity.

The three men waited for Davidson to appear with Tommy Cogon. DI Bruce broke the awkward silence. 'I must say sir; this so far is the easiest arrest we are ever likely to make.'

'As I said earlier, Tommy will not give you any trouble. He will be glad to co-operate and give you a full confession, unless he has had a complete change of mind since yesterday,' Chris Paxton replied.

A knock sounded on the door. 'Come,' Chris Paxton called. The door opened, and Tommy Cogon walked sheepishly into the room. Davidson had escorted Tommy as far as the study but then returned as fast as possible to the kitchen. She was concerned about Alice, but she also sensed scandal and could not wait to hear Alice's version of the goings-on now unfolding at the Hall.

'Come in Tommy. These two men are Detective Inspector Bruce and his assistant Detective Sergeant Hepplewhite. They would like you to assist them with their enquiries. I have briefly told them that you were expecting someone coming to see you concerning the death of a man found recently at High Gosforth Park. I have explained to them the subject of our conversation yesterday. Remember to tell them everything, exactly as we discussed it,' Chris Paxton said, putting emphasis on the word *exactly*, hoping his groom had got the gist of his real meaning.

'That will be enough on your part sir,' Hepplewhite said. His policing instinct gave him a feeling that Paxton was grooming his man prior to their interrogation.

DI Bruce approached Tommy with a pair of handcuffs at the ready. 'Thomas Cogon, I am arresting you for the murder of Jed Smyth and would like you to accompany us to the station to help us in our enquiries.' He was about to place the handcuffs on Tommy's wrists when Chris Paxton intervened. 'I do not think that should be necessary inspector. I am sure Tommy will not give you any trouble.'

'That may be your opinion, sir. Nevertheless, we have a job to do, and we will do it my way,' he said as he locked the handcuffs about Tommy's wrists. He continued by formally cautioning Tommy as he clicked the handcuffs closed.

Tommy looked in bewilderment in the direction of Chris Paxton. He hoped for a sign of assurance from Chris Paxton, that what he was doing was for the best, but his master did not give him a glance of any description. Instead, he averted Tommy's eyes and looked toward the floor. As the two officers led him off to Newcastle, Tommy turned to Chris Paxton and asked, 'Will you look after me Mam for me sir?' But no words of comfort left Chris Paxton's lips. As he closed the study door behind them, he maintained his silence. Tommy left Shinwell Hall a prisoner and as he walked away, despite the advice given by Chris Paxton the previous day, he felt his master had duped him and he wondered if he would ever be free again.

Left alone, Chris Paxton agonised over his actions. He was acting completely out of character by misleading his groom into confessing his crime.

What is happening to me? I am a changed man. It is so unlike me to abandon Tommy Cogon in his hour of need. What alternative do I have; I must protect my darling wife even if she has transgressed her marriage vows. I love her too much to allow her to bear the shame that exposure of the truth would bring. I have always considered, and indeed striven to be an even minded person offering a helping hand to my fellow being, even at times when my peers, especially other coal owners, would have me act otherwise. I have never had it in me to exploit my workforce at the pit; yet here I am now prepared to be instrumental in sending a man to the gallows to keep silent about my wife's adultery.

*

Back at the Police station, Tommy was fingerprinted then placed in a holding cell while the police conducted further tests. Later, the fingerprint experts confirmed that Thomas Cogon's prints matched those on the piece of wood found at the scene of the crime. With their latest piece of information, DI Bruce formally charged Tommy with the murder of Jed Smyth, alias Harry Appleton.

Chapter 35

The trial of Thomas Cogon for the murder of Jed Smyth, took place at the Durham Summer Assizes. James Outram KC, a philanthropic lawyer with socialist principles who operated on the north-eastern circuit, had worked his way up from being a humble solicitor. He had made his wealth from representing the Durham and Northumberland miners' associations in all legal matters and in the early days of his career, he had been the legal representative for the Daniel Swain Hospital, but he had moved on since then. Now a rich lawyer, he would occasionally take on a case, waiving his fees, where the accused was unable to pay. Unbeknown to Tommy, James Outram, as a young solicitor, had tried to represent the families of the victims of the 1884 explosion at the West Fell colliery at the inquest. Daniel Dean, the coroner that day, had refused to recognise him in his court. The young solicitor vowed then that he would have his day with pompous coroners and arrogant coal owners. He had remembered Tommy Cogon who had been down the pit when his father had lost his life that fateful day.

*

The trial was short since Tommy had admitted responsibility for the murder. James Outram KC had defended his client not on what he had done, but why he had done it, pleading mitigating circumstances. He described vividly how Thomas Cogon had fought for his own life before gaining possession of Jed Smyth's gun. He also pleaded provocation saying Smyth had taunted him about the death of Tommy's lifelong friend, Robert Anderson in 1902.

When questioned in the dock, Tommy had told the court that Smyth had confessed to drowning Bobby Anderson in the millpond at the old mill house on West Fell and he described Smyth's modus operandi. He also explained that Smyth had revealed these facts at the point where he was about to pull the trigger and had he, Thomas Cogon, not acted the way he did that day, he would not have been here to tell the tale.

Chris Paxton's lack of concern for Tommy's wellbeing following his arrest, made him realise his master had totally misled him. Therefore, he had nothing to lose by telling the full story of what really happened. After all, he felt his was now a lost cause and that he was the only person alive other than the Paxtons who knew of the famous singers lapse of integrity. They would be the main benefactors from his death on the gallows. Therefore, he called for a meeting with James Outram, to whom he related the full story, chapter, and verse; including Chris Paxton's advice to Tommy, that when interviewed, he should withhold the truth about Bobby's suicide letter and Jed Smyth's admission of drowning Bobby in the millpond.

In addition, he told James Outram of Jed Smyth's attempt to blackmail Chris Paxton through the fact that he knew she had committed adultery with Bobby Anderson. He also revealed to his counsel how Bobby Anderson and he, had been responsible for the aborted attempt at the pay-out of the blackmail money.

Furnished with this fresh evidence, Tommy's counsel called him back into the witness box to give further evidence. On facing the court, he noticed that both Chris and Jemima Paxton were present, seated close to the prosecuting counsel's team. He took from this that they were here to give evidence against him. Evidence he knew, coming from such celebrities as a world-famous singer and her landowner and public benefactor husband, would have more impression on the jury than a modest nondescript groom who they would see as someone clutching at straws to save his own neck.

*

Prosecuting counsel had indeed torn his new evidence to shreds, suggesting to the jury that it was nothing more than a figment of the imagination of a desperate man trying to exonerate his actions that day at High Gosforth racecourse. He emphasised dramatically, his version of what happened, saying, *'You have heard the police pathologist state most categorically, that forensic evidence proved; the barrel of the gun was pressed hard against the temple of the victim, when he pulled the trigger'* and he emphasised dramatically, *'an action that blew the brains out of poor Jed Smyth.'*

In evidence given by Chris Paxton, under oath, he refuted most emphatically, any involvement on the part of his wife with his former jockey, Robert Anderson. He even gave false evidence by saying Tommy sold bags of horse manure to locals for their vegetable plots and pocketing the money without declaring this little enterprise to his employer, thus corrupting the minds of the jury into thinking Tommy was not to be trusted.

Jemima Paxton, when called to the witness box by James Outram, reiterated what her husband had said earlier.

*

The jury found Tommy guilty of murder, but they recommended that mercy be shown, as they were not convinced that the evidence given by Christian and Jemima Paxton was totally dependable. Despite this, the judge passed sentence and as he did so, he placed a square of black cloth upon his head and pulled on a pair of black gloves. He looked straight at Tommy and pronounced sentence. 'Thomas Cogon, the sentence of this court is that you will be taken from here to the place from whence you came and there be kept in close confinement until a date to be established, and upon that day, that you be taken to the place of execution and there hanged by the neck until you are dead. And may God have mercy upon your soul.'

Tommy stood; his head bowed. He raised his head and looking

straight back at the judge he said, in a clear voice, 'Ah did it for Bobby. God rest his soul. Ah'm ready to meet him in Heaven. As for the Paxtons, ah doubt ah shall meet them again anywhere.'

The judge replied, 'That, be as it may – take the prisoner away,' and two constables led Tommy back to his cell.

Despite his promise to Tommy that he would 'look after' him, Chris Paxton never set eyes on him from the time he left Shinwell Hall on the day he was arrested until today when he and his wife appeared in court as witnesses for the prosecution.

It appeared to Tommy Cogon that Chris Paxton was hell bent on Tommy going to the gallows and he had certainly played his part by lying under oath.

Chapter 36

The date for Tommy Cogon's execution was set for the first of September, six weeks hence and James Outram had put no time off in appealing to the Home Secretary for a stay of execution.

In the appeal he reiterated the provocation that Thomas Cogon had experienced, brought on by the taunting of Jed Smyth, by describing verbatim to Tommy, how he had drowned Bobby Anderson. He also claimed Christian Paxton knew Bobby Anderson had cuckolded him before his client's arrest for Jed Smyth's murder and indeed Jed Smyth had blackmailed him with the threat of exposing to the entire world, his wife's infidelity.

Tommy lay on his bunk, contemplating what was looming ahead of him and wondering when his appeal date would come through. He suddenly jumped from his bunk and began walking up and down within the confined space of his cell, thinking as he did so. *Ah have been a fool all this time; ah have the evidence to prove that what ah said in court was true. Ah must get to see me lawyer.* He banged furiously on the door of his cell. 'Get me my lawyer, now,' he yelled at the top of his voice.

The aperture on the door was opened swiftly. 'Shut that row will y.' What's up wi' y'?' The burly prison warder shouted in. Tommy found this warder a bit of a gentle giant who he usually found a likeable fella' compared to some of them he had encountered during his incarceration at Durham jail. 'Howay man Tommy, settle down. What's got into y' to make y' agitated? Y' not usually like this.'

'Ah must see James Outram, Mr Staff. Ah've just remembered something that is vital to me case; something that could save me life.'

'Well now Tommy that does sound important. Ah'll make no promises understand, but ah'll see what ah can do.'

*

Mr Staff was true to his word and two hours later James Outram entered Tommy's cell. 'Now Tommy, what is so important that you have caused me to leave my dinner and come to see you?'

Well sir, ah'm sorry about that, but ah've remembered what it was that made Jed Smyth claim he had proof that Jemima Paxton had committed adultery with Bobby Anderson.'

'And what was that Tommy?'

'Jemima Paxton has a birthmark on the inside of her right thigh, right at the top. Ah'm certain. Old Andy Thompson, my old boss told me. He was the one who saw it for himself. He told me all about it, over a couple of whiskies in 'The Fleece' in Newcastle. Caught the two of them at it, he did. Just off the five-furlong gallop, in the woods of Shinwell Hall.'

'Is this Andy Thompson still alive?'

'Ah'm afraid he's been dead for some time now. Ah'm the last to know this fact, other than the Paxtons themselves. They think they are alone in knowing this. All they think is that Bobby told me about their affair.'

'This is something that could make such a difference in your appeal. It is enough to get you a stay of execution at least. We need to get the Home Secretary to insist on Jemima Paxton settling finally, whether she does or does not have such a significant birthmark. Chris Paxton should be the only person alive with such knowledge. On the other hand, Tommy, if she has no such mark, then I am afraid it would mean the exoneration of the Paxtons and the scuppering of your appeal. We have no alternative but to take that risk.'

If it is true that the mark exists, then we stand a good chance of getting your sentence commuted from death to life imprisonment, and that being the case, Chris Paxton must stand trial for lying under oath, and we will both have our day with them, Tommy.'

'What ah don't understand is why Chris Paxton would turn against me like he has, when up until my arrest, he was supportive; or so I thought. He even lied in court; all that business about me stealin' manure of all things was a pack of lies. Ask any of the people in West Fell, they'll tell y' the truth.'

'You believe me Tommy; I intend to do just that. It is a fact that the landed gentry, when up against it, they can swiftly switch allegiance to save their own necks. Once they find themselves in a position of exposure resulting in scandal, in desperation they see the members of the working class as commodities, to dispose of at their behest, like lambs to the slaughter. I promise you Tommy; I will fight tooth and nail to make sure Paxton does not use you to his advantage. We both have good reason to see him get his just desserts.'

*

The next weeks were frantic for James Outram. Time was running out and he was desperately attempting to get Jemima Paxton to prove or disprove the vital fact that she was born with a mark on the inside of her right thigh. His tenacity bore fruit when news came through that Jemima Paxton had received a summons to appear for examination by a doctor appointed on behalf of the Home Secretary.

'There is a Bill going through parliament now Tommy which, if passed will allow people like yourself, to appeal through appeal courts instead of through Parliament. In the meantime, we have to make do with the law as it stands.'

The examination proved conclusively that Jemima Paxton did carry a birthmark as described by their former coachman, Andrew Thompson. Moreover, the fact that Jemima Paxton did indeed, have such a birthmark, substantiated what Andrew Thompson claimed to have seen in the woods that Sunday morning in 1890. His intelligence, given to Jed Smyth and later to Tommy Cogon for the price of a couple of free drinks in 'The Fleece Inn', proved that he had indeed, seen Jemima Paxton and Bobby Anderson *in flagrante delicto*, could be enough reason for the Home Secretary to order a stay of execution. Thomas Cogon gave his account of how he knew about the birthmark; how Andrew Thompson had shared his knowledge with him of what he had seen in the woods that Sunday morning all those years ago, in exchange for a couple of free whiskies. He also told James Outram that Andrew Thompson had also told his scandalous tale to Jed Smyth who, when armed with this knowledge, had attempted to blackmail Chris Paxton.

Bobby Anderson and Tommy Cogon had thwarted Jed Smyth's attempt at blackmail on the night he fell from the cliff edge at South Shields and how he had survived his fall from the cliffs. Tommy also told James Outram that Chris Paxton had refrained from making his wife aware that he knew of her adultery with Bobby Anderson. Tommy Cogon went on to explain how he had overheard the conversation between Bobby Anderson and Chris Paxton from within the stable block when Chris Paxton approached Bobby concerning his affair with his wife.

*

James Outram KC, campaigned relentlessly throughout West Fell, questioning everyone who had a plot of land for a garden, and he got each person he interviewed to sign a petition confirming that no one had done a deal with Tommy Cogon. Now armed with all this fresh evidence plus the petition from the people of West Fell, James Outram KC returned to the Home Secretary's office.

Meanwhile, at Shinwell Hall, Chris Paxton was agonising over the outcome of Tommy Cogon's death sentence. He had not been able to face Alice Cogon since the trial and he had suspended her on full pay and taken on a replacement. He and Jemima sat at dinner, and she could see the effect this business was having on him.

'You have hardly touched your dinner darling. If you go on like this, you will be ill.'

'Being ill is the least of my worries Jemima, the thought of

Tommy Cogon hanging by his neck in Durham jail, is far more important. I must speak out and reveal the truth. I cannot have Thomas Cogon's death on my hands. If I can be instrumental in saving his life, then I will do everything in my power to do so. I will speak out truthfully and admit my mistake. I did what I did for you darling, my love for you clouded my judgement and I acted in folly.'

'What about the consequences? You will surely go to jail. Whatever will I do if they take you from me? I will surely die.'

'Come now Jemima; let us not behave dramatically over this matter. You will not die, and you will have Miles and Jeanie to support you. What is certain is Thomas Cogon will die and I cannot have his death on my conscience; it will destroy me. By admitting my wrongdoing, they may look upon it with clemency and pass a lighter sentence, but I know I must tell the truth, which is the driving force behind my actions. There have been far too many lies told already. Now it is time for the truth.'

Chapter 37

The Home Secretary granted Thomas Cogon a stay of execution giving James Outram more time to fight for Tommy's death sentence to be commuted to life imprisonment and to investigate further the evidence given against him by the Paxtons.

Because of James Outram's persuasion, a three-man Commission of Enquiry was set up to determine the validity of the evidence given by the Paxtons at the trial of his client, Thomas Cogon. The fact that Jemima Paxton did indeed bear a birthmark high on her right thigh, was in the eyes of the law enough evidence to prove that what Andrew Thompson had seen, that Sunday morning, was indeed accurate and that she had committed adultery with Robert Anderson. The recommendation of mercy by the jury at Thomas Cogon's trial added weight to James Outram's determined efforts to have his client's sentence commuted.

*

The three-man enquiry summoned the Paxtons to attend, and the proceedings took a surprising turn, when they called Chris Paxton to address the enquiry. Faced with questioning, Chris Paxton produced a sheet of paper on which he had prepared a letter in advance. He asked the three-man commission if he could read its contents. Granted permission, he began reading from what turned out to be a total admission of guilt.

My wife and I do apologise to both the court at the trial of Thomas Cogon, and to your good selves seated on this enquiry, for lying when we both gave evidence that day. My wife was guilty of concealing the truth in as much as she claimed she had not committed adultery with Robert Anderson. She would now like this enquiry to know that she indeed had sexual intercourse with Robert Anderson on the one occasion described by Andrew Thompson. I stand guilty of lying under oath on several counts. When under oath, I denied any knowledge of Jed Smyth's attempted blackmail and the part my employees played in the termination of that attempt.

Secondly, I admit that when I stood in court, I had full knowledge of all the points made by Thomas Cogon in his defence. All the evidence he gave in his trial was the truth. He had told me all those details when we had a conversation in the library of Shinwell Hall when he off-loaded all his troubles that had built up over a long period. In short, all my evidence against him that day was a pack of lies, especially the story of the horse manure. They were all lies, for which I beg his forgiveness; if indeed, he can find it in him to forgive me. If not then I do not blame him, for I know my behaviour that day was abominable.

I also beg his forgiveness for my wife. In her defence, I engineered the whole of this pathetic plan to try to save my wife's reputation. I know it was her only transgression and I know that she thought I was not aware of her wrongdoing. I love her implicitly, I always have, and whatever the outcome for us both, after this admission, I always will.

Thomas Cogon told me of a letter he found at the dwelling of Robert Anderson, declaring his intent to commit suicide. Tommy burnt it without revealing its contents. The reason for his action that day was to conceal the truth, which if made known to the world, would have tainted the memory of his lifelong friend. A friend, whom he loved almost as much as I love my wife and as much, I have since learnt, as Robert Anderson loved my wife. A fact, which Thomas Cogon told me Robert Anderson, had declared in his suicide letter.

Eventually, Robert Anderson did not commit suicide although he did attempt it. While Jed Smyth watched Robert Anderson's actions that day in 1902, he realised he was watching Robert Anderson commit suicide, thus depriving him of his revenge. As Smyth dived into the water, he saw his prey rise to the surface, thrashing frantically to abort his attempt at suicide. He pressed Anderson's head down below the surface and held it there until he drowned.

Bearing in mind Thomas Cogon heard all this at the point of Smyth's gun the day he killed Smyth at 'High Gosforth Park'. Taunted and provoked by his victim as he was, it comes as no surprise he acted as he did. This, in my humble opinion for what that is worth, is the only action for which Thomas Cogan should stand accused.

Thomas Cogon and I have similar reasons for doing what we did. I love my wife so much; I wanted to protect her reputation. Thomas Cogan's love for Bobby Anderson was the reason he pulled the trigger that day. I thank you gentlemen for your tolerance in hearing me out and in conclusion, all I have to say is that I place myself at the mercy of this enquiry.

Chapter 38

Following Paxton confessing to lying under oath, the three-man Commission of Enquiry found him, guilty and sentenced him to two years imprisonment. They allowed Jemima Paxton to go free on the grounds she had no charge to answer on her act of adultery and with regards to her perjuring the court that day; they decided she was acting under duress from her husband. Chris Paxton impressed the chair of the enquiry and his colleagues with his great remorse, and they admired his complete openness.

It made such a difference to Thomas Cogon's case of appeal, the result being, the Home secretary commuted his death sentence to that of manslaughter. Considering the mitigating circumstances in his testimony, they sentenced him to twenty years in prison.

*

At Shinwell Hall following the imprisonment of her husband, Jemima sat in the withdrawing room discussing the future. 'What will I do for the next two years?' Jemima Paxton asked of her son and daughter-in-law, Miles, and Jeanie Paxton. Also, in the company was Sally Binney. 'I cannot face the people here in West Fell. I shall not be able to continue my work with Lily Collingwood and the mothers of the village, which I so enjoyed. I am not complaining as I brought it all upon my own head.'

'Do not torture yourself mother. At the time of your sole act of indiscretion, you were in a dark place in your life. You were struggling to fill the void left after you retired from the stage. You were not yourself and Anderson took advantage of your vulnerability,' Miles Paxton said, sympathetically.

'I will not have you condemning Bobby Anderson, as I said it is my own fault.'

'You will not be the first to do such a thing under similar circumstances and you certainly will not be the last,' Jeanie replied, pragmatically.

'I wish your father were here Miles, to plan our future together. He has stood by me in all this. I do not deserve such devotion after what I did to him.'

'You are doing it again, mother, taking yourself to task for one moment of folly. Father by his very actions has forgiven you, if indeed you needed forgiving. The whole business has proved his love for you,' Miles said.

Sally Binney remained silent during these exchanges, apart from moving her eyes from one person to another, as each in turn spoke; when her eyes were open that is. She was now at the ripe old age of eighty-five and well into her dotage. She chose instead to keep her counsel. Keeping her counsel was not always a conscious decision, these days she often snoozed through the proceedings when it came to family matters, especially matters as delicate as the one under discussion.

'I have already considered some alternatives, but I would need to discuss them with your father first before I get carried away with my own thoughts.'

'What have you in mind mother? Please share your ideas with us, will you?'

'Oh, just whimsical ideas that flew to mind when your father's prison sentence was passed. Ideas totally conceived in a state of panic and certainly not in the right frame of mind. I must admit I have given them a little more thought of late and I think there may be some substance in what I have in mind.

'Please Mother, share your thoughts with us,' her son asked.

'Remember, for the moment, this is nothing more than an idea and without your father here to air his views, which is what it remains. I have been thinking it might be a good idea, if your father and I should move away somewhere, to the Northumberland coast say. I do not mean in total isolation just far enough away, to some place smaller than this huge pile we are in now. This would become yours and Jeanie's home if you so wish. Someplace where it matters not that we are, Mr and Mrs Christian Paxton of Shinwell Hall; and less still that I am the famous 'Mimi Martin.' Early in my musical career I wanted the entire world to know of 'Mimi Martin.' How times have changed. Here we are now; I am sixty-nine and your father almost seventy-five, with your father only halfway through his sentence. I worry about him every minute of every day he is away. We are both getting older, and I agonise over his well-being whilst in prison. I wish the next year were over. I miss him so much.' Salty tears stung the inside of her eyes when she thought of her husband incarcerated in Durham jail.

After Jemima had finished speaking, Jeanie was the first to break the silence. Jemima dabbed her eyes as Jeanie spoke, 'It may not be a full twelve months he has left to do. With good behaviour they may set him free earlier.'

Miles Paxton was engrossed in thoughts on his mother's idea for moving away, 'I know there are some very respectable houses in the Alnwick area which is not too far from the coast; and you could enjoy the facilities that a town can offer. We will think more positively once father is with us again. I agree with Jeanie; he could be home sooner than we think. Do not worry Mother; he is as tough as old boots. He is very resilient, even in a place as dire as Durham jail.'

'God speed the day we have him back,' Jemima Paxton replied.

'I never thought when we took on the young solicitor as the legal representative for the West Fell hospital scheme, that one day he would be challenging my father in a court of law. I bear him no grudge; he has developed into a fine lawyer, and we are lucky he has stayed as a member of the committee. Moreover, thanks to his prowess in and out of court, Thomas Cogon got off lighter than he might have done. Good luck to Cogon, it was a messy business for all of us and Jed Smyth was a nasty piece of work. The world is a better place without him, thanks to Tommy. By the way mother, what is happening to his mother Alice in the future?'

'I have not forgotten about her Miles; she is included in my plans. She will be invited to accompany us to wherever we decide to go if she wishes. She is fifty-five years old now. Dear me Miles, we are all getting old are we not?'

'That is a fact Mother. It does not require one to be a holder of a medical degree to subscribe to that view,' her son replied somewhat sarcastically.

'I think your idea is splendid Mother,' Jeanie Paxton said. 'We are considering buying one of those motor vehicles that are becoming so popular these days. If we do, we could drive up to Alnwick and visit you. Even drive down to the coast on a day trip while we are with you.'

'Remind me Jeanie, when we go shopping for such a vehicle, it must have four seats,' Miles Paxton said. Turning to his mother, he said 'Mother dear, your idea has got me speculating on the future. For some time, the hospital scheme committee has talked of setting up a convalescent home for injured and sick miners. It would be a place which would offer accommodation and succour to help them back to full recovery. The trouble being, up until now, there are few places available for such a project and the cost to build such a place would be inhibitive. If Jeanie and I took over the Hall from you and father, we could turn the whole of the west wing into a convalescent home and we would still have plenty of room for our own private quarters. It is something I have wanted to do ever since I left university. These people are such hard working people that they deserve something in return when fate has dealt them a cruel blow.

Part of the house could be set aside for palliative nursing where the miners, suffering from incurable disease such as pneumoconiosis and silicosis, could spend their last days with dignity, but that is for the future. My enthusiasm is running away with me. Better we walk before we run.'

Jeanie Paxton jumping to her feet ran and threw her arms around her husband. 'Oh! I love you so much; you are so full of great and wonderful ideas.' She remembered how her own father, after spending all his working life hewing coal in the pits of Fife in Scotland, died coughing his lungs up at the age of forty. How he would have benefited from such a place as her husband had just described.

'What a magnanimous idea Miles. I would love the Hall to be used for such a noble cause. I could not agree more. You have my wholehearted support, and I am sure I speak also for your father on the matter,' Jemima Paxton said, enthusiastically.

'Well let us say, we are all agreed that the idea will hold water and it is something which we can look forward to once father is returned to us,' Miles said.

Chapter 39

Chris and Jemima Paxton were returning from the funeral of Sally Binney in Renton, Norfolk. She had died in her sleep at Shinwell Hall the age of eighty-five and her wish was that they bury her in Norfolk with her late husband George. After the interment, the couple were leaving the churchyard when a grave situated close to the path, caught Jemima's eye. The headstone read, *Robert Hart, born 1818, died 1888 aged seventy years. Also, his wife Mary, born 1828, died 1890 aged sixty-two.*

'Look Chris, it is the grave of my infamous stepfather; he survived my mother by twenty-three years. He must have married Mary sometime after the death of Mama in 1865.' They stood together reading the headstone.

'He never did come after your mother or her money; he must have genuinely loved Mary Harrison,' Chris Paxton commented.

'Had Mama known that, at the time she fled to Durham, she would have had a more pleasurable journey,' Jemima stated.

*

Chris Paxton dozed to the rhythm of the wheels of the train bringing them back to Shinwell Hall. While her husband slept, Jemima, uninterrupted by conversation, her thoughts returned to her childhood in Norfolk. The fact she had stumbled on Robert Hart's grave, made her wonder if he ever realised, after she became famous, how instrumental he had been in her success story. After all, it was thanks to him for getting her singing lessons from Professor Henri Colbert. She also remembered the Christmas's they shared with him. With the passing of time, she felt she had mellowed towards him, and she was pleased. *Bearing grudges does nobody any good. Let bygones be bygones,* she thought. Now he was dead, it mattered naught what he may have done in the past.

*

As the train pulled into Darlington station, the screeching of the brakes and the hissing of the steam roused Chris Paxton from his slumber. Blinking rapidly, he said, 'are we there?'

'Not yet Darling, we are coming into Darlington. A stop at Durham, then Newcastle and home,' Jemima said, relieved that their journey was almost at an end.

Her husband rubbed his eyes and said, 'Oh yes, I recognise that old locomotive on the platform.' The old locomotive Chris Paxton had alluded to was Locomotion No.1, the first to pull a passenger train on the Stockton to Darlington railway in 1825. Now on static display, it occupied pride of place on the platform alongside their train. Fifteen minutes later their train was chugging across the railway viaduct on the approach to Durham railway station, offering the passengers an excellent view of the city spread below them, before pulling into the station. Jemima scanned the panoramic view of the city below as the train, its speed now decreasing, approached Durham station. 'Look Chris you see the rooftops of the houses in South Street where our old home was; we were happy there.'

'Why do you say that Jemima; are you not happy *now*?'

'Well so much has happened in our lives since we left Durham City for Shinwell Hall; happenings that brought us so much heartache, all brought on by my stupidity. Why you did not kick me out of Shinwell Hall I will never know. You should have divorced me and let me suffer the consequences. I would have deserved your wrath. I am unbelievably fortunate to have you Chris.'

'Well thankfully that is all behind us now my dear,' her husband said, rather glibly. 'I have an idea: what say we return to Durham City to live when we leave Shinwell Hall.'

'How I would love to live once more in South Street. I suppose it is expecting too much, to think we would be able to buy back our old home. I would be ecstatically content if that was a possibility.'

After a brief halt at Durham, the train continued its journey north to Newcastle. Once underway again, they soon left Durham City behind them, and Chris Paxton took up the conversation on the possibility of a move to Durham. 'You never know darling; we could be lucky; it is something we will investigate. You never know, if not our old home, then possibly another property in the street is available. I would prefer Durham City to Alnwick. We know Durham and Alnwick would be new to us. Moreover, it would be easier for Alice to visit Tommy in jail.'

Jemima Paxton's thoughts returned to her life after leaving the stage. 'I would go as far as to say that since my retirement I have come through the worst period of my life; a period which challenges even the nadir in my life, when as a child. In saying that I refer to the year I spent living in the workhouse in Norfolk. The time we spent living in Durham City I would say was the zenith of my life, not surpassed even during all the successful years of my stage career.'

'I agree darling but let us not forget there were times when things were not easy for me. I have had *my* share of hardship, especially recently, what with the time in Durham jail but I am not complaining. That was my own fault entirely. What I did was foolish, but at the time, I was desperate to protect your reputation for I love you so much and I always will. Let us not dwell on the past, for it will eat away at us like a canker. Let us look to the future with optimism. When we return, we will expand on Miles's idea on what to do about Shinwell Hall. I agree with you; the place is far too big for us; we are no longer young.'

'I agree wholeheartedly dear, we will make firm plans at the first opportunity, with Durham City in mind.'

Shortly afterwards, the train was crossing the newly opened King Edward VII bridge over the River Tyne, before pulling into Newcastle Central station.

Chapter 40

The search was on for a property in South Street, Durham City. The place where Jemima said she had felt at her happiest. They had discussed the possibilities of a move from Shinwell Hall, where the establishment of a convalescent home in the west wing for the Durham miners was underway. A contribution from the fees paid by every member of the miners' union throughout the Durham coalfield would help finance the scheme.

Miles Paxton was the main architect of the scheme, ably supported by his wife Jeanie. With internal alterations completed, and living quarters established, for example a dormitory, reading room, and a recreation room for internal pastimes. Men who were recovering from mental illnesses would help in the gardens on a voluntary basis. Those who were recovering from lower limb injuries were encouraged to take part in the manufacture of wicker baskets, hampers, and trugs for cut flowers. The convalescent fund contributions and the proceeds from the sale of the goods produced in the workshops, helped pay the wages for the staff needed to conduct this venture and the produce from the gardens supplied the kitchen. A further magnanimous gesture on the part of Thomas Mays played a large part in the development of the convalescent home.

*

Miles Paxton and his wife Jeanie, together with Chris and Jemima Paxton, were having dinner and the conversation turned to the senior

Paxtons' move to Durham. 'I have been in touch with Craddock and Spinks, Estate Agents of Durham City, to look for a property in South Street, preferably near our old home before we moved to Shinwell Hall. Well would you believe I have heard back from them, and I am delighted to say they have been in touch with the present owner, who has informed them that a lecturer at the university presently occupies the house. On further research, they have discovered that the occupant is leaving Durham for Oxford at the end of the Michaelmas term and the owner is prepared to sell the freehold property to me. He is asking ten per cent above the market value.'

'That is wonderful father; you have spoken rapturously about that view across the river to the Cathedral and that must be worth ten percent of anyone's money. You cannot put a price on a view of the cathedral, like you describe,' Miles Paxton said enthusiastically. 'So, I have instructed the estate agent to proceed on our behalf with a view to buy. To say we are ecstatically pleased with the prospect of returning to our old home would be an understatement.'

Miles Paxton rose from his seat, walked round the table, and kissed his mother on the cheek. 'I am so pleased for you, Mama. I am so pleased for you both. I know how much this means to you, especially you Mama. I know how happy you will both be back in Durham City, and you will be pleased to get Jeanie and I from under your feet.'

'Nonsense, it has been our pleasure having you here with us since you returned from University and then when Jeanie joined us, well that was a bonus. Moreover, with the addition of our granddaughter, she was a double bonus. This place needed more occupancy and your idea of founding a convalescent home makes the best use of it,' Jemima stated.

'Can I propose a toast,' Jeanie Paxton suggested, 'to the convalescent home and your new, old home in Durham City.'

They all raised their glasses and echoed Jeanie's words.

Chris Paxton was next to speak, 'I have another announcement to make. I have decided that when we move to Durham, I plan on relinquishing my share in the West Fell pit and I am offering it to you as a gift, Miles. I know in advance what your response will be. Like me, you do not like getting your hands dirty, well not with coal dust. I have still not been underground in the mine. I doubt if I ever will. I think now is the time to put my feet up. The time I spent in Durham Prison had a bad effect on me and I am not getting any younger. If you have no interest in getting involved with West Fell pit, you can sell it, with the provision that the connection with the hospital scheme and the convalescent home is maintained.'

*

The purchase of their former home in South Street went through without a hitch. Jemima's happiness living back in Durham was short lived. Barely a year after the move, Chris Paxton died from heart failure. The time he spent in Durham jail had, as he predicted, contributed greatly toward the rapid deterioration in his health. The family had decided that Chris Paxton's final resting place would be in the churchyard of Saint Mark's in Standale, were his mother and father were buried.

*

'Hello son, how are y' bonny lad? Are they still lookin' after y' in here? You look a bit pale to me.' Alice Cogon was visiting her son Tommy, serving a twenty-year sentence for manslaughter in Durham Jail. The death of Chris Paxton had made her more anxious about Tommy Cogon's health while in prison.

'Don't worry Mam, ah'm fine, believe me. Ah'm dealin' with things better than ah ever expected when ah first came in here. Ah'm doin' a lot of readin' and ah'm preparin' meself for when ah get out of here. Ah'll be much wiser when ah come out than when ah came in, that's for sure. Ah'm studyin' motor mechanics so ah can maintain them new-fangled motor carriages that are becomin' so popular with the upper classes. There won't be many horses by the time ah'm out of here. Ah'll struggle to get me old job of groom again, but ah might get set-on as a driver or mechanic.'

'The young Paxtons have bought one, Tommy. It's a four-seater Armstrong Siddeley tourer, so ah'm told. For now, young Miles drives it himself, but no doubt, he'll be takin' on what they are callin' in posh circles, a chauffeur. If you get a job as a chauffeur, you'll have a new uniform, complete with peaked cap,' his mother informed him, hoping it would give Tommy some hope for the future while he whiled away his incarceration in Durham Jail.

'A peaked cap y' say; that sounds very fetching, ah'm sure,' Tommy replied. 'How Bobby used to play up about the coachman's uniform, when he first came to work at Shinwell Hall, after he hung up his riding boots,' he added. Thinking of Bobby again, stirred something inside him.

Seeing Tommy's face change at the mention of Bobby Anderson, Alice quickly tried to take her son's mind off his late dear friend. 'Ah've got to tell y' Mam, I often think about Jemima Paxton's betrayal of her husband while ah'm in here, but she was not the only one who loved Bobby Anderson. Why do y' think ah never had a girl friend? I too loved Bobby, but ah could never tell him, so he would have blown his top if ah even brought up the subject. He would never have understood a man could have such feelings for another man. So, it was, I had to love him from afar and that's the way it always was between us.'

Alice Cogon, on hearing her son's revelation, realised the implications such a relationship could have provoked, and wanted to change the subject of their conversation. Realising she had not told Tommy of Chris Paxton's death she said, 'Ee ah forgot to tell y' our Tommy. Chris Paxton has died. Fancy me forgettin' somethin' as important as that. That's because ah noticed how pale y' looked when y' came in... He died three weeks ago, of heart failure. They think his time in here played a big part in his poor health since his release. That's how ah was so taken up with how you looked soon as ah came in. Are y' sure y' really feel all right son?'

'Ah told y' Mam, ah'm grand and that's the end of the matter.

What's Jemima doin' for the future?'

'Following' the funeral, at Standale, she's back at her South Street home here in Durham for the time being, but she intends her and me will be back at Shinwell Hall as soon as possible, she's missin' Chris Paxton and she doesn't like bein' in that house on her own.'

'Times up!' shouted the warder standing at the back of the visitors' room.

'By, that went quick, ah have just got started,' Alice Cogon said and gave the warden a questioning look. 'Ah'm sure he wants to get his watch sorted out Tommy.'

'Don't worry Mam; he'll have his watch tellin' the right time. Don't forget, it's the same watch he finishes to, and no doubt, he'll be off for a pint in the Court Inn when he's finished here.'

Mother and son said their goodbyes and Tommy disappeared through the door, which led back to his cell and solitude. Although he was happy to see his mother, he was pleased that he did not have many visitors other than his mother. Too many visitors reminded him too much of what he was missing in the outside world. He was coming to terms with his solitude and his quiet studying and the loss of his lifelong friend, Bobby Anderson.

*

Following the death of her husband, Jemima was back at Shinwell Hall for a while, until she got over her loss. Alice Cogon had accompanied her as her companion. At the reading of his will, Chris Paxton's solicitor revealed its contents. His client had left the house in South Street to Alice, with the proviso that she resided there caring for Jemima for the rest of Jemima's lifetime. He also left Alice an annuity of three hundred pounds. To Tommy Cogon on his release from prison, the handsome sum of five hundred pounds, the sum of money demanded by Jed Smyth when he attempted to blackmail Chris Paxton; an attempt thwarted by Tommy Cogon and Bobby Anderson. His share in West Fell Colliery he bequeathed to Miles Paxton, to dispose of at Miles's own discretion. Because of the colliery's important association with both the hospital scheme and the convalescent home within Shinwell Hall, he had hoped his son would not sever the connection with the colliery. A trust fund was to be set up in the name of his granddaughter, Frances Jeanette Paxton, to mature on her reaching the age of twenty-one years. The rest of his estate he bequeathed to his wife Jemima, instructing her to make a payment of whatever size she chose, to their daughter-in-law, Jeanie Paxton.

Chapter 41

1914

Four years had passed since the death of Chris Paxton, and it was seven years since Tommy Cogon began his twenty-year jail sentence for the manslaughter of Jed Smyth. Throughout Europe and beyond, the word 'war' was on everyone's lips and on 4 August 1914, Britain declared war on Germany. Men all over the country were volunteering to serve King and country. Some were barely men others had been men for more years than was good for them, but still they came forward. The image and the demanding finger of Lord Kitchener emblazoned throughout every town, village, and hamlet, psychologically emboldened the men of the country to take the King's shilling. The outstretched finger pointed at the observer like a loaded revolver, had the desired effect on the males of Britain.

The War Department had commandeered the hospital and convalescent home at Shinwell Hall, as an Army hospital for injured British troops returning from the battlefields of north-eastern France and Belgium; the theatre of war known by the allied forces as 'The Western Front'. Miles Paxton had volunteered for the army as a field doctor. But both he and Jeanie were exempt from serving over in France as they were required here in England, at Shinwell Hall. The turn of the year saw the war, which everyone said would be over by

Christmas, escalating, not abating. The medical staff at Shinwell Hall was working all out in preparation for the forecasted increase in the number of soldiers, scarred both physically and mentally, returning from the war across the channel. Jemima and Alice were making their own contributions by lending a hand doing simple tasks like washing and folding bandages and bed sheets. Everyone at the Hall was working long hours, some almost sleeping on their feet, especially the doctors and nurses Miles and Jeanie Paxton.

*

It was June 1915 at Shinwell Hall and Jeanie Paxton was enjoying a rare lull in the activity at the hospital. She came out onto the lawn in front of the big house to take a breather for what seemed to her to be the first time since the commencement of the hostilities. Seeing her daughter-in-law, Jemima hurried to join her. 'You have a moment at last, when was the last time you were able to take a break?' Jemima asked.

'It is vital to these poor souls returning from France. Most have life-changing injuries. Some are beyond recovery; here to spend what is left of their blighted lives in peace and quiet away from the battlefield, with someone to bend a sympathetic ear while they slowly sink into eternal sleep, the guns finally silenced,' Jeanie said dolefully.

'Talking of sympathetic ears and slowly slipping into eternal sleep, could I indulge you to listen to my tale of woe. I feel I must talk to somebody before I meet my maker,' Jemima Paxton said.

'Come now Mother, let us have none of that talk, you are as fit as a fiddle.'

'That may be so, but the truth is, I am getting no younger and since the war started, the days here at Shinwell Hall are so hectic it is difficult to catch anyone with the time to talk anymore.' Realising immediately that her words could be misconstrued, she offered an apology. 'Please Jeanie, please, no offence meant.'

'None taken Mother and you are absolutely correct in your observations.'

'There is a period in my life of which I am not proud, and I would like to talk to someone about what is troubling me.'

'Well, believe me if you will, things have quietened down at last at the hospital. I was about to have a break and a cup of tea, but I can forego that for now, so get it off your chest.'

'Let us take a short walk in the grounds while we talk. The rhododendrons will be in all their glory at this time of the year and I have not seen them yet this season; it will be a pleasant change from all this death and destruction surrounding us. There have been too many deaths already, even without the war,' Jemima suggested.

The weather was beautiful – a glorious June day. They talked as they went along, their arms linked. Jemima was the first to speak. After all, it was she who had so much to say, and Jeanie was there as the listener.

'Do you think you can love two men at the same time, Jeanie?'

The abruptness of the question took Jeanie by surprise, and she pondered it for a little while before answering.

'It depends on what kind of love you mean. There are many different types of love. The love of the man in your life for example, the man you married, then there is the love you have for your father and your brothers, and the love a mother has for her son even after he has reached adulthood. Therefore, Mother, in my opinion, it *is* possible to love different men for different reasons and with different intensity. Does that answer your question?'

'What you say makes perfect sense. Nevertheless, your explanation does not cover my own personal experience.'

'In what way do you mean?'

'I have concealed my true feelings for far too long. Now is the time to tell someone the truth. I am sorry that it should fall upon your shoulders Jeanie, to hear my confession. I am getting old, and I am running out of time.'

'Nonsense Mother, you have many years left in front of you.'

'Not if I have to carry the burden of truth any longer. I have carried it now for over twenty-five years. I cannot carry it a moment longer; it is killing me, and I feel I must act now. Although I claimed, my involvement with Bobby Anderson was nothing more than a mere distraction and I let people believe it was due to my being at a low point in my life, but I knew then, and I still know now, it was more than that. I have spent every living hour since, trying to suppress it as nothing more than lust. I knew I loved him then, I know I still do and since his death, I miss him so much. Feelings I had for him then have never diminished and I can say even now, after all these years; they never will. The strange thing is, while playing out this episode in my life, I still loved Chris. All through my stage career, he was my mentor, my rock and I knew I would always love him.'

Just then, they reached the entrance to the five-furlong gallop. 'Let us stroll down here, a little way; the rhododendrons will be at their best. I am sure you will agree Jeanie when you see them for yourself. I cannot wait to see them once more.'

In her mind's eye, she could see an image of Bobby Anderson as he was that fateful Sunday morning all those years ago. They reached the place where the tall rhododendrons arched, forming an arbour of pink and white. The large blooms, some as big as tea plates, were vivid purple, others were white as snow each petal tinged with a warming flush of pink. 'Let us go through here Jeanie where we will enter a beautiful clearing with dappled shade; it is much cooler in here.'

Jeanie led the way, her mother-in-law in her wake. Sure enough, on entering, Jeanie felt totally at one with nature. 'It is indeed a magical place, Mother. It intensifies one's senses. I have never felt so aware of nature before.'

'I will let you into a secret, should I?' Jemima said pausing as she reminisced about the last time she visited this place, savouring once more that delicious moment, lodged permanently in her mind; her memory sharpened by the aromatic nutmeg scent of the large rhododendrons.

'Please, tell me, do not tease me any longer,' Jeanie pleaded.

Jemima looked up to where the broken beams of sunlight penetrated the canopy high above her. The ground beneath her feet was wet with dew, as it had been the last time she had entered this place; only this time Bobby Anderson was not there to gallantly take off his hacking jacket and provide her with protection. A single beam of sunlight found its way through a gap in the trees, its glow magnified intensively until she could no longer make out the trees above her. Although the glow almost blinded her, she could see clearly within the radiance, an image of Bobby Anderson smiling down on her. Without further hesitation, she made her confession to Jeanie.

'This is where Bobby Anderson and I made love.' She had said it to another human being for the first time, and she felt relieved and pleased she had.

'This is the first time I have visited this place since that day twenty-five years ago. Oh Jeanie, I am so glad you came with me today. I just had to visit here one more time and I am glad I was able to share it with you. Thank you for listening to the ramblings of an old woman. I have always thought about Bobby even though I tried to appear outwardly that he meant nothing to me. We were kindred spirits in a sense. We both came from humble beginnings, he the son of a Durham miner; I the daughter of a Norfolk ploughman. I even spent a short part of my childhood in a Norfolk workhouse.'

'I never knew that Jemima.'

'Oh yes my mother, my three brothers and I spent a short time in the Durham workhouse following the death of my father in America. My youngest brother Daniel, was born in the workhouse. That is where Bobby and I had much in common. We had both known fame and in both our cases that was down to the man who led me throughout my career, my late husband Chris, the same man who had launched Bobby's riding career; and we both betrayed him. That is why I need to clear my conscience before much longer. I was desperate to find something to replace the boredom I suffered on my leaving the stage. I was taking an interest in the emancipation of women, but I was not brave enough to join the Pankhurst movement. They showed too much violence for my liking. They could not have had love in their hearts as I had. I caused enough commotion when I tried to enlighten the women of West Fell about contraception. It took me all my time to carry that through, let alone throw myself in front of the King's horse in the Epsom Derby. I am not sure whether Emily Davison was brave or foolhardy in doing what she did two years ago. My love for Bobby was always destined to be a covert emotion. Someone else's love for Bobby has gone on suppressed by law for more years than my own. I will not mention his name, for that would be a betrayal. It was a one-sided passion not shared by Bobby.'

Without any revelation from Jemima, Jeanie knew that she alluded to Tommy Cogan. Jeanie noticed Jemima's voice begin to crack; it was getting weaker, and her eyelids were half-closed almost trance like.

'Are you all right Mother?' Jemima's face creased into a soft smile as she remembered Bobby Anderson. The smile developed into a little laugh, as her mind filled with the pleasant thought of twenty-five years ago, the laugh soon stifled as she clutched her chest. Jemima's voice got thinner before she finished her last sentence, and tears burned the inside of her eyelids.

'Please Mother; do not get upset; who am I to judge you? Under the circumstances I see no shame in what you did. You were not the first and I doubt very much that you will be the last woman to have an extra marital affair. On hearing your story, I do believe a woman in similar circumstances to yourself, could love two men at the same time.'

Jeanie recognised the sudden change in her mother-in-law's condition, and she acted quickly to save her from falling.

'What is wrong Mother? Are you all right?' Jeanie cried.

Even though she acted quickly, she failed to support her mother-in-law's body weight as she slowly slipped through her hands and collapsed to the wet ground. She made Jemima as comfortable as possible and did what she could to revive her. With her doctor's expertise, she recognised immediately that her mother-in-law was dead.

The Lark, her wings composed, her music still.

THE END

ABOUT THE AUTHOR

I was born in Coxhoe, County Durham. The son of a Durham coal miner.

I attended Durham Johnston Grammar School. On leaving school I studied mining engineering and spent ten years working at the coalface.

I have lived in Wiltshire since 1964, following the closures of the coal mines in the UK. Since then, I have worked in general engineering, in the QC laboratory and in the final six years before retirement I worked in research and development.

I have had a keen interest in horse racing from a very early age, attracted as I was by the aesthetic pleasure it gave me to see these beautiful animals in action. In writing this book, I have drawn on my own personal experience and in doing so, I hope the reader finds it a good read.

By the same author also available on Amazon:
A LARK OVER NEW YORK

Printed in Great Britain
by Amazon